HAND IN THE FIRE

Also by Hugo Hamilton

Disguise
The Sailor in the Wardrobe
The Speckled People
Sad Bastard
Headbanger
Dublin Where the Palm Trees Grow
The Love Test
The Last Shot
Surrogate City

HUGO HAMILTON

Hand in the Fire

FOURTH ESTATE • *London*

First published in Great Britain in 2010 by
Fourth Estate
An imprint of HarperCollins*Publishers*
77–85 Fulham Palace Road
London W6 8JB
www.4thestate.co.uk

Visit our authors' blog:
www.fifthestate.co.uk

1

A catalogue record for this book
is available from the British Library

ISBN   978-0-00-732482-8
TPB ISBN   978-0-00-736556-2

Typeset by Palimpsest Book Production Limited,
Grangemouth, Stirlingshire
Printed in Great Britain by Clays Ltd, St Ives plc

Mixed Sources
Product group from well-managed
forests and other controlled sources
www.fsc.org Cert no. SW-COC-1806
© 1996 Forest Stewardship Council

FSC

FSC is a non-profit international organisation established to promote the
responsible management of the world's forests. Products carrying the FSC
label are independently certified to assure consumers that they come
from forests that are managed to meet the social, economic and
ecological needs of present and future generations.

Find out more about HarperCollins and the environment at
www.harpercollins.co.uk/green

For Maria

1

You have a funny way of doing things here.

Like friendship, for example.

Nobody does friendship like you do in this country. It comes out of nowhere. Full on. All or nothing. I've been to places where friendship is cultivated with great care over a longer period of time, like a balcony garden. Here it seems to grow wild.

You could say that I did him a small favour. I found his mobile phone lying in the street and contacted his girlfriend. Her name was Helen and there was a picture of her on the phone, laughing into the camera. I could have read through all her messages, but I didn't want to be intrusive. I contacted her and arranged for him to pick it up that same evening. It was nothing more than that. Anyone else would have done the same. I waited outside a late-night shop and saw him walking towards me with a big smile as though we already knew each other. He thanked me and stood there, refusing to let me go. Before I knew it, he was returning the favour, shaking hands and leading me away into a bar for a drink. He gave me his name, Kevin. I knew it already but he made it more official. Kevin Concannon. He told me that he was a lawyer and the phone was his life and he was glad it didn't fall into the wrong hands.

He was curious about me and asked me what I was up to. When I told him that I was a carpenter looking for work, he said he would keep his ear to the ground. There was a chance he could set me up with a job, if I was interested. He stored my name and number on his phone. Vid Ćosić. He repeated the surname a number of times phonetically to make sure he got the pronunciation right. Ćosić. Like *Choz-itch*.

'Where are you from, Vid?'

'Belgrade,' I said, just to keep it short.

I was trying to avoid all those long explanations about why I came here and what I left behind.

'Serbia,' I added. 'Former Yugoslavia.'

What do you say when the country you grew up in can only be remembered for one thing? I told him that I left after a bad car accident and wanted to travel, see something different.

'Fair enough,' he said.

What does it matter where you come from? You could say it's irrelevant. I wanted to forget about my own country and start again. I wanted to get a foothold here, get to know the place and the people. I already knew some of the most famous names, like James Joyce and George Best and Bono and Bobby Sands. I knew the most important landmarks, like the GPO, where the Easter Revolution took place, and Burgh Quay, where the bus to Galway leaves from. Right next to the immigration offices. I was beginning to understand the way things are done here, the way you have of saying 'how's the man?' and 'what's the craic?' I was starting to pick up the jokes, trying not to take everything so seriously. I was working on the accent, learning all the clichés – at the end of the day, nine times out of ten, only time will tell. I was eager not to be misunderstood or misled, so I stuck to the expressions that would give me least trouble. I was reluctant to abbreviate. I never allowed myself to use puns or play with people's names. I tried to limit the amount of times I used words without meaning, such as 'like' or 'you know'. I was cautious with terms like 'mega' and 'sketchy' and 'leggin' it' and 'literally glued to the television'. I didn't trust myself saying things like 'will you go away' or 'would you ever fuck off' because I'm always afraid people might take it to heart. Besides, I can never pronounce the word 'fuck' properly. I make it sound too genuine. You have so many different ways of saying it in this country, I've given up trying.

We got talking about where I had been so far and what places around the country I had visited. I told him I was planning to travel out to the west, but then he sent me on a detour down south instead.

'Have you been to Dursey Island?'

'No,' I said.

He had a commanding way of speaking. His eyes were intense, looking right at me. He stepped into my life quite easily, offering advice and making decisions for me.

'Don't go anywhere,' he said, 'until you've been to Dursey Island.'

'Why?'

'There's no place in the world like it,' he said. 'Hardly anyone living out there now. Just yourself and the ocean, that's all.'

Was there a reason for sending me there? Did he have some connection to the place? They talk of six degrees of separation, but here in this country you only have one or two at the most. He looked away towards the door of the pub as though he could see right across the landscape and all the people in it. He told me how to get there, right at the tail end of the country, off the coast of Cork.

'You go over by cable car,' he said. 'The only place I know with a cable car crossing the Atlantic.'

'You're not serious,' I said.

'I am serious,' he said. 'You can look it up, Vid. It's a fact.'

'Dursey Island.'

'Dursey Island,' he repeated. 'Don't tell anyone that you haven't been there.'

He clapped me on the back and got up to leave, thanked me once more, then disappeared.

Two days later I found myself taking up his advice, knowing that unless I went down there to see it with my own eyes, I would never believe it.

I followed the map and got lost. I dropped into a pub along the way for directions and the man behind the bar started pointing with a knife. He was cutting a lemon into slices and stopped what he was doing in order to show me the way. I could not really understand his accent and kept staring at the filleting knife in his hand. The words came spilling across the counter and I was so distracted by the way he was stabbing the air that I hardly picked up anything he was saying to me. I smelled the tang of lemon and waited for him to finish. He must have noticed my confusion because he began to repeat the whole thing from the beginning. But again, my concentration failed, watching only the silver blade flashing in his hand. He pointed the knife directly towards me, giving an almighty stab, forward and upwards. Straight all the way, he said. If I had been standing any closer I would have got it in the neck. He waited for me to repeat these directions back to him like a schoolboy, so I nodded, more out of politeness. Rather than forcing him to go through the whole frenzied attack all over again, I thanked him and told him it was all perfectly clear to me now. But as I turned to leave, I could not help thinking he was going to throw the knife at my back. A dark stain seeping through my clothes as I sank down to the floor.

And then I went on a shaky journey by cable car out to Dursey Island, high over the water with my heart in my mouth, as they say, and my stomach falling into the ocean below. Once I got there, I wondered what was so special about the island. It was a beautiful place and full of history, but I didn't really know what I was looking for. I walked around for a while and took a few photographs. Some of the seabirds were new to me. Some of the clouds, too, faster, lower down, more eager to reach land on their way in off the Atlantic. I heard the waves crashing on the rocks, like the door of a giant freezer being slammed shut repeatedly. I kept thinking there were better places to visit, more start-ling, more empty places such as Skellig Rock, rising up out of the sea in the shape of a solid black fin. There were patches of sunlight shifting across the water. It looked like it was going to rain, but didn't. A strong breeze flapped at the back of my jacket making me think there was somebody behind me. But there was no one around and I felt like the last man on earth.

After an hour or two I wanted to get back to the main-land. As the cable car swung across towards me, I could see a young boy inside. The door opened and a dozen sheep came bursting out as though set loose from a trap, their hooves banging and scraping at the steel, jumping over one another in the rush to get at the grass.

One of the sheep got its front leg caught in between the cable car and the pier, so the boy tried to dislodge it. The animal was in great fear, eyes wide, struggling to get away. I gave him a hand to release the sheep and he told me the island was used mostly for grazing now. Some people owned holiday homes there, but they were absent most of the year. The sheep were already ripping lumps of grass as though the perilous trip over was not worth another thought. On the return passage, I was overpowered by the smell of sheep shit and sheep fear and possibly my own fear included, until I stepped on solid ground again. I watched the boy's sister whistling and herding more sheep on to the cable car with the help of their dog. Then they all travelled across to the island together in the same compartment. At one point, I imagined the door opening and the sheep falling down into the sea, one by one, with their legs pedalling frantically as they accelerated towards their death. But that never happened and there was little or nothing else to remember except the fact that I had been there.

So there you have it. Dursey Island. It does exist. As much as I exist. It has become part of me now, like a stored photograph. I can boast about being there and tell everybody that it's not just a place on the map where people once lived and God knows where they all are now. But what about all the places I never managed to visit? How could I go around verifying every headland and town in the country? Most of it has to be taken on trust. I take your word for it.

There were plenty of other things I had to find out for myself. And maybe I needed a different sort of map altogether. Some kind of rough guide on how to fit in as much as possible. The rough guide to friendship. The rough guide to betrayal also. The rough guide to rage and hatred and murder.

I had to verify all those things as well.

Don't get me wrong. It was good to be here. I loved the place right from the moment I arrived – the landscape, the wind, the change of heart in the weather. I didn't want to live anywhere else in the world. I loved the easy way you have of making people feel at home. All the talking. The exaggeration. The guesswork in the words. I wanted to belong here. I wanted to take part in this spectacular friendship.

2

At the time I was still employed in security. My first job here was working as a night watchman in a nursing home. Not bad for the time being, I thought. Not a bad introduction to a country either, because it gave me some idea of the back story. All the hopes and disappointments collected under one roof.

The nursing home was situated around an ancient castle by the sea, on the outskirts of Dublin, with extensive grounds overlooking a small harbour, used mainly for pleasure boats and fishing. What a great place for the old people to spend their final days, watching ships coming and going in the bay. Those that could still see, in any case. At night, the lighthouse shone across the water and there was a string of yellow city lights going all the way around the edge of the coast. My job was to take the guard dog out to patrol the grounds once every hour and to deal with any emergencies, which amounted to a few drunken shouts, no more. The dog was an old Alsatian who had a peculiar sense of obedience. He had been trained to obey your command as long as you stayed on the inside, between him and the buildings. If you strayed on to the far side, he would see you as an intruder with no business being anywhere near the place. I spent the first night sitting on top of the oil storage tank with the dog below me, waiting to tear me apart. After that, I learned to stay on the right side of him.

It was clear that I was never really cut out for security work. I was a bit of a walkover. I didn't have the confidence of an enforcer. What I really wanted was to get into carpentry, even boat building, if possible, but there is no such work available. It was just a dream really. The best I could hope for was some kind of restoration work on old boats. In the meantime, I was glad to make any contacts that might get me into the building trade.

The nursing home was administered by nuns in brown habits, though they didn't take part in day-to-day caring any more. Those duties were carried out by lay nursing staff. The few nuns that were left over came out from their residence early in the morning to walk the grounds with their head-gear blowing vertically in the wind. I got to know one of the nurses on night duty. Her name was Bridie and she had red hair. She was much older than me, in her fifties, but she kept winking and calling me the love of her life. She would laugh out loud and repeat a few of the things I said, not just the accent but the vocabulary. She said I sometimes sounded like a letter from the bank, using words like 'complete' and 'commence' and 'with regard to', words I picked up from the newspapers and which were not suited to everyday use.

'I'm going to commence laughing,' she would say.

It took me a while to get the hang of the ordinary words. At first I couldn't see any difference between start and commence. My sentences must have sounded more like trans-lations, asking people if there was any rumour of work going for a carpenter.

The problem at the nursing home was not so much people breaking in as people breaking out. The 'inmates', as Bridie called them, had no valuables to speak of, only books and pictures of their families, packets of shortcake, tins of exotic mints and butterscotch. The rooms all smelled of apple cores and rubber sheets, sometimes banana and leather. There was no alcohol allowed on the premises and some of the patients were going mad with abstinence. One night the dog caught an old retired doctor by the name of Geraghty trying to sneak away across the lawn. He had no socks on and his shoelaces were undone. He stood with his hands up, pleading with me, saying that he had permission to go to the pub. What could I do? I tied his shoelaces for him and let him go. Some time later, Nurse Bridie came down to raise the alarm and he was eventually found sitting on a seafront bench, singing to the waves.

The ground-floor windows were fitted with special bolts after that. Then Geraghty asked me to buy him a half-bottle of whisky and Nurse Bridie knew I was responsible. She came down to the office and sat on my lap, putting her hands around my throat, pretending to strangle me. Doctor Geraghty had run amok through the corridors upstairs with his clothes off, declaring love to every woman in the place. He had forced his way into one of the rooms and refused to leave, hanging on to the metal bed end where a terrified woman sat up with the blankets under her chin, asking for a mirror so that she could fix her hair. When I went upstairs to help escort him back to his room, he turned on me. He could not remember that it was me who had given him the whisky. I took hold of his arm and he went from being drunk and spongy to being rigid and defensive. I was surprised by his strength as he ripped his arm away and stared at me with stony eyes, full of anger or only joking, I wasn't quite sure at first.

'Don't touch me,' he said. 'Where are you from? You have no right to interfere in my business.'

'Now, now, Doctor,' Bridie said in a firm voice.

Then she led him away quickly, no nonsense, just by sheer willpower and authority. Within minutes she had him back in bed, kissed the top of his bald head and told him to be a good boy. I could never imagine having that command over people here. I had no way of telling an old man what to do in his own country. I was like a child ordering the adults to go to sleep.

Most of the patients drank tea all day and couldn't sleep at night. One old woman came down to see me regularly and Nurse Bridie told me to 'go along' with her. Which turned out to be good advice in general. The woman was dressed elegantly in a green cape and drooping earrings, ready to go out to the theatre, so she claimed. The only thing out of place was that it was well after two in the morning and she was wearing slippers. She asked me to call a taxi and I pretended to do that, lifting up the phone and dialling an imaginary number, speaking to an imaginary person on the other end of the line.

I suppose you could say that everyone is an actor, to a certain degree, but I sometimes found it hard to enter into the character I had been given to play here. I was still learning the lines, while everybody around me seemed so sure of their roles. They were born for the part.

I couldn't help being myself most of the time.

While the woman in slippers waited for the taxi, she produced a silver cigarette box from her handbag, telling me that it belonged to her father who had fought in the War of Independence. She asked me to place my index finger into an indent left by a bullet. But for that cigarette case, she said, her father would have been killed as a young man and she would never have been born. Holding the silver case in my hand, I thought of the man whose life it saved. I could even imagine the night of the ambush as if it happened only recently in my own country, when the war was going on. The faces hidden in the grass. The empty landscape. The well-chosen bend in the road. The hours of boredom and the clothes of men stinking like soup after rain. All the imaginary noises in the distance until the sound of the real truck driven by enemy soldiers came along at last with headlights stabbing across the bog. The fear vibrating in the turf and, eventually, the crack of shots and the shouts of men and unforgettable silence after it was over. Men lying dead on the road and the echo of gunfire still singing in the brown bog pools for weeks and months, even now.

As she placed the cigarette box back into her bag, she revealed that her father was not the kind of person who owned a cigarette case, let alone a full packet of cigarettes. He had taken it from a dead British officer after an ambush. He had inherited the charm of the silver cigarette case and passed it on, like so many other monuments left behind in this country from that time, so she told me, like the railway tracks and the granite harbours and the obelisk in the shape of a 'witch's hat' on the hill which was built for no reason during the famine times.

My first history lesson. I was grateful to her for it. It gave me the feeling of belonging here, a feeling of friends and enemies going back a long time. It made me think I had lived here all my life, with uncles and aunts talking about me and waiting to hear from me. You can read as many history books as you like about this country, but it all sounds like fiction unless you have something tangible to link it up to.

The taxi never came. As she got up to leave, she told me it was nice to have got the chance to meet me. The next time she came down, she had no idea that we had met before, which allowed me to pretend I never heard her story and I could be welcomed all over again.

More often it was Nurse Bridie who came down to get away from the 'insatiable maniacs upstairs', as she put it. I recognised the squeak of her white shoes on the floor. She sat down and tried hard to get me to talk. She asked me why I had come to Ireland and what dark secrets did I have hidden behind my eyes. She wanted to know if there was anything I missed about home, apart from the weather and the cakes. She wanted to know if I had a girlfriend, and when I shook my head, she didn't believe me.

'You're so innocent,' she said to me a number of times, which made me think I was completely transparent.

She told me lots of things about the nuns in Ireland. She said they were savages, most of them. She had gone to school with the sisters of 'no mercy'. She said the nuns had always employed the most vulnerable. There was a young boy working in the kitchens who got a pot of boiling chip oil spilled over him. 'You should have heard him screaming,' she said. 'Blisters the size of cups on his neck. When they tried to remove his shirt, the skin came off like red silk lining. Mass. That's what they offered him as compensation.' Then she warned me to leave before it was too late.

'Get out before they pour boiling oil on you.'

She blew me a kiss each time, just as a joke. Then I heard her shoes squeaking away again. I knew there was a sadness being suppressed by her laughter, like a cut under the skin that would not heal. But it was hard for me to ask her what it was.

When I stopped working there she said she was not surprised that I would break her heart and walk away, it

13

was the story of her life. She invited me for a farewell drink. We met in a pub close by and she seemed older out of uniform, or younger, it was hard to say. More motherly, perhaps, and also more fragile, more like a girl. Sitting with her coat on and her handbag beside her, she stirred her vodka and tonic with a plastic stick and did all the talking, because I had nothing to say and didn't know what questions to ask. She placed her mobile phone on the table beside her drink and watched it for a while to see if it would ring. She started crying and I could not work out what to do in a situation like that where she was not my mother or my sister. She ended up putting her hand on my arm to comfort me instead. She opened her handbag, searching for a tissue to wipe her tears, but then produced a letter which she asked me to read.

Dear Bridie, it said, *it is with a heavy heart that I write you this letter.*

It was written by her fiancé around thirty years earlier. I read it slowly all the way through, moving my lips across every word. He was breaking it off with her, so I gathered. They were intended to get married. The date had been set for the wedding and the families notified. At the last minute, he changed his mind and explained that he was not ready for it, because he was still drinking too much. He was not fit to be married to her. He didn't deserve her love and the only thing left for him to do was to leave the country and emigrate to America.

I suppose each country has its own rules for love and dishonesty. Different ways of disappearing and walking away from the past. Different measurements for loneliness and happiness. I wanted to track down the man who wrote the letter and tell him that he had made the biggest mistake of his life. But it was no longer possible to intervene because time had turned us all into distant observers.

She told me that she had a baby shortly after he left, but that she had been persuaded to give it up for adoption. She had tried to make contact with her son in recent years, but he had not wished to meet her. She asked me if I thought he would be good looking and intelligent, so I said yes, of course. She wanted to know if he might have red hair like her and then she answered all her own questions, assuring herself that her boy was happy in his new family and better off not looking back. Even though he was grown up by now, living his own life, she still spoke of him as a baby. Staring straight into my eyes, she said she hoped he turned out a bit like me, in fact, which made me think of myself as her son, promising to do my best.

She'd been holding on to the farewell letter ever since, refusing to get off the bus at the terminus, dreaming back and forth along the same route for ever.

'Go for it,' she said to me, putting the letter back into her handbag. I wondered if these were the exact same words she had spoken to her fiancé, just to be big-hearted and to make sure they parted as friends with no hard feelings. She pushed me with her elbow, unable to sit beside me any longer. Then she stood up to embrace me.

'Come back and see me sometime.' She smiled through red eyes. Then she sat down and looked at her phone to see if anyone had left a message. She waved with both hands and told me to take care of myself, so I walked out the door, away across the street, not even watching for the traffic on the wrong side of the road, as though it was impossible for me to get killed.

3

To be honest, I never expected to meet him again. The city was full of carpenters, so it was a surprise to get the call early one evening saying he wanted to discuss a small job at his mother's house. What was even more strange was the urgency. We had to meet right away. And then it was all quite informal, with no clear lines between work and friendship. Normally you keep those things separate, so I thought. You might go for a drink after the job is finished, if everybody is happy. But he started everything in reverse. He wanted to go for a drink even before I had time to prepare a proper estimate.

By then I was working full time for a small building company. My plan eventually was to get into business on my own, so I was happy to take on small jobs in my spare time. I had got to know a Lithuanian carpenter by the name of Darius who had his own workshop and a van. My own range of tools was very limited and he lent me some of his whenever I needed them.

Kevin picked me up and brought me over to his mother's house. A beautiful, spacious family home on a terraced street leading down to the sea, not far from the nursing home where I had worked. It was clearly in need of some repair and as he parked the car, he called it Desolation Row, after one of his mother's favourite songs.

He left me standing in the kitchen while he went upstairs calling his mother. But then she came in from the back garden wearing gloves and holding a pair of shears in her hand, looking at me as though I had just broken in and couldn't find my way out again.

'And who are you, if I may ask?'

The confusion was soon cleared up when he reappeared and introduced us. She took her gloves off to shake my hand.

'Vid Ćosić,' he said and she repeated the name slowly: *Choz-itch.*

Next thing we were standing upstairs in his mother's bedroom, talking about fitted wardrobes. I asked her what she had in mind and she mentioned black ash.

'Black ash,' I said, trying to warn them off with a smile. 'In a bedroom. Might end up looking a bit like a funeral parlour.'

There was silence in the room. I had said something wrong. His mother sighed like a slashed tyre. She wore a very serious expression and perhaps she was in mourning, I thought to myself. In fact she hardly smiled even once during the meeting.

'Black ash is very dignified,' Kevin said, helping me out.

'Of course,' I said, as soon as I realised my mistake. 'It depends on how it's done. Like, what kind of ash were you thinking of, veneer or solid ash, stained?'

I thought it was a travesty putting any kind of fitted wardrobes into a room like this. It was an old period house and they would never look right. But that's something you learn after a while. You couldn't be honest. You had to make allowances for taste and be prepared to say that black ash

17

was an elegant choice, even when it was the most revolting material you ever had the misfortune to work with. Besides, there was no changing her mind. She had seen something in a magazine. Floor to picture rail in black ash veneer was what she wanted.

They must have known I would be very competitive, because they didn't seem to have anyone else in mind for the job. The cost was not much of an issue, or the timescale. I made it clear to them that I could only take it on in my spare time.

'I'll need a bit up front for the materials,' I said.

'Fair enough,' he said. 'How much?'

'I'll have to price the stuff and get back to you.'

'Just let me know.'

'Fair enough,' I said, because that seemed like a good, neutral sort of phrase to me.

And that was it. He was already rushing me away to the nearest pub for a drink. While he was waiting for his girlfriend to turn up and go to dinner with him, he filled me in on his mother's personality. You could see that he admired her and also feared her a little, like a schoolboy. She was a schoolteacher, he explained, so you had to earn your smiles. She could be a bit severe at times, but she was actually very funny underneath the exterior, so he claimed. Quite street wise, too.

He gave an example which sounded more like a warning. His mother had been attacked in the street recently by a junkie who was after her handbag. She managed to distract him by saying the next thing that came into her head. 'They knocked down the wall,' she said. Her attacker looked all around in confusion. Who? What wall? By then he had completely forgotten about the handbag and fled empty-handed.

'Don't worry,' Kevin assured me. 'You'll get on great with her.'

It was not the kind of job you could easily price for, because there were other factors involved. Payment in kind. He knew I was trying to get a foothold in this country and encouraged the idea of me getting into business on my own. He started explaining the rules, telling me how to run my own future, giving me all kinds of advice on how to get started.

I felt so accepted. You see, when you're not from around here, it often feels a bit like gate-crashing, like you're at a party and people are wondering where you come from and who invited you. You take everything at face value and you can easily get people wrong. It's often hard to make a call between good and bad. So it's great to have somebody looking out for you. Somebody on your side who's going to let you know what's coming your way.

He even introduced me to his girlfriend, Helen. She shook my hand and recalled talking to me briefly on the phone. It was good to see her in person. You could understand why he would have fallen in love with her. The energy in her eyes. The open smile. She started asking questions as soon as she discovered where I was from.

'Belgrade,' she said. 'I love Balkan music. All those high-speed trumpets and drums.'

It made me feel homesick for a moment to meet some-body who was so interested in my country. She said she had a few CDs from that region and that she would love to go there sometime.

'I'd give anything to hear the music live.'

They were quite well informed about Yugoslavia and what happened during the war. There was nothing much that I could add to their knowledge, only to confirm that Milošević and Karadžić and all these people had fucked up the place and left a terrible stain on the map. What more can you say than that?

They wanted to know about my family. So I told them how my parents had died in a car crash. Long after the war was over, we were on our way to the wedding of my sister when the accident happened, somewhere in the countryside. Both parents were killed instantly and I was very lucky to be alive, if that's how you would put it. I was able to attend the funeral, but I suffered head injuries which had me in and out of hospital for months afterwards. I was having great trouble with my memory ever since.

The truth is that I didn't want to remember anything. I've read stories about women who suffer from voluntary blindness after repeatedly witnessing terrible things in war. They cannot bear to see any more horror and lose their sight as a form of sub-conscious self-protection, so it seems. Their faculties close down in an attempt to shut out the worst. Maybe it was a bit like that for me. There were certain things from childhood that I didn't want to know any more. You could say it was voluntary memory loss. Except that it was much simpler to tell everyone I had received head injuries in a serious car accident and suffered from amnesia.

I liked to think of myself beginning all over again here, with a clean slate. I had no life before I arrived and could hardly remember a thing.

'Why did you pick this country, of all places?' Kevin asked, though I don't think he meant it like that.

'It's a very friendly place,' I said, trying to say the right thing. 'And quite neutral.'

'Neutral?'

I hesitated and told them I had been to Germany for a while, but it didn't suit me there. Not that I had anything against Germans, just that I was under pressure to say something good about this country. I said I found people here less judgemental, more forgiving perhaps, more open to mistakes in history.

'Leave him alone,' Helen said, smiling.

They fell into a brief argument among themselves, as if I was absent. Some older debate which I could not fully understand. Only in the tone of her voice could I tell that she was defending me, putting words into my mouth. Then they stopped, as if it didn't really matter all that much. He laughed and put his arm around my shoulder.

'Another quick one.'

It struck me that I had forgotten to mention my trip down south.

'By the way,' I said. 'I took your advice and went down to Dursey Island.'

She seemed surprised by the mention of the island. I saw her staring at him, but he was turning something over in the back of his mind and didn't want to look up.

'Dursey Island,' she said. 'You sent him out to Dursey Island?'

'Where else?' he said, finally answering her eyes.

'Out on the cable car with the sheep?'

'Not exactly with the sheep,' I replied, just to clarify that point.

'And was it raining with the sun shining at the same time?'

But she was not really waiting for an answer from me. She was looking only at him. I remained silent, because they might as well have been sitting alone together, on the edge

21

of a cliff, overlooking the ocean. They continued staring at each other and I felt as though I had walked right into their bedroom.

4

Some days later I phoned him to agree a price for the job at his mother's house. He laughed at one of my linguistic errors. I said it would cost 'twice as less' as I had initially estimated. He pointed out the mistake and offered to meet me later on that same evening with the start-up money so that I could buy the materials and begin the job the following morning.

It was a Friday night and I was out drinking with some of the lads from the site after work. The building company I worked for was a medium-sized operation with about a dozen or so core workers. Home renovations. I spent my time hanging reconditioned doors, putting in new saddles and repairing architraves, replacing damaged floorboards and skirting boards. The builder kept getting my name wrong and called me Vim. I corrected him a number of times and told him it was Vid, but he insisted on changing it back to Vim. Some of the workers had other names for me, like Video. Because my first name was so short and they were unable to shorten it any further to, say, Pat or Joe, the only thing they could do was to lengthen it, giving me versions like Viduka, or Vidukalic, or Videolink, sometimes Vid the Vibrator, or Vim the most effective detergent against household germs.

The builder said he was keeping me on, not because I was a good carpenter but because I finished things. He could find any amount of carpenters who were better skilled than I was, but I had a way of completing the job that made it look done. I think some of the other workers were irritated with me for being so neat, but that didn't stop them from bringing me with them after work on the razz, as they called it.

I was sucked into the rush-hour of their celebration. It felt like the world was going to come to an end at any moment and they were compelled to make the most of it, like a big farewell party. They had a store of phrases and excuses to justify being young and not dead yet. They were determined to live it up by any means, to make up for all the bad times behind them and maybe all the bad times ahead of them as well. They kept predicting the amount of drink they would take and how much fun they would have. There was no question that they were having the time of their lives, but I always had the feeling that, instead of living in the moment, they were more interested in getting away from the real world, stepping back and talking everything up into a big story, like people watching their lives pass in front of them.

Don't ask me what the name of the place was, I can't remember. It was a traditional kind of bar with three men standing on a small stage with guitars, belting out songs which most of the people in the pub knew by heart, old and young.

There was a song about a woman called Nancy Spain. It had to do with a ring she had been given, but which seemed to have gone missing. Every time it came around to the chorus, the whole pub joined in to ask the big question, where was the ring that had been given to Nancy Spain? Did she lose it? Did she give it away? I asked some of them around me who she was and what happened to the ring, but they had no idea. They were on the same level of ignorance with me, though they knew instinctively the question could not be answered. Some things exist only in the form of enquiry. They could relate to the idea of the lost ring and were just very happy to mime the action, pointing at the ring finger and repeating the gesture of giving it away each time the chorus returned.

I ran into an electrician who had been working on the same site with me for a while, rewiring. He was a cool character, in his late fifties, with a goatee beard. He spoke to me in a casual way, indirectly, looking away towards the band. He started telling me about a guy called Dev, saying that he had 'totally fucked up the place' and I thought it was somebody working with him on one of the sites. Was he another electrician or what? They all laughed when I asked the question. And that's how it often is, you say something without even knowing that it's funny. Until it was explained to me that Dev was the short for De Valera, a tall figure from history that some of the older people talked about as though he was still alive and likely to walk into the pub any minute and order himself a drink.

The electrician was glad to step in and give a summary of Irish history. I listened eagerly, accepting the facts about internment camps and hunger strikes. He mentioned place names and dates which meant nothing to me but which made some of the women flinch. I suspected that there was still a strong level of sexual attraction revolving around national sorrow, not just where I came from but here as well. They talked about how bad things were 'up there' in Northern Ireland. One of the women said it was great to have no more checkpoints and no more dawn raids, not to mention car bombs and kneecapping. But she felt there was something great about those times as well. Lots of passion. Lots of men on the run. She said there was a smell of disinfectant in the air since the Peace Process began, and within seconds they were all laughing again.

I tried not to ask any more stupid questions and they claimed me as their friend, temporarily at least.

'Anyone gives you any trouble, we'll burst them.'

The word 'burst' confused me at first. I could only associate it with the phrase 'bursting out laughing'. They were making me laugh all the time. Everybody was bursting out and cracking up, and I had no idea that I was walking myself into trouble. It came as a complete surprise to me that the electrician would end up trying to burst me a little while later.

All through the evening, they called each other 'knackers', which I first thought was some kind of joke. It was a reference to travellers, people on the move, like the Roma back home. Unlike the settled people who lived in houses, the travellers lived in caravans by the side of the road mostly, or used to, before it became illegal to do so. I had seen them on my journey around the country and was told that they had been displaced by a man named Cromwell, another hated figure in Irish history. 'Knacker-drinking' was a term which they used to describe those who consumed their alcohol outdoors in public places.

From what I could work out, the top most despised people in this country were Dev, Cromwell and Margaret Thatcher. After that it was knackers and scumbags. After that it was people like junkies and drug lords and clampers. Further down the list were the environmentalists and the artists. The person they hated most of all, it seemed, was an old woman in a shawl who was long dead, a woman by the name of Peig Sayers who lived in very poor circumstances on the Blasket Islands and forced everyone to speak the old language, Irish. The most dangerous people of all according to them were the bi-polars, because they could not be easily identified. It was not as though they conveniently lit up green at night like Zombies with their hair falling out. You never even knew when you were in the company of a bi-polar. But none of them were despised half as much as spongers. They could not be trusted for one minute.

I had no idea which of these categories I would fit into. My problem was not knowing how to judge people here. I tended to trust everybody equally. I didn't know who to avoid or what streets to stay away from.

At some point in the evening I started getting on very well with a girl called Sharon. Her hair was streaked with highlights. The trunk of her belly was showing with a diamond stud in the navel. She had quite a few tattoos, on her arms and around the small of her back as well, all pointing downwards. She wanted to know if I had any tattoos or piercings, but I was embarrassed to say I didn't. There were plenty of guys around with tattoos running up along the side of their necks, but they didn't seem to interest her.

Whenever she laughed it was like the sound of gunfire going off and I mistook her initially for an old woman. She kept making me laugh until I had to tell her at one point not to burst me any more. She said my English was very good and started dragging me outside for a cigarette, even though I didn't smoke.

That's when the misunderstanding arose. She turned out to be the daughter of the electrician I had been talking to and he was not really in favour of what was going on between us.

'Don't get any ideas,' he whispered to me in passing.

I think I had more to drink than I could cope with. I completely misread the signals and saw no sign at all of danger.

The band was playing the Bee Gees number about a man on death row, and maybe I should have taken that as a warning. There was a TV on in one part of the bar with an old movie playing silently without anyone watching because they all knew the story. *The Godfather*, I think it was. Al Pacino lying to his sister about having her husband killed.

There I was, being pulled out the back door of the pub to a small grotto which had been erected for smokers. Sharon called it a pagoda. We sat down and instead of smoking she took out a small sachet of pills, wrapped in silver foil. She took one herself and offered me one as well, but I didn't need it.

She got up and started dancing to an imaginary techno beat which was far more energetic than the pop ballads coming from inside. She seemed not to be aware of me. Then she came over to kiss me, grabbing the back of my neck and rushing her tongue right into my mouth like a jeep. The other hand reached for my balls.

'Show us your prick,' she demanded.

I delayed long enough until she got impatient and searched for my zip. I was totally out of my depth and couldn't tell if it was more of a rescue than an interference when her father suddenly appeared with two of his friends standing next to him.

'Sharon,' he roared. 'Get in here.'

'Ah fuck off, Da.'

He came over towards us while the other two remained at the door in case they were needed. Sharon had a screaming argument with her father at that point, with me as the main focus. She claimed she was old enough and entitled to screw anyone she liked and that this was not 'Holy, Catholic Ireland' any more with people placing an armed guard on their own daughters.

'You've got a six-month-old baby, Sharon,' he said.

'Look, it's OK,' I interrupted, beginning to edge away towards the pub door. What I wanted most was for everyone to go back inside and enjoy the music again and be friends. But it wasn't up to me to make a move.

'You fucking stay where you are, you Polish cunt.'

'I don't believe it,' Sharon said.

'He's only a knacker and a sponger.'

The electrician threw a punch which sent me right out of the grotto, into a line of bins. Before the full panic set in, I had time to get offended. I wanted to tell him that I have never been to Poland in my life, but my nationality was hardly the issue here. The mistake suited me in many ways because I didn't really want people to know I was from Serbia. I picked myself up and looked around to see where I should run to.

But by then it was already over. Sharon was walking away with her father and the two other men, like a team of escorts leading a pop star in through the back door of an arena. She must have been thrilled to be rescued like that. From inside, I heard the sound of applause and whistling and people cheering and the band starting up a number by the Gypsy Kings.

That's when I got the phone call from Kevin. It couldn't have come at a better time and we agreed to meet in a bar across the street, well away from the electrician and his daughter. It felt a bit sneaky, doing a bunk on my work mates, but I didn't want to drag Kevin into any of this trouble.

He arrived with Helen and they immediately looked at me with some concern.

'Are you all right?'

There was a bit of blood on my shirt and they kept asking me what happened. I played it down and told them I had simply miscalculated the situation in the bar. I had no idea that Sharon had a six-month-old baby or that her father was her chaperon for the night, not to mention the other two bodyguards.

'I wouldn't be seen dead in a place like that,' Kevin said.

'The lads at work brought me there,' I said.

'Trust me,' he said.

They were no friends, he assured me. A true friend was somebody who would put his hand in the fire for you. He explained what was more likely to happen and what it meant when somebody got burst. Briefly, it meant losing teeth. It meant footprints on your face.

He handed me the money for the materials and bought a round of drinks. He got quite drunk and told great stories which made Helen laugh out loud. Me as well. I liked him. I liked them both together, because they gave me this great feeling of being at home.

5

There we were, later that same night, Kevin and Helen and myself. The three of us walking together. Him in the middle with one arm around her and the other around me. Our feet shooting forward in unison. A strange animal with six feet and three laughing faces, two parts male and one part female. Once we reached the car and broke up, each of us stumbled away in a different direction. We lost the balance we had as a unit and had to regain our stability as individuals. He leaned into her, pushing her back against the side of the car to kiss her, but she shrugged him off, saying she was going to concentrate on getting home first. He fell away with his hands against the bonnet in a worshipping gesture. She laughed as she searched for the keys in her bag. She got into the car and turned on the engine while he sank down on to his knees, speaking to one of the headlights. His face lit up white. His eyes shut. Grinning. She shouted at him to get in, and then he cast an enormous shadow into the street as he stood up again.

'Look, I can get a taxi,' I said.

There were plenty of empty taxis heading back into the city centre.

'Hang on, I'm bursting,' he said.

His back was turned, hunched over as though he was counting out some money. Beyond him, the shutters of some shops, sprayed with graffiti. Then he spun around laughing and began to piss against the side of her car.

'You bastard,' she shouted.

I stood back on the pavement trying to pretend I was not part of this. I was embarrassed for her because he started pissing right across the bonnet. She was calling him a fucking animal, but I was not sure if she was really that angry and whether it might all be nothing more than a bit of fun in front of me. She must have known that he would pay to wash the car. He would even try and convince her later that it was an expression of affection. It was his trademark way of doing things in great waves of raging love and generosity. And maybe this was what she liked so much about him, his explosiveness, his talent for surprise. One day they would settle down and get married. Then all this madness would have to come to an end.

He began pissing right across the windscreen at her. She cursed again, but that only seemed to encourage him. She put on the windscreen wipers and sprayed two jets of soapy water in a counterattack, spreading the mixture of soap and piss across the glass.

Then I wondered if she was crying because she just backed down and remained silent, looking away into the street because this was not a very good sign for the future.

Was he consecrating her car or desecrating it? Quite possible that he would not be doing this without me present to witness this balancing act between them. They seemed to be appealing to me like a referee.

But who was I to judge?

Hard for me to know where the boundary lay between a joke and an insult. It was only a bit of a laugh, I kept telling myself. They have different rules here that I had not figured out yet. Or was it something else? Was he showcasing his power over her? Over me? Including me in this insane, intimate public act, but also letting me know that I had no right to take part?

A car sped past with all the windows open and three female occupants in the back seat singing along to the radio. They left a fraction of a familiar hit song on each part of the pavement, in doorways, in alleys, like cats hiding under parked cars.

And then the electrician turned up out of nowhere and pushed me against the shutters of the shops.

'Where is she?' he shouted.

It's possible that he said other things. 'You Polish bastard.' You tend to add things in reconstruction, when it's all so difficult to believe. The electrician seemed to think that I was alone in the street, because he began to swing punches at my head and claimed that I had abducted his daughter.

It didn't take long for Kevin to react. He came rushing over and pulled the electrician away by the collar.

'Get your hands off my friend.'

There was a struggle on the pavement. Not even a fight but more of a dance. Kevin kicked the electrician right in the groin and forced him to bend over, following it up with a strong punch in the face.

'Kevin,' I heard Helen screaming.

Maybe she thought she knew him better than that. She was tied to previous assumptions of his character, unable to understand where this violence had come from. To her it must have looked like something happening far away, beyond her control. Kevin swung the electrician around and sent him falling back against the shutters. The sound resembled the clap of a shotgun, followed by the scattering of pigeons.

I got the impression that the electrician was being lifted up off the ground. His feet were left hanging in the air. The first part of his body to land was the hip and I could hear it crack on the concrete, like a rare piece of porcelain shattering inside a velvet bag.

His head was the final part to descend, perhaps in self-preservation. There may have been another boot added at this moment, though I would still like to believe it's not true. It was quite possible that the addition of this final kick to the head fractionally delayed it from reaching the ground. Perhaps it provided a vital alteration in the angle of fall, bringing it down to the pavement sideways, with the corner of his forehead as the last point of contact. A phase tester came clattering along the pavement.

There were several more urgent kicks to the head, but then it was over. The electrician didn't stir after that. The whole thing lasted only a few seconds, as far as I recall. Kevin pushed me towards the car and roared at me to get in. Then he got in himself and slammed the door as if that was still part of the momentum.

'Drive,' he shouted.

But instead, Helen got out. She ran over to the man lying on the ground, quite peacefully. Blood had come creeping out of his nostrils. His right hand stretched out on the pavement in a begging gesture.

'Come on,' Kevin shouted through his teeth, getting out of the car again.

She kneeled down with some obligation to care for the man on the ground. But Kevin pulled her away, forcing her back into the car, this time into the passenger seat, while he ran around and took the wheel.

'No,' she said. 'You can't drive.'

As if being over the limit had become the main problem now.

'We can't just leave him there.'

The car accelerated away. I looked behind me, not sure if he was dead or alive any more. Then I heard her shouting at him and telling him to stop.

'You're a fucking lawyer, for God sake!'

Kevin continued driving at great speed. After a while he stopped and parked the car in a place where we were looking out at the sea. The lighthouse in the distance, blinking lazily. Some stationary ships out there, waiting to go into port on Monday morning. The usual orange necklace of city lights and a thin drizzle making it look like the ships were drifting away. We sat there breathing, listening, not doing anything but trying to sober up and figure out what to do.

'What's come over you?' she said. 'You just beat the shit out of that man for nothing.'

'I only tipped him and he fell over.'

'And now you're doing a runner.'

'Racist bastard,' he said. 'He brought it on himself.'

'We have to go back,' she said.

'No way.'

'You've got to call the guards.'

'It was a split-second thing,' he said. 'I had to protect Vid here.'

There's a pause, but it didn't seem right to express gratitude.

Nobody moved. Each one of us trying to roll back what happened. But you might as well try and turn history into reverse. Soldiers taking crimes out from underneath their pillows and carrying them off to secret locations. Bullets popping out of people's heads. Dead people jumping back to life and walking away backwards.

35

We were parked right on the verge of the quay. Any further forward and we would have ended up in the water. They would be lifting us out with a crane in the morning, out from among the floating condoms and beer cans.

'You've got to be able to walk away,' he said. 'Big mistake to retrace your steps.'

'Did your mother tell you that?'

She stared at him, extracting a forecast from his words, as though he had become a stranger to her.

We sat there, looking out at the black water of the port, the dark eyes of deep water staring back at us. We heard the sound of small waves going up and down the granite steps. We waited for the future to come, wondering if he was going to drive over the edge. We might as well have gone underwater as it was, driving away along the floor of the sea, through fields of brown seaweed, with mullet and luminous prawns swimming across the windscreen before us. Speeding through a silent landscape of rocks and bar-nacles and anchors and suspended lobster pots. I had the feeling that we were only waiting for the electrician to come and join us, limping or crawling up to the car, getting in beside me and putting his seat belt on. Dark worms of blood going in and out of his nostrils. Breathing clogging up in his chest. We would never get rid of him now, I thought. I imagined him speaking calmly, with moisture in his voice, getting ready for this long underwater journey that we were about to embark on together. 'I was only having the craic,' he would say, because he really wanted to be friends and keep the conversation going.

The engine started up again. I can remember thinking that he was going in the wrong direction, reversing instead of going forward. He drove in a rage once more, this time parking outside her place, rushing us away inside, into her basement apartment.

'Stay there and don't move,' he said.

Then he disappeared again. We heard him walking away. Where to, we had no idea. We stood looking at each other. After a moment, her hospitality returned and she asked me to sit down.

'I'm sorry,' she said.

I didn't know what to say to that.

'I've never seen him do anything like this before,' she said, more to herself.

To calm things down she started making tea. Then she put on some music. Balkan wedding music, of all things. She was trying to make me feel at home, but the music was so familiar that I was overwhelmed by homesickness and horror simultaneously.

I was instantly reminded of my sister's wedding, the wedding that never took place because of the car accident on the way. The violence in the street had brought back everything I had been trying to leave behind. Now the music was returning me to the same fatal scene in which my parents had died, repatriating me to the country I had just escaped from. But how could I explain that to her? In any case, neither of us were really listening to the music, only staring at the floor, silently going over what had just happened and wondering what was laid out before us.

She said it was probably best for me to spend the night there and prepared a place for me to sleep on the sofa.

When Kevin finally returned, he looked at the two of us with great suspicion, as though we had been talking about him all this time.

'What's that music?' he asked.

'Where the fuck were you?' she demanded.

It took him a while to answer. He went to the fridge first and took out a beer, then began to open it with his teeth, just to annoy her, it seemed, because she flinched and said, 'Jesus, will you get an opener, Kevin.' Then he took a long drink before he finally spoke.

'The less you know, the better,' he said.

'I want to know what's happened to that man,' she asked.

'He's outside, waiting for you,' he said to me.

'Christ,' she said.

'Only joking,' he laughed. 'He's alive and well. In the best of health, as a matter of fact.'

She turned and disappeared into the bedroom. He went in after her and they continued arguing, occasionally shouting at each other, sometimes mentioning my name.

I hated being involved in all this and felt like slipping out, making a run for it. I imagined the police arriving any minute. I even thought of leaving the money that he had given me to start the work.

They were arguing for a long while. At times they went silent, but then she raised her voice once more, calling him a thug and telling him not to touch her.

'It's the pissing,' I heard him say to her. 'That's what's getting to you, isn't it?'

'You don't fucking care, do you?'

'Come on, Helen. Admit it. You're only worked up because I did a wee-wee on your car, isn't that so?'

'Wake up, Kevin,' she said. 'Think of what you have done. Assault, that's what they will call it. You have just put your entire career in jeopardy and you think it's funny.'

He paused. He seemed to be reflecting on what she had said.

'Look, Helen,' he said, finally, 'I'm sorry for doing a wee-wee on your car.'

'Asshole,' she shouted.

Then he came out grinning while she slammed the door behind him. I suppose you could say it was a victory for him, sort of. Even though he got kicked out of the bedroom by his girlfriend, he was still able to claim that he had won. The world was falling apart around him, but he was happy holding on to the last laugh. He didn't say anything more to me, just sat down in an armchair and dozed off, buried in sleep with a smile spreading across his face.

6

Next morning he stood above me with the sun behind him, ready to leave. He had a glass of water in his hand, which he drank down and put on the table with a clack, the equivalent of saying, 'Come on, let's go.' There was no looking back. No retracing steps. No time to reflect on what had gone by.

'Mental, last night,' he said.

I couldn't make out why he was not more concerned. But this was a new day and it was time to put everything behind us. Within minutes I was sitting in his car, speeding over to his mother's house.

'Listen, Vid. What happened last night – don't give it another thought.'

My reading was that these things never go away.

'I work with them,' I said. 'They know me, those guys.'

'He's not dead,' he said with great confidence. 'There's nothing to worry about.'

'What if they go to the police?'

'You've done nothing against the law, Vid.'

'Yes. But what about you?'

'Look. This is important,' he said, pulling in to the side of the road for a moment. 'You cannot mention my name. I can't be dragged into this.'

He had done me a favour and now it was my turn to return the favour, to put my hand in the fire for him.

'You're doing a job at my mother's house, that's all you have to say. If they come looking for information, you call me. Say nothing. They cannot force you to answer any questions until you have your solicitor present. You understand that?'

He drove on with the windows open and his elbow out, coaching me, assuring me that everything would be fine.

'You remember nothing, right?'

He smiled at me, placing his hand on my neck.

'OK, my friend.'

We were tied to each other now, though I couldn't work out whether he needed me or whether I had become a dead weight around his shoulders.

He stopped to buy a newspaper, flicked swiftly through the pages, then showed me a small report on the incident which described the victim as a man in his early sixties who was the subject of a serious assault. He was recovering in hospital and the Garda were appealing for witnesses. They were looking for two attackers, believed to be non-national, of Polish extraction.

'They have it all arse-ways,' he laughed, throwing the paper into the back seat.

As he moved on again, I noticed that he had time to examine every woman we passed on the street. He spoke quite openly about what he liked and disliked, what turned him on and what he would never touch in a million years. He started telling me about his life, about Helen, about his family. Disposing of his biography, so to speak, in a single breath, like something he needed to leave behind rather than something he had grown into over the years.

I heard somebody once say that your childhood runs after you like a little dog. He started telling me things about his family that he wanted to get away from, confiding in me as an outsider who could be trusted, knowing that I would keep it all to myself.

His parents had met in London. They were probably hippies who couldn't find enough drugs and rock music in Ireland and left the country. They were the last generation to leave on the boat, he explained, before cheap flights took over. People who felt stifled and compelled as much by the habit of leaving as by the excitement of arriving anywhere else. It was in the blood. They just did what so many did before them. He began his life growing up in England and only returned when he was around nine years old. With the troubles going on in the North, he explained, and the mistrust of Irish accents on the streets of London, his mother decided to make a go of it back in Dublin. Over the years, he had lost any trace of his English accent. And maybe this was why he understood my position so well. At school, he learned what it was like to be excluded and tried to mix in and camouflage himself. He did his best to be Irish. He was aware of the inadequacies that come with being a stranger and denied the early part of his own childhood, ignoring the dog running after him.

'Never look back, my friend.'

He would repeat this phrase many times more. It was inscribed on every thought, on every decision he made.

'You've got to be able to walk on out of it,' he said. 'Believe me. You can't let yourself be dragged down.'

He was speaking out of my mouth, as they say. I agreed with everything he said for my own personal reasons, which had all to do with leaving and never going back again. He must have seen something in my situation that could perfectly explain his own, the story of his life described in mine. Like me, his aim was to escape. Only, he made it look like fun. All the bad things erased. Everything full of optimism and enterprise. Everything converted into a laugh. You could tell what made him so attractive to women, for instance, not only his striking good looks but also his ability to magnify the world around him into a great story.

His mother's name was Rita, and right from the beginning I could see that he adored her. She was a born schoolteacher and you could hear the chalk grinding when she spoke. Her word was always final, with no remission. End of story. She had seen everything in life, including drugs and sex and anything young people could invent. It was all being repeated over and over down through the generations, just a new treatment, new lingo, new energy and new boredom. She took in the news and current affairs as though she could see it all coming. She reacted in the same way to her own misfortunes with stoic detachment, as though they were happening on the far side of the world.

He told me that she had a long memory. If you did something to her, she would never forget. For example. His little sister was initially called *Eilish*, after his aunt Eilish. But there had been a falling out, something unforgivable was done, and his mother changed the baby's name to Ellis.

He said his father was a 'waster' from Connemara who had 'fucked off', leaving Rita to bring up three children on her own back in Dublin. She'd had the good fortune to inherit a house and was helped out by her brother, a priest, but it had not been easy to keep the family going. His father was the classic emigrant, the person who walked away but kept on singing about going home.

'Homesickness,' he said. 'It's like a disease. A psychiatric condition that people used to pass on to their children at birth.'

He could remember his father coming back from time to time on a visit. The family had tried to make a go of it once when Kevin and his sisters were small, but he left again, back to London. Kevin could recall him singing with his eyes closed. Speaking the old language, talking in Irish to his friends. But then he finally disappeared for good. The only contact after that was talking to him on the phone once or twice, before the money ran out in whatever coin box his father stood in. The line would go dead and all he would hear was the crackle of the rain on the other side.

'Thing of the past, really,' he said. 'Homesickness. All that seeping nostalgia. It's like polio. Or tuberculosis. Very rare these days.'

His father had written himself out of the family history. I was being written in. And maybe that's what I longed for most, to be pasted into the family scrapbook, whatever the consequences. He was claiming me as his friend, offering me this precious information, but also conscripting me as a foot soldier, sworn in by an unspoken oath of loyalty.

When we arrived at the house, he introduced me to both his younger sisters, Jane and Ellis. His mother made a pot of tea and put some fresh scones on the table for us. I felt more like a guest than a worker. Kevin gave them my biography so as to avoid too much interrogation from his mother. Belgrade, parents died in a car crash, memory loss after the accident, came to Ireland to get a new start. No further questions.

'Tragic, what happened there,' his mother said, being polite.

Then he disappeared again and I began working upstairs

44

in the bedroom. First of all I smashed up an ancient free-standing wardrobe which was listing to one side. I stacked the broken pieces in the back garden to be used for firewood. After that, I ran around to the local building supplier's to collect some batons so I could start framing up for the new wardrobe, which was simple enough. It was not such a big job. The black ash panels were to be delivered during the week. I reckoned the whole thing would not take much more than a week or two in my spare time.

Later, while I was fixing the batons to the wall, his mother brought me a mug of tea and some biscuits. She was curious to see how I was getting on. And when I was finished, I made certain to clean up after myself, so that she would not end up walking on splinters in her bare feet at night. I brought the plate and the mug back down and placed them in the sink.

'You're a bit of a perfectionist,' she said to me. 'I can see that.'

'Thanks,' I said.

'Not often you get that around here.'

'Ah well. I do my best, I suppose.'

She owned a collection of tin, wind-up toys. A little boy on a bicycle. A duck on wheels with a windmill on his head. Tin mice. Tin frogs leaping and a tin carousel with tin children swinging. She showed them to me and allowed a few of them to spin around the kitchen table. I had to stop the duck on a bike from falling over the edge. We got talking, because these toys were not sold in the shops here on safety grounds, because of the sharp metal parts, bits of blades bent over to hold them together. But they were still found in markets and shops all across Europe where I come from. For adults only. Parental guidance, that kind of thing. I promised her that if I was ever back home in the near future, I would buy her one to add to her collection.

During the following week, I worked away at the shelving and began to discover a little more about the family. I'm not the kind of person who pries into other people's business. I'm quite discreet. I do my work sort of blindfolded, you might say. But when you're in somebody else's house, you can't help noticing things.

In the bedroom, her stuff was all temporarily stored on the floor. It wasn't just a wardrobe she was after but a place to keep her documents. They were stacked up on top of each other against the bay window in boxes and large envelopes and folders tied with ribbon. Bits of newspapers from another time. Photographs. Wedding albums. All the evidence of her life, which she possibly didn't want to look at very often but slept with every night, alone in the same room. It was now exposed on the floor, waiting to be put away again as soon as I had the new wardrobe finished.

I didn't look at any of her personal things. I swear, it's not like me to do that. But one evening, a bundle of letters fell down. The ribbon around them must have come undone and they were scattered all over the floor. It looked as if I was nosing through her stuff, and I had no option but to pick them up and put them back so they were in exactly the same order, as far as possible. Letters with her name on them. Rita Concannon. His mother came from the time of letters, before all the new technology took over. Even though she still looked quite young, the letters seemed to put her way back into an ancient era of handwriting and lots of time between things being sent off and delivered.

The letters, I could not help noticing, were sent from England, all sealed, all unopened, all unread.

What is it about letters in this country? I asked myself. An email or a phone message could be easily ignored. But letters seemed to have such substance. They were real. You could hold them in your hand, as I did, briefly. I wanted to know more about the person who sent them. I wondered if they had come from the absent father, the man who had excluded himself from the family. What terrible words did they contain and why were they never even opened? All those far-away things inside your head that can only be written down in a letter.

What a cruel archivist she was to keep them unread. She was the perfectionist, I thought, storing these precious hand-written letters, gagged and sealed, with no right of reply.

Anyone who lives in a foreign place must ask themselves that question all the time: Have they been forgotten? It made me wonder about myself. I was hoping that my presence here was not like this one-way correspondence, that I was not just a worker and that they would miss me, if I had to leave for some reason and not return again.

7

The Garda officers came looking for me on site around lunchtime. With all the other workers eating their take-away food and staring at me, they asked me to confirm my name and address. Was my real name Vid or Vim? Was I a Polish national? They suspected I was trying to conceal my identity and wanted to see my passport, evidence of my work permit, which I did not have with me at the time and which I agreed to provide as soon as possible. But they needed to see it immediately. They were polite and took me to my apartment and then on to the station for further questioning.

At the station, they asked me to cast my mind back to a particular night and tell them whether I had been involved in an assault in which a man had been seriously injured. They gave me the date and the location and an approximate band of time in which the assault had taken place. They wanted to know about my movements on the night in question and asked me if I had made an anonymous phone call to a particular Garda station alerting them to the crime. They informed me that a man with a foreign accent like mine had reported seeing the victim lying in the street but then refused to identify himself. I told them I had not made any such call and that the incident had nothing to do with me.

'That's very strange,' one of the officers said. They explained that the victim had claimed I was known to him, that we had met in a nearby bar on the night in question and that I had been seen in his company by several witnesses. It was reported that I had accosted his daughter and then subsequently, on the same night, assaulted him on his way home. He was recovering from multiple injuries, including a broken hip and a broken jaw. He was pressing charges against me, as well as another unknown Polish national who had yet to be identified.

'Was it your friend who made the phone call?' they wanted to know.

They asked their questions too quickly for me to think. It was a shock to discover that I had become the main suspect. I had no idea what to say to them. I denied that I had assaulted anyone. They asked me if I needed legal aid, but I let them know that I was already fixed up with a lawyer, so they allowed me to make a call.

Kevin arrived as soon as possible, dressed in a dark suit and carrying a brown case. He knew some of the officers and spoke to them in an informal way as though they were friends. He winked at me and we were given a chance to have a few words alone.

'I know this is a bit of a shock, Vid,' he said. 'But listen, don't worry. They'll never get anywhere with this line of enquiry. They're only groping around in the dark. You simply deny everything. You didn't assault anyone. You have no recollection whatsoever of what they are alleging, am I right?'

'I will have to tell the truth,' I said. 'I can't lie.'

'Nobody's asking you to lie, Vid.'

He smiled at me and placed his hand on my shoulder. It was good to see him. His presence brought a great surge of confidence back to me.

I didn't want to let him down either. He had stood by me. At last I had a friend and was beginning to feel at home here, so I couldn't afford to lose that. But I felt so inadequate in front of the law. I was too honest. I didn't have the knack of out-staring the questions and sneaking up on the facts. You had to be born with that kind of gift, like a good card player. I was a newcomer to the table, all nervous and unsure of myself, ready to bet everything on one hand and blurt out the unabridged truth.

'You have the right to remain silent,' he reminded me. 'You understand that, don't you?'

'I'm afraid they will turn everything around with their questions.'

'You don't even have to say yes or no.'

He seemed so relaxed, slipping his phone in and out of his inner pocket to check messages. His sandy hair fell naturally across the corner of his forehead. His nose leaned a tiny degree to the right and his smile moved across with it, very openhearted, I thought.

'They're asking me who I was with that night,' I said.

'I know what you're talking about, Vid.' He nodded calmly. 'But the fact is, you don't remember anything, am I right in saying that? You have a very poor memory, isn't that so? You were involved in a bad car accident back home in Serbia. You sustained head injuries which caused severe brain trauma. With the result that you are now left with bouts of prolonged amnesia.'

'That's right,' I said.

'Show them the scar on your head,' he said. 'You suffer from memory loss, short term as well as long term. You have big gaps where you cannot remember much about growing up. Nothing about school, not even much about your own family.'

'Well, yes.'

'You can hardly remember where you come from, isn't that so?'

'Just about.'

'Explain that to them,' he said. 'Make it clear to them what a painful condition this is, not to be able to remember your own past. You don't even recall much of what happened in your own country and who was brought before the European Court or anything of that sort.'

'More or less,' I agreed.

'Some days are a complete blank,' he said. 'How does that sound?'

He went over the details of the night again, shaping it into a brief and unambiguous synopsis. I could remember being in the pub and meeting the victim. I could recall having a friendly chat with his daughter outside the back door while she was smoking, but I had no recollection of anything after that.

'Will I tell them that he hit me?' I asked.

'I wouldn't mention it. That would only give you a motive.'

He was so convincing. I admired the way he could see things with such clarity. He had the ability to think on his feet and look ahead while he was speaking. He knew where each sentence would end before he even began. In contrast, I spoke almost entirely in beginnings, or endings, with nothing sounding in the least bit finished or credible.

'Just a bit of advice, Vid. Don't let them put words in your mouth. And don't be the big storyteller. Doesn't suit you. Best to remember as little as possible.'

That was it. He spoke to the officers again and told them it was clearly a case of mistaken identity. First of all, I was not Polish, so they appeared to have the wrong man. They discussed this for a moment and then insisted on taking a statement. A woman Garda typed it up on a computer, then printed it out and produced a pen from the back of her hair for me to sign. Kevin later said to me that she was quite pretty, despite the fact that she was in uniform and that she was so small, not even the size of a milk carton.

'That's very convenient,' one of the officers remarked at one point, referring to my memory loss, but Kevin objected quite vigorously to that suggestion, saying it was completely out of order. Calling somebody's disability convenient, that was not on. They had the wrong man, he reiterated, and I liked that idea. It was so good to have him by my side. There was no progress made with the enquiries. At the end of the interview, they told me that I would need to come back in order to be formally identified by the victim, but in the meantime I was free to go.

Two weeks later I had to show up again for the line-up, which was made up of immigrants like myself mostly, with a man from Nigeria at one end and a man who turned out to be a plain clothes policeman in the middle, just to mix things up a little. The electrician was still on crutches, but he had no hesitation in pointing to me right away, without even wishing to look into my eyes.

To me it felt like I had been picked out as the only person who didn't belong here.

On the same day, I was brought before the court and charged with the assault. I don't even remember the words that were used because I was hardly listening to what they were saying. I think my mind shut down completely and refused to hear anything. I suppose I was clutching at the familiar things in my life, images of home which I was running away from but which might still give me some comfort. I was thinking of the streets of Belgrade, the trees in summer, the sound of the language, the Cyrillic writing we learned in school. The people in the cafés, the wasps around the cakes. None of those things had prepared me for what was happening in court. I was concentrating on the shape of the houses on Washington Street, my route to and from school on the bus. I could see myself passing by the cinema and I could even remember some of the movies I had watched there, the posters outside on the wall, the excitement of paying the money at the box office, getting the ticket stub and walking into the cool, darkened auditorium on a hot day, like the only refuge from the heat. I could see my life condensed into a number of key memories, like the sound of the bus doors clattering as they closed and the bus pulling away and leaving diesel fumes behind, mixed with the smell of coffee and leather goods and a million other things. I could remember the stalls with vendors selling bootleg merchandise. I could feel the heat of the summer lying across the lazy streets when I emerged from the cinema, hitting me in the face like a cushion, even though it always took a long time to step out of the story of the movie back into reality. I could remember the face of an old woman who begged on the corner, next to the bakery, still sitting on a small wooden box at that very moment, in her own city, while I was in court a thousand miles away, completely out of place.

I wondered if it was a mistake to leave your own country. My first impression here was of everything being so wealthy and inviting. The shop fronts were new and the goods on display were neat and ordered, with lots of choice. Belgrade seemed so dull by comparison. I could recall passing by a ladies' fashion shop with the mannequin of a woman with one amputated arm. She had rosy cheeks, but her nose looked like it had been bitten off and the plaster inside her nostrils was showing as though everything had been affected in some way by the war.

I heard my name being called out a number of times, badly pronounced. Next thing I was standing in the street again, free to go, awaiting trial. The whole thing was over so fast that I had no time to pick up what had been said. It would have been so much more depressing if it hadn't been for Kevin encouraging me, clapping me on the back as though I had won a prize. He was doing everything in his power to sort this out.

'We're in this together, Vid. I will not let you down, I swear.'

He reminded me that I was doing him an enormous turn and that he would see me right. He would engage the best legal minds in the city to work on this case. He got me a cup of coffee and told me to put it out of my head for the moment, but I could think of nothing else and even thought of leaving and going back home to my own country to escape from this, as if that would solve my problems.

'We'll get you out of this,' he assured me. Once again, I felt the rush of confidence coming from his words. I felt safe and welcomed, as always, until I was on my own again, walking home.

It was lashing all afternoon after the court appearance. Nothing could be done about the weather. Even when the rain stopped, the trees were dripping and the gable ends of houses were stained with watermarks. I could feel the moisture at the back of my neck, inside my sleeves. I could see it hanging across the streets. The whole earth sagging under the weight of unhappiness, with more clouds, like heavy curtains being closed. Cars hissing along the streets as if we were all living in a fish tank. Passengers floating away on buses with steamed-up windows. The swings in the People's Park were wet. The benches were wet. The lawns saturated like a green sponge. Nobody wanted to be out and nobody wanted to be in either. The faces of children at the windows, waiting for something better. I wondered if I could ever get used to it. The dampness seemed to affect everything here. Children got curls in their hair. Hall doors swelled up, causing trouble closing. Rusted railings. Rusted bicycle chains. You could hear people coughing. You could hear them complaining that it was impossible even to get the clothes dry.

At one point, while I sheltered in a doorway, a woman came along the street saying 'rotten' to everyone she passed by. I was in a trance, staring through the rain in front of my eyes, just hearing the word 'rotten' echoing again and again along the street. I listened to the water, like the sound of wheels spinning inside my head. Water running down the drainpipes and gurgling away into the sewers. Herringbone patterns rushing into the drains. Broken gutters where the water came spurting out in a fountain across the pavement until the whole city was turned into one great water feature.

I was angry. I even had time to feel betrayed. There were so many unanswered questions in my own head. Who made the anonymous phone call on the night? I refused to even think that Kevin would have done such a thing, calling the Garda station and putting on a Polish accent. A friend would not do that.

The following day, I quit working for the building company I was employed with. It was important to avoid running into the electrician or any of his mates. I got a job sanding floors instead, which was not ideal, and it made more sense to get out of the building trade altogether. It was best to lie low for a while, until this was all over.

I went back to security work. But it was not my style, standing around outside bars and night clubs in a black suit, looking people up and down and refusing entry. Not much better hanging around the door of a pharmacy all day. I decided to stop that and took up a job in a restaurant. I kept my hand in, doing a bit of carpentry work here and there with my friend Darius. But it was Kevin who really helped me out in the end, bringing me back to his mother's house. She was so happy with the black ash wardrobes that she wanted me to do more work. The back door to begin with. It was falling apart and totally unsafe from a security point of view. You could almost walk in without even having to turn the handle. So they wanted me to put in a decent hardwood door with a proper three-lever mortise lock.

That kept me going for the time being and made me feel I was still part of the family at least.

8

It would take a good nine months or more for the court case to come up, so there was lots of time to sit around and agonise over the situation. Better to go out and have a good time while I was waiting, Kevin advised me. What helped to take my mind off things was that I found a girlfriend. Her name was Liuda and she was from Moldova, working here as a beautician on a temporary visa. I got talking to her at the pharmacy where she was promoting some skin-care products and we started going out.

I felt badly not telling her that I was charged with assault, but she was better off not knowing anything about that.

We got on very well together and maybe immigrants were better off sticking together, I thought, because we might have more in common. Put it this way, we both knew what it was like to live away from home and what a comfort it was to float around in each other's arms. When it came to sex, you could say that we spoke the same language. Some of the things she did with her body gave me such a rush of blood to the head that I forgot everything. She was so full of stage-craft and imagination that I could never think of anything else but the act of making love itself. Her legs. Her mouth. Her breasts pointed slightly upwards at the tops of trees somewhere. Everything about her in bed demanded such full attention that I could not concentrate on anything other than the specific details of her body. The incredibly soft areas on the inside of her thighs. The brush of her nipple against the side of my face. All those breathy voicemail sounds in my ears. The encounter with her seemed to prohibit all memory. For instance, I could not remember any old people. I could not get myself to remember any dead people either. She distracted me from thinking about the news, about war and climate change, disasters of any sort, like famine and poverty and people dying of AIDS. She produced such a powerful urge in me, pulling me so vigorously inside herself that I became truly blank. In other words, we were fucking to forget. We created this little enclave of love and sex which inhibited us from getting a proper foothold in the real world.

Yes. You could say it was love, but there was no future in it. Under the circumstances, with my court case coming up and her being here on a temporary visa, it seemed pointless for us to accumulate too many memories together.

We did all the right things. We went for picnics in the Phoenix Park. We spent time at the Zoo. We went walking along the pier together. We took photos of each other with all the local landmarks in the background. Her eyes caught the sunlight – glossy, hazel-brown pebbles at the bottom of a stream. She came from a place where they still had bears and wolves and numberless trees, where nature might still make a big comeback some day. We heard the sound of the accordion coming and going on the breeze. We passed by the man from Romania playing a gypsy waltz and wondered why we had left home in the first place. We remembered the same kind of things, the sight of villages and church spires and headscarves and open shirts and unshaven smiles in the fields. We felt close to each other – same nostalgia, same tug of self-loathing, same shock of familiar tastes and images from which we had walked away.

In the long run, we were only preventing each other from integrating and moving ahead. It was there in our eyes, in the kind of choices we made, the places we went to, the kind of things we purchased that didn't cost too much, like ice-cream cones.

For instance, one day I brought her to a place called Howth. It's meant to be beautiful out there. Famous too, because this was the location where the writer James Joyce first made love to his future wife Nora, something which is commemorated publicly on the sixteenth of June every year in a national celebration of sex and literature and first love. People told me that Ireland used to be sexually repressed, but you'd never think it now, would you?

Howth was just another hill, basically, with a big golf course and some wealthy villas and gates and planes landing nearby at the airport. It didn't really mean anything to us. When I gave Liuda the relevant tourist information, she shrugged as though I was talking about a past lover. We walked around and sat on a bench. We felt the dampness in the air, rising up into our shoulders. We gazed at the clouds moving fast overhead, which made us want to hold on to the bench with our hands. We kissed and touched, but we couldn't really connect to the place. It was a mistake to bring her out there because it already belonged to somebody else. We were the latecomers. She looked lonely and pale, so we didn't stay very long.

'Come on, Vid. I'm cold,' she said.

There was quite a breeze blowing and she started rubbing her arms. As we got up and walked back, I spotted a used condom hanging like a pink piece of stripped fruit in the gorse bushes. I deflected her attention, pointing eagerly like a child at the lighthouse, but I think she had seen the condom before me and didn't mention it out of courtesy.

We were both dragging our feet. When you come from somewhere else, you develop all these prejudices about the people of this country being superior, more funny, more gifted with language and jokes. She said Irish women were strong and very independent. She wanted to learn that. Every time we stared into each other's eyes, we were reminded only of our own inadequacies. We had to be realistic, I suppose. We were both on the lookout for something better. There was something missing, something preventing us from committing fully to this love in a damp climate.

We stuck it out together for about six months, but there was never any mention of us moving in together permanently. And the idea of setting up a family seemed completely out of the question. Think of it. We would remain strangers to our own children. We would be like two homesick parents, living in a fantasy. Lacking essential local knowledge. Routine stuff that everybody knows around here. Our children laughing at us and correcting our mistakes. Talking to us like we were deaf and blind and had no idea what was going on in the real world outside. We would speak to them in a foreign language and they would never get used to what we sounded like in our own mother tongue. It would remain a life of confusion and contradiction and naturally occurring blasphemies.

I tried to integrate her as much as possible into my life, but it never worked out. One night, I brought Liuda with me to meet Kevin and Helen, but that was a bit of a disaster. Nobody knew what to say except Kevin. He couldn't take his eyes off Liuda all night. Kept talking only to her as though myself and Helen were not even present.

Liuda was very shy in his presence and hardly said a word. Helen was even more silent, almost aloof. The only thing she said all night was to mention Dursey Island.

'I believe the cable car is down,' she said, and Kevin looked up with great surprise, wondering where this thought had slipped out from. 'They have a new one ordered from Germany,' she added. 'So I read in the paper.'

We had more fun on our own, Liuda and myself. At least we had love and sex, like living on our own island. We could also talk about our observations as outsiders, without offending anyone. We spoke about some of the funny things, the contradictions we experienced here. I loved listening to her talking about her clients and how envious they were of her complexion. She told me how Irish women often hated their own skin. They wanted the make-up lashed on thick. 'Does my face look like a plate of chips?' they sometimes joked. And how could you answer that? Beauty therapy was not about being honest but about making the customers feel good.

We agreed that people here didn't want the straight answer all the time. They needed lots of praise. They loved exaggeration. They used compliments like mind-altering substances. She was on commission for skin-care products, so she got used to telling people that they looked gorgeous, cool, brilliant, absolutely amazing – out of this world.

She told me the story of how she came here. She met an Irish businessman who was in Moldova sourcing timber. She ran into him in a bar and he offered to get her a job. Paid for her flight over and put her up. She was nervous because she had heard about girls getting their passports taken off them when they arrived. But her passport didn't matter as much as her visa, which put her at the mercy of her employer. She could not work for anyone else. So she lived with him and slept with him and cooked for him and worked in the office of his joinery firm.

Once he got tired of her, he allowed the permit to lapse. When he came back from another business trip with a new woman from São Paulo and a consignment of hardwoods that he swore were not from the rainforest, Liuda had to move out and find herself a new employer who would apply for a new visa. Asshole, she called him, and it made me laugh to hear her putting the emphasis in the wrong place. Ass-HOLE.

Inevitably, she was taken out of my hands, as the saying goes.

We were in a bar together one night and this guy came up to me in the jacks, talking about her. He was staggering around the place, pissing dangerously beside me in his urinal, chasing the green, pine-smelling dice around in circles with the force of his flush.

'Come here,' he said, zipping up. 'Is that your girlfriend?'

'What?'

Out in the corridor, he held my arm and smiled with great sincerity. He had something important to tell me.

'I just want to let you know that your girlfriend has the most beautiful arse I've ever seen. I'm not joking you. I've never seen such a beautiful arse before in my whole life.'

What was I meant to say? Thanks?

'No offence, like. I'm just saying, in case you haven't noticed.'

He had me cornered.

'Come 'ere. Is she a model or something?'

I smiled and tried my best to walk away, but he insisted on shaking my hand to congratulate me.

'Look, I hope you don't think I'm coming on to her or anything like that. I'm just telling you the truth, that's all. Her arse is only fucking amazing. You should be proud of yourself.'

He was right of course. Liuda was wearing incredibly tight jeans with zips across the back pockets like long, silver eyelashes, fast asleep. And knee-high boots. I could never really understand the boots, or the jeans for that matter, but that was the whole idea, wasn't it, attracting lots of attention to herself.

'Only messing,' he said, putting his arm around me. 'I'm just having the craic, that's all.'

He leaned on me all the way back towards the bar. I could hardly interpret this as a form of aggression, because he was being so friendly.

'I was just remarking to your man here,' he continued, nodding to me but speaking directly to Liuda this time. 'You have the most perfect arse that ever came into this country.'

He waited for her to smile.

'There's no woman anywhere around here to match you.'

I thought she might have been offended, for my sake. But this was really her opportunity to land on her feet at last, so I could not allow myself to stand in the way.

I became a has-been. I felt like shit. All my inadequacies like a tray of cakes on display in front of the world. I tried telling myself that she was the traditional sort of woman, expressing her femininity, enjoying the attention she got, not only from men but also from the jealous eyes of women who wanted to tear their false nails across her face. I told myself that I was the more progressive type, adjusted to the give and take of love, while she was still nostalgic for the time when men were men and women were women. I think she expected me to be more of a man than I appeared to be. Protective. Knowing what to do in case of emergency.

Look, I'm a lover, I wanted to say to her, not a fire-fighter. I didn't know how to stand up for her in a row.

'He's only messing,' I tried to warn her.

'Look, Vid,' she smiled, 'we both know this is going nowhere, you and me. We're in the wrong place.'

It didn't help that I was working in a restaurant at the time, in the kitchens, coming back home every night with a heavy film of grease on my face and the stink of chicken breasts in my clothes. Early bird all night. No matter how much I showered, it would not remove the toxic residue of cooking. Each plate with criss-crossed potato wedges built up like sleepers in a railway yard. And the amount of salt they piled on to make it taste better. Then one night the manager, who must have been only nineteen years of age and looked more like fifteen, came up to me and said it was my duty to clean the toilets. They were covered in vomit. You could read the menu in small print all over the floor and the walls. I told him I wouldn't do it. He said he under-stood my position. But then he told me that refusal was not an option and threatened dismissal. He informed me that everyone took their turn cleaning the toilets, so I told him he could have my turn and left.

I walked out along the pier at Dún Laoghaire harbour. I had a small apartment out there, not far from where Kevin's mother lived. It was handy, because he was giving me more and more work at the house, so I could walk there from my place.

The wind was quite strong that night. The sailing boats

were being tossed around and the guy ropes made a ringing melody against the masts. All kinds of things banging and squeaking and set loose. I was wondering if Liuda had already deleted the photos on her phone, taken at the bandstand by the accordion player from Sighişoara. The sea was churned up and as I walked around by the elbow of the pier, the wind was like a hand on my chest. A big bouncer preventing me from walking any further, pushing the words back into my mouth.

9

As the date of the trial began to come closer, Kevin called me over to his mother's house to discuss a bigger job. Something quite substantial. His mother had been complaining for years that the floorboards in the front room were running in the wrong direction. She wanted them turned around so they would run lengthways, towards the front window rather than laterally across the room towards the fireplace. The original builder had made a right mess of things. It made the house feel small and claustrophobic.

I was the first to agree with them for aesthetic reasons, but I knew immediately that it was not worth correcting at this point, purely on financial grounds. I told them so, but the cost was not really seen as a barrier any more. Apparently she had inherited money lately from a relative in the USA, so they felt it was the right time to get it done.

I was thrilled to get back into serious carpentry again, especially a big job like this where I could really prove myself. But I was not sure it made sense. The thought crossed my mind that I was possibly being re-employed each time because of the imminent court proceedings. He was utterly calm about the outcome, but he needed my absolute allegiance to the family. He knew the Garda would never come after him at this point, unless I lost faith and brought the whole story out into the open in the witness stand. He needed me to be completely on his side, and maybe this was a kind of payment in advance for the favour I was doing him.

He reminded me from time to time not to say a word to anyone. And maybe he needed to isolate me a little from the threat of new friends who might start asking questions. He explained things to me about this country, how friendship often masqueraded as curiosity. He tried to teach me the art of answering a question with another question. He told me there was a secret language here, not the old, Irish language or the English language, but something in between the lines, like a code.

'This is an island,' he pointed out to me once. 'You can never completely trust what you hear. You have to forecast what's behind the words. You have to be able to read people's inner thoughts. You have to be able to think on your feet and keep ahead of them.'

Perhaps he was speaking as much to himself as he was counselling me. I listened to his advice eagerly. But you can't learn all that street-wise acumen like a faculty. You can't pick it up like chess or tennis. So he felt it was his duty to protect me and look out for me.

His mother must have known nothing about the case, otherwise she would not have wanted me in the house. She had her arms folded as we stood in the front room looking around. Kevin half sitting on one of the radiators, allowing the full force of her tenacity to work on me.

'It's a shocking waste of money,' I repeated, but then I heard her big sigh gathering once more, like a gale coming.

I tried to put her off with a rough estimate. I told her it would take months to get finished. All the floorboards taken up. All the joists underneath would have to be turned around. There would be a lot of wastage, new joists, broken floorboards to be replaced. All the noise. Sawdust all over the house.

I was doing myself out of a job, but my instinct was to tell her straight out how insane this was. I didn't have the nerve to say it so bluntly. That was something else I hadn't learned yet. How to say no. How to prevaricate. How to play the long finger. How to make people think you said YES when you're actually saying NO WAY, out of the question. It's impossible to learn that stuff because it usually sounded so false coming from me. You must be out of your mind, Mrs Concannon. Turning the floorboards around. Are you serious? I searched hard and came up with a borrowed phrase which I had heard on one of the building sites.

'Ah, go easy on me, Mrs Concannon.'

But that didn't scare her off either. She only stared at me with great disappointment in her eyes.

'I would prefer you to be honest with me,' she said. 'If you don't want to do it, that's fine.'

'You'll be well looked after,' Kevin added.

How could I refuse? She had her heart set on it and there was no turning back. She asked me to name the price. I told her I would have to come back and measure up first. I tried to backtrack. I tried to tell her that I was not really qualified to take on such a big job. But that only made them both smile. The wardrobes and the back door and various other small jobs I had carried out in the meantime had already given them more than enough proof of my qualifications. I reminded her how long the project would take.

'You'll never get rid of me,' I said, as a joke.

'That's fine. We're not in a hurry.'

There were thousands of carpenters around who would love to take on the job. With her kind of money, she could pick the best in the country. But they had singled me out, because I had become a loyal and trusting friend.

'You're like part of the family now,' Kevin said. She nodded and I was so overwhelmed by the welcome that I even imagined myself receiving a certificate, rolled up with a ribbon, stating that I belonged here.

And that's how I took up semi-permanent employment with the Concannons. I became self-employed and even began to pay my own taxes to keep everything straight. I was getting on like a house on fire, as they would say, given a key and told to come and go as I pleased.

I began by removing the furniture from the two living rooms, front and back. I was very glad to be able to call on Darius to come and help me clear the rooms, lifting out sideboards and book cases and sofas, storing them around the house with sheets draped over them. The dining-room table was placed away into the conservatory. I made sure to carry all the porcelain service and other precious objects myself.

Darius had been here in this country a lot longer than myself. He was married to an Irish girl and had one child, though they were separated. He saw the boy once a week, but that was the height of his participation. You could see that he was upset about it, but he always remained cheerful, always suppressing his sadness and making jokes while working, using Irish phrases that didn't make any sense to me.

'Game ball,' he kept repeating for no reason.

Like everyone else, Darius wanted to know my biography, pre-arrival. He asked what my father did and I told him he worked in import–export of some sort, before he died.

'Import–export,' he said, looking at me. 'You mean he was in the secret police?'

There was nothing I could say to deny that. He laughed and said his own family were also in with the secret police.

'My mother turned out to be the village informer,' he said.

We left it there. We had plenty of other things to talk about. I would need Darius later on for some of the tricky parts, but in the meantime he went back to his work while I began the job on the floor in earnest, on my own.

I got to know Kevin's two younger sisters, Jane and Ellis. Ellis was not getting on so well with her mother, I could not help noticing. She was meant to be preparing for her final exams in school, but she was doing nothing. They were constantly fighting and I tried to avoid overhearing some of the shouting between them. Ellis had a large diagram of male genitalia on her wall. I had seen that while I was working on the wardrobes. Now I could feel the intensity of her gaze whenever she saw me in the house. I could also smell the distinct scent of weed, or whatever, coming down the stairs from her room whenever her mother was out. The older sister Jane had a masculine appearance in her face, but she was far more studious, more balanced and normal, maybe.

In the afternoons, it was back to cups of tea and chats with Mrs Concannon, after she came home from school. It even got to the point where she asked me to call her by her first name, Rita. But I had difficulty with that much familiarity, since I was still, basically, an employee.

One afternoon, while I was in the kitchen, I came across a number of personal items belonging to her, lying on a chair. Since the discovery of the unopened letters in her bedroom, I was sometimes afraid of what I might find around the place. Things which I might not be able to conceal once they entered into my head. Folded on the chair were some items of underwear, a pair of her stockings and a brassiere. I could not help noticing that one of the cups in the bra had been filled with silicone. A false breast.

I got on with the work and later that afternoon, when she made a cup of coffee, the items were gone. She stared at me and brought the matter up.

'I'm sorry that you had to see those things,' she said.

'What's that?' I said.

'What I left on the chair,' she said. 'I must apologise.'

I tried out the rules of silence which I had learned from Kevin. I pretended not to know what she was talking about and I think she got impatient with my stupidity.

'The bra, for God's sake.'

'Oh that,' I said.

'You see, I had cancer.'

'I'm very sorry to hear that,' I said.

'My friends from school brought me on a pilgrimage to Lough Derg.'

She told me that she had gone to boarding school in Dublin, a convent school. Her friends from class still met for a book club each month. She was kept in the loop with emails informing her of deaths and marriages. Every week, somebody's mother or some former nun was dying. She received messages about girls in her class who were ill or in difficulty. Then it was herself who was diagnosed with cancer and became the subject of the emails. They brought her to Lough Derg for a day. Not that many of them were very religious any more, but it was a nice way of keeping in touch and doing things for each other in times of need.

It was all the cigarettes she smoked in her early life, all the 'fags', as she put it, which her husband had forced on her

71

while they lived in London. It was the first time she mentioned her husband, and then only in the past tense. She said he was a great smoker and a great singer, which was not really intended as a compliment. A man whose life evaporated with smoke and songs.

I had noticed a packet of Marlboro cigarettes in a glass case in the living room while I measured up for the floorboards. It was there, she said, more as a symbol. A deterrent. The last, un-smoked packet of cigarettes in her life, perhaps also keeping him away.

'Are you going to be fine?' I asked.

'I haven't got the all-clear yet,' she said. 'But the prognosis looks good.'

She said the worst part of it was the initial tests and all the worry it caused in the family. She was afraid not so much of dying but of leaving her children, who still needed her. Once the diagnosis had been made, it was easier to fight it and be strong. And once she had fought this off, she could fight off anything that came her way.

She said she felt lucky to be still among the living and I agreed with her. It was good to be alive.

She was still young and beautiful and strong. It happens sometimes that I think of the most inappropriate things, maybe because I feel so out of place and away from my own rules. I thought of the phantom silicone breast wobbling in my hand. I could not help seeing her naked in front of me, with one breast missing completely as though it had been ripped away. A surgeon's gash like a red zip across the left side of her chest. For some reason, I thought one breast was as good as none. It was only as a pair that certain things worked. Only in companionship that breasts mattered, like two eyes or two ears or two hands. It was a question of

72

balance. These were some of the absurd thoughts I had in my head but which I didn't express, even though we were looking at each other in such an awkward way and there were plenty of silent moments for me to fall into with words that were not fit to be said.

'I hope,' I said nervously, 'I hope you will get the all-clear soon.'

'Thanks, Vid,' she said.

And maybe that's the true certificate of belonging, when somebody allows you to worry about them and be happy that they're still alive.

10

The big job on the floor was well under way. It was a change from working in restaurants, I can tell you, or standing around as a security guard in a pharmacy all day, trying to keep a gang of children from storming the place. Even worse when there was nothing going on and I had all this time to think about myself and what was about to happen.

Even if the work at the Concannon house didn't exactly make sense to me, I was happy to be doing it. Turning around the floorboards was not what the house needed most. I could have suggested a million other improvements on which she could have spent the Irish rancher's money, like insulation for example. The casement window downstairs was like a sieve, letting the gale straight in from the sea across the living room. The house had great charm, though it could be a big, draughty place. And cold. And damp. The walls could have done with dry-lining to improve the energy efficiency rating. Not to mention the touches of mould, black patches left behind the book case, at the backs of the sofas.

I got on with it and forced all doubt out of my head. Sometimes it's better to carry on and not ask too many questions, otherwise you'd never even get started.

There were two large rooms in question, with interlinking

wooden doors. Out of curiosity, I asked some of the neighbours on the terrace, like the old woman next door, for instance, if they also had the floorboards running the same way. It turned out the Concannon house was unique. A one-off. It seemed that the original builder must have acted on a specific request to run the floors laterally in the rooms downstairs. The hallway was done as normal, lengthways up to the front door. Upstairs also, running towards the casement window. The houses were over a hundred years old and took a decade to build. And here I was, almost a century later, soaking up good money to put things right.

I began with the skirting boards and then loosened the floorboards at the edge of the rooms, working in reverse order. Reading history backwards, you might say. Retracing your steps. You could not avoid doing some damage to the outer boards. But that didn't cause me too much concern, because this was all going back in a different order. You should have seen the savaging the plumbers had already done to some of the boards when they put in the central heating pipes and the radiators. They should have been brought back by the ears to look at what they did. No need for that kind of destruction.

Once I got the outer boards up, it was easy to get a hammer underneath to lift the next one with minimal damage. Even better with a small angled crowbar.

I de-nailed each plank as I went along. It was great to hear the squeak of nails, like the cork coming out of a bottle. Some of them were almost fused into the wood. It was hard not to do some damage because it was tongue and groove, gone quite dry over time, breaking off in big splinters. In any case, it could all be repaired and filled in later. I stacked the planks carefully in the hall, by the door. I found all kinds of stuff under the floor, like a bit of domestic archaeology. Ancient cartons of cigarettes that the original workmen must have left behind. Craven A – such an appropriate brand name. Nibbled at by rodents. Old beer bottles. Some coins. A black dice. Hairclips and combs and a knitting needle which had fallen down through a hole in the floor. Empty cement bags from long ago. A dead rat that had dried out with time and looked more like a dusty leather glove.

The biggest part of the job was getting the joists out and turning them around. The simplest thing was to cut them along the wall. They were set in across little supporting walls built up in the middle, which was great, because it meant some of the wood could be re-used. The outer walls were full of granite boulders, so I was not going to touch them, apart from injecting damp-proof fluid into cavities. Ultimately, I would have to construct a new foundation, an inner wall up to floor height, just inside the main walls, leaving sufficient room for ventilation. Otherwise they would have serious problems with condensation.

It was all new to me. I needed advice. Darius had never done a job like this either, so I decided to check it out with some of the local builders who knew these old houses.

There was a bar in Dún Laoghaire where I could discuss the matter casually with experts. The advice centre is what I called it to myself, because you could find experts on all subjects there. It was like an Almanac, run by three elderly brothers, frequented mostly by older men sitting on the bar stools and women in the snug, singing songs on a Sunday night. They left the Christmas lights up all year round. They had a portrait of Jack Charlton behind the bar and also a plaster cast of Laurel and Hardy joined at the shoulders. The men's toilets were out in the yard. Follow your nose, they said to me. Apparently the women's toilets were in the house next door, where two of the brothers lived and where they had a full-size snooker table upstairs in the living room.

There was an expert on everything from rat catching to cleaning materials – leather, tiles, linen, you name it. Experts on all kinds of bygone practices such as stippled ceilings and embossed wallpaper. The women were experts on jiving and Sinatra lyrics and celebrity data going back decades, before I was even born. They could still remember darning socks and seeing horses on the streets. And periwinkles. One of them remembered a woman selling periwinkles on the main street, something only the Chinese people eat now and which you saw them collecting on the shore sometimes.

They were all experts on soccer and current affairs and history, and they had a way of reducing world events down to size.

'Do you see those bar stools?' one of men said to me one night. 'They've survived two world wars.'

When it came to building matters, the advice could be conflicting. Once I outlined the project to them, turning the floorboards around in a house that was constructed over a hundred years ago, the entire pub got into the discussion, barmen and all, even the women.

'God love you, son.'

'They want me to run them back to front,' I explained.

'Ah here, you need your head examined.'

They could only assume that I was getting handy money for it. Some of them said they wouldn't touch it for love nor money.

'It's a folly,' one of them said.

'Better you than me, Gunga Din.'

I wondered if that was meant to convey something else.

A message about the family I was dealing with, more than the job itself. Some hint that what I had undertaken, nobody else in his right mind would even attempt. As a warning, one of them began to recount a story of doing a job in a house nearby where he was treated 'like one of the family'. Everybody laughed. I didn't know what was so funny, until I realised that being treated like one of the family was maybe not always the best thing you could hope for.

'Jesus, can we not talk about something else for a change?' one of them eventually muttered. Because they were also experts on other things like scandals and corruption and crime, solved and unsolved murders going years back, serial killers, in particular DNA evidence and sexual crimes which they read about in the newspapers and seemed to know off by heart. They could reconstruct the details and the time-line in each case with forensic precision.

At times I felt that I had crossed over to the other side. Whenever they started talking about a particular crime, describing some mutilated body or the mysterious circumstances around a death, I felt I was a suspect. I kept nodding, letting on that I was just as concerned about the crime rate as they were, but I always felt guilty and ready to confess.

Kevin reminded me from time to time not to reveal anything about the Concannon family in public, because the news had a way of travelling ahead of you in this country. You said something in one bar and it was there before you reached the next bar. The big gossip jump, he called it. Besides, with my position working at the house, I was entrusted with some very personal information which was best kept close to my chest. The rules of friendship included a code of client confidentiality.

'And don't let my mother interrogate you either,' he said.

He made it sound like a security issue and I assured him I was not likely to spill anything.

But it was hard to sidestep his mother's questions. In the afternoons, Mrs Concannon, or Rita, as she wanted me to call her, would sometimes make a pot of tea and put scones on a plate in the kitchen in order to get information out of me. It was worse than being at the Garda station because there you had the right to remain silent.

I think she was a little disappointed because I had so little to tell her about myself. As if the family trust into which I had been received had not been reciprocated on my part.

'Both my parents were killed in a car crash,' I told her, but it sounded like a prepared statement at this stage. 'I survived the crash, but I spent months under observation for brain trauma.'

'But you must remember something about your family, your childhood?'

'I wish I could.'

'Nothing at all,' she said. 'That's incredible.'

'I can remember getting my first job in a petrol station,' I said. 'I remember somebody asking me for a litre of petrol in a can that held only a half litre, so the petrol went all over the street.'

'Everybody remembers the smell of petrol,' she said dismissively.

The information was of no value to her. She stared at me, hoping I would crack under the pressure. I could have told her about coming home from school on the bus when I was a boy, falling asleep and waking up with an erection when it was time for me to get off. The unwanted erection. Every time it came to my stop, there was this thing I had to hide with my schoolbag in front of me.

'You must have relatives back home. Are you in contact with them at all?'

'I have an older sister, Branka,' I said. 'We keep in touch by email.'

'Don't you need to go back and see her?' she asked. 'Go and visit your parents' grave? See where you grew up? Your friends?'

'I had good friends in Belgrade,' I said. 'It's a great place for the night life and the music.'

There was something utterly irrelevant about my answers that frustrated her. It seemed to make me less trustworthy. What person has no family and no memory at all of his background, like there was a fire and all the archives got burned? I didn't like making her angry, but you have to understand, she was still on chemo treatment.

'I think there's something you're not fucking telling me,' she said.

'Honestly, Mrs Rita,' I said. 'I really have no memory of anything.'

'Vid, there's obviously something you don't want to talk about.'

'I swear. My sister keeps telling me things but I have no recollection at all myself, I'm afraid.'

'What you need is a girlfriend,' she said, smiling bitterly at her own failure to extract anything. 'She'll make you remember, all right. Wait till you see. Some nice young Irish girl will get it all out of you.'

There was something very stern about her eyes that looked almost masculine. What made her angry was my inability to enter into the common trade of personal information. The practice here is to give a bit and then you receive a bit in return. People tell you their misfortune, like a short-term

80

investment, expecting immediate returns. I could see that I was a big let-down, because I possessed so little by way of family calamities, only the obvious fact that my parents were no longer around and that I had left my home country behind.

I tried to make up for my lack of gossip by doing her other small favours. I went out of my way to fix a silver teapot which she had got as a wedding present. Even if the marriage had not lasted, the silver teapot was still in existence. But the wooden knob on the lid had cracked and broken off, making it impossible to lift the hot lid, except with the aid of a spoon. So I fixed it temporarily. I screwed in a replacement knob, made from the black dice which I had found under the floorboards. It looked a bit funny, I would admit, but it had the number six facing up. She laughed and gave me the word for that part. The finial, she called it. Originally, it was made of pear wood, same as the handle. I asked Darius to turn a new finial for me, but for the moment, she had the dice coming up lucky each time she made the tea.

We got on fairly well together. She came in occasionally to check my work and asked me to take a look at a spot in the foundations to see if it was dry rot. I put her mind at rest. It was nothing but white dust emerging from the cement.

Then she laughed at me because I had black marks all over my face. The floorboards were covered underneath in a fine black fur from a hundred years of coal fires, smoke and soot which was sucked down by the ventilation.

One day, I noticed that she had changed her hair and thought it would be impolite not to mention it. The colour was a more sandy shade, and she looked really well, I thought. So while I was in the kitchen later that afternoon, I remarked on it discreetly and told her that she had picked a good colour, very natural.

'Thanks,' she said.

As we were talking, I told her that my mother once changed her hair colour when I was a boy and I couldn't recognise her. The only way that I could be sure it was my own mother was by going up close to her and closing my eyes and smelling her arm.

'I thought you couldn't remember anything,' she snapped.

I had gone too far. Her hair was none of my business and I returned to being a worker again. She was making it clear that I was not really invited to take part in the free trade of information. She stared with her schoolteacher eyes, scaring the living daylights out of me, as though she already knew everything about me and was only waiting for me to come clean and confess the whole thing. She was not going to stand there with her backside to the cooker listening to me blathering all kinds of innocent stuff from my childhood that was of no use to her. Hard facts, she wanted. The full story, with no lies or half-lies. She didn't want excuses. She didn't want compliments. She didn't want me begging for sympathy and saying I was in hospital and had a valid reason for not remembering anything. She wanted the cold blue information laid out before her. If there was any conversation to flow between us, it would be strictly on her terms. Not something given freely or volunteered, but more like minerals extracted from a mountain.

11

Coming up to the date of the trial, Kevin appointed a senior counsel to the case and brought me into an office in the city centre where I was introduced to a man named Barrington. He was older and more weary. We were left alone together and he asked me to sit down while he examined the file for a couple of minutes, then looked up with his eyes wide as possible, frowning like an accordion across his forehead.

'Vid,' he said, shaking his head as though he would have a problem with my name in court and needed something more respectable. 'Is that the short for something?'

'No, it's just Vid.'

'David, maybe?'

'If you like,' I said.

'We have a problem, Vid. The prosecution say they have another witness.'

'That's impossible,' I said.

'Why's that?'

'He was alone,' I said, with great certainty. 'The electrician. There was nobody else around, just him and us.'

He stared at me, then dropped the file out of his hands. I realised that what I had just said was self-incriminating.

'We'll see how things go in court and make a decision on whether to call you as a witness.'

He pointed out to me that I could not be compelled to give evidence.

'My understanding is that you're from Serbia and that your memory isn't the best.'

'That's true,' I said.

He glanced down at the file again in despair, assessing the severity of the charges and the extent of the electrician's injuries.

'We'll do our best,' he said. 'It's hard to predict how this will go. You could end up facing a jail sentence, Vid. We would apply for the Probation Act, of course, but who knows? This is a very serious case.'

'What about my residence permit?' I asked.

'That will not be affected. If convicted, you may serve time in prison, and you will have a criminal record. But you won't be deported, if that's what you mean.'

'So I'll be free after that,' I said.

'Yes. Unless the victim comes after you for damages, but that's very unlikely. You have no money, no property?'

'No,' I said.

And that was it. The meeting was over and I was back out again walking down the street with Kevin. I felt the outcome of the trial had already been decided, but Kevin remained upbeat. He wanted me to show more confidence on the day.

'Take the sad immigrant look off your face, Vid. That's never going to work.'

He said this in an invented accent, somewhere between Polish and Russian. It made me wonder whether he really had made the anonymous phone call to the Garda station in that accent. What else was he doing when he disappeared that night and left us waiting? I put these suspicions out of my head. I didn't want to believe it. I went back to work and tried to concentrate as much as possible on the job.

Now and again I had short conversations with his sisters, Jane and Ellis, while they were coming and going. Jane kept to herself a bit more. She was stern and very studious. She was at university and had already received notification of a research fellowship in Limerick and would soon be moving out altogether. Ellis was just about to finish school. She was friendlier and also prettier, like her mother, with great dark curls falling around her face.

Ellis was meant to be studying for her exams, but she seemed to spend most of her spare time smoking dope in her room, as far as I could gather. She also got very depressed from time to time, her mother once told me. I was making a terrible noise, cutting the joists with the electric saw and sending the smell of sawdust all over the house, but Ellis took the volume even higher. She blasted off something simultaneously depressing and uplifting by Curt Cobain or even Leonard Cohen, just to piss her mother off. At other times she would sit silently in her room and it was only the radio in the kitchen, beaming obscene doses of happiness back up the stairs with boy-band lyrics, somebody appealing to his girlfriend to keep her mouth shut because it was far better for everyone concerned when she said nothing at all. Music wars all over the house, until Ellis eventually couldn't take it any more and came halfway down, leaning over the banisters, breaking a self-imposed vow of silence and shouting at her mother to turn off that 'fucking shite' immediately. It was wrecking her head and there was nothing as depressing as those Irish boy singers.

Another time, Ellis came to inspect my work and told me

right out that what I was doing was utterly useless. She walked across the joists, balancing like a tightrope walker. How could I stop her? She said the fireplace looked funny, out on its own, built up on blocks like a doll's house. She sat on the beams with her bare legs dangling, asking really stupid questions, like why did I come here and why did I decide to become a carpenter and get stuck working in this fucking house?

One evening, while her mother was out at a book club and Kevin and I were having a quick beer before going out drinking, Ellis made a lunge at me. Without warning, she came straight across the kitchen to embrace me.

'I love you,' she said, clasping her arms around my neck.

What could I do? Difficult to push her off me as if she was disgusting. Even more difficult to sit there and do nothing. I felt she was calling for help, begging me to save her from something.

'I love you. I love you. I love you.'

Kevin stood up and prised her away.

'I'm sorry about this, Vid.' Then he took her upstairs, gently but forcefully leading her by the arm.

He spent over twenty minutes up there talking to her. I could hear her crying.

Did she expect me to liberate her? Escape with her out to the west of Ireland and live a sustainable existence, all organic and home grown? Getting stoned on nature, with the curls around her face and the sound of Nirvana?

'She's only a child,' he said to me later on.

'I'm sorry.'

'Not your fault, Vid.'

In the pub, he explained to me that she missed her father. She was tormented by the fact that she had been abandoned by him. She had gone for counselling all through her teenage years, but none of it helped. The absence was destroying her. She had built up dream images of him in London. Fantasised about him coming back with toys for her. Waited for him by the window at night, listening out for his footsteps in the street.

It struck me that, apart from the wedding photos which were stored away upstairs in the bedroom, I still had not come across a single photograph of their father anywhere in the house.

'You see, Vid, we're afraid she will throw herself at any man in the hope of finding a father.'

What was that saying about me?

I've never liked asking questions. I think the main reason for this is that it might invite too many counter-questions. I prefer to wait for people to tell me things, because the information has a way of finding you in the end.

And sure enough, later on that night, as we went for a late walk after the bars were closing, the real revelation came in its own time. It came looking for me as we stood on the pier together.

We were on the lower ledge. We passed by people drinking and some girls screeching like herons, as he put it. We passed by the bandstand where I had taken some photos of Liuda. We came past a brass plaque on the wall which had been erected in commemoration of the writer Samuel Beckett but which didn't mean very much to me until Kevin told me about it. The plaque was there to mark the place where the writer was supposed to have had an epiphany, but which he may have had somewhere else altogether, only that the pier seemed more convenient. He read out some of the writer's words, which were inscribed on the plaque, and pointed out some of the features mentioned in the text that were very close to us, such as the lighthouse and the wind gauge. The extract ended with the words 'clear to me at last . . .'

'They missed the point,' Kevin said, with some irony in his voice. 'They left out the most important part of all. Either they didn't understand what the writer meant, or else they were afraid to put it in because people walking up and down here in the summer would be freaked out.'

'. . . *clear to me at last that the dark I have always struggled to keep under is in reality my most . . .*'

He spoke about the dark and how it was kept under. We walked all the way up to the lighthouse.

'There is a place on the Aran Islands,' he began. 'It's called *Bean Bháite*, which is the Irish for drowned woman.'

We were not facing each other but standing side by side, an easier way of coming to the truth. He spoke straight out across the water, in the same wide arc as the light of the lighthouse, swirling around the bay in a circle.

'I've been there,' he said to me. 'On Inishmore, the largest of the islands. It's in a place not far from the harbour at Kilronan. A woman's body was washed ashore there once and they remembered it ever since by calling the place after her.'

He told me that he was related to the drowned woman on his father's side.

'She was an aunt,' he said. 'From Furbo, in Connemara, where my father is from. Nobody knew if she drowned herself or whether she was drowned by somebody else. She was the subject of controversy at the time. She was pregnant and not married. The priest in the local church denounced her from the altar. He said that if the men in the area were not men enough to drown her, then perhaps she would have the decency to drown herself.'

He didn't want me to talk to his mother about it, but it was possibly an explanation for the darkness in his family. All the trouble with Ellis came from their father's side. But was it also an explanation for himself, I asked myself.

The place where his aunt was found was not signposted or written down on any of the maps. Not like the Black Fort on the edge of the cliffs, he explained, where visitors went. The spot remained pretty much anonymous, remembered only in folklore by the event itself rather than by the name of the woman whose body was found there. Something unspeakable about her death which entered into the memory of the landscape.

'If you look at the maps,' he said, 'you can see how the tides would have brought her body from Furbo directly across Galway bay, out to the eastern coast of Inishmore.'

I imagined the parish priest speaking from the pulpit on a Sunday morning to denounce her. I remembered some of the things that Nurse Bridie told me and what happened in her lifetime, giving away her baby and never seeing her own son again. The story Kevin told me seemed not unlike the way the secret police operated in my own country and the paralysis that people felt in the face of authority.

If the men were not fit enough to drown her, then perhaps she would have the decency to drown herself. The words would have been spoken in Irish, he told me, sounding even worse in the old language.

From what he knew, the sea normally returns a drowned body nine days after it enters into the water and goes to the bottom. There is another likely time for it to be found, at twenty-one days. The returning body is often badly damaged, at times even partially decomposed and attacked by sealife. There are tests that could be done now to establish whether a person died before they entered the water, but these were not conclusive either. It was also difficult, even now apparently, to prove with complete certainty whether injuries to the body were suffered before drowning or after. People searching for drowning victims often kept an eye out for birds congregating in one place on the water. Was it possible in this case that the tides brought her across the bay more swiftly and that she was spared this mutilation?

'The sea shows no mercy,' he said.

I thought of her lying on the rocks where she was found. Her hair possibly the same colour as the seaweed, jumping with sea-lice. Her face, translucent and green as marble. Her dark eyes enlarged, maybe missing already, black cavities staring out with terror at the sky above her. The wind creating a sad, hollow note across her open mouth, her lips also perhaps the first to go missing and her teeth showing in a crying grimace. Her body cut from the rocks where the sea finally delivered her back to land. Raw bites and flesh-wounds which no longer bled. Her clothes torn. Bare feet swollen. White limbs laid out by the tide in a design of further disgrace.

Who knows? Perhaps there was one final touch of dignity, with one protective arm held lightly across her round, exposed belly with the child inside.

The big question remained unanswered after all this time. Did she drown herself or was she drowned by force? Was this a case of suicide or a case of murder, in other words? Because she seemed to have been drowned by force of the priest's words.

These things could only be answered by their absent father.

12

The day in court went like this. First of all Kevin and I met in a café nearby because he wanted to give me some encouragement before walking up to the Four Courts. I was nervous and distracted, unable to concentrate, looking away at the giant basket of freshly baked, steaming scones on the counter. I was wondering why the staff didn't let them cool down on a tray first, because they were turning back into dough under the soggy weight of each other. Then I saw that most of the staff were immigrants, like myself, so they must have been following the way things were done here for years without questioning.

'Barrington is going to blow this thing out of the water,' Kevin said with such confidence. I felt a lump in my throat. I couldn't speak, so I coughed instead.

What the prosecution claimed was absurd. Unable to identify who actually assaulted him in the street, the victim had picked the easiest target available and accused me, along with another unidentified non-national, of jumping on him in an unprovoked attack. He would claim that his daughter had rejected me and that I had used this as a motive to seek revenge against him. It was easy for him to find out my name and address from other workers in the building trade. His witness would testify that he saw me grab the electrician by the throat and hurl him against the hoarding, then kicking him repeatedly in the head and chest. After breaking his hip in the fall and spending weeks in hospital, he would give evidence that his quality of life had been seriously compromised as a result.

Our defence would be to insist that his identification of me was flawed and that I had no motive for the assault.

'It's riddled,' Kevin said, but he was only giving me false hope.

He winked at me and I became aware once more that I was doing him an enormous favour, standing in for him as a substitute. He would never forget this sacrifice. It placed our friendship on to the level of soldiers in action, ready to lay down their lives for one another. How many million medals were handed out for bravery to people who had no choice but to lose their lives in defence of their comrades? I felt the knot of friendship tightening and could not allow myself to forget that it was he who defended me on the night in question, that without me there would have been none of this trouble in the first place.

He was wearing a beautiful suit. I had never seen him look so handsome before. Helen turned up as well, though he seemed surprised by this and asked her what she was doing there. He made it clear to her that they could not sit side by side in court or even pretend that they knew each other.

'If he takes the rap for you,' she said to him in a low voice, 'we'll never be able to forgive ourselves.'

I was so happy that they had come to support me, separately, even though neither of them would play any part in the hearing itself. Helen wore a light brown linen jacket and a matching skirt which allowed you not to think too much of any movement underneath as she walked ahead of us.

My own suit was bought on eBay for half nothing. Made by Savile Row. The fit was not entirely right, but who was going to notice? By the time we walked along the quays and approached the entrance to the court, the suit began to feel too big. Passing by the people standing in anxious groups outside, smoking and whispering, staring at everyone in order to read their own future, I could only imagine what countless other lawbreakers had worn the suit before me, sweating at the crotch and answering to God knows what terrible crimes.

We met up with the defence lawyer in a consultation room. My mind went blank as Kevin and Barrington discussed the chances. They talked about the character of the presiding judge and Kevin seemed to be very optimistic. He said the judge might be on my side, but Barrington was not so sure. He looked grim and didn't seem to hold out much hope at all.

'We have significant difficulties,' he said.

The case before mine drew a lot of attention. It dealt with two young intruders who had broken into a villa overlooking the beach and terrorised the occupants, hanging the family dog in an execution ritual. The defence claimed that the men were not responsible for their actions because they had taken too many drugs. It was quite sensational, judging by the presence of reporters from the newspapers and by the severity of the sentence and the reaction in the public gallery.

There was an Irish harp on the wall of the court. It was there to remind those present what country they were in and under what jurisdiction this court was convened. It seemed to reinforce the understanding that any person outside the law was an enemy of the people, excluded from their respect. Floating above the judge's head, the harp was basically saying

93

that there was nothing better in the world than being Irish and anyone who brought this into disrepute was an offender and would be removed from the community.

From what I was told, the Irish had always been the innocent people who had things done to them in the past. They had never meant any harm to anyone else. They were loved by everybody all over the world. So it was a shock each time a crime came before the court that the Irish were now doing things to themselves that no oppressor would ever have dreamed of. All the people in court seemed Irish to me, the men in suits, the judge, the prosecution, the victim and his family of supporters in the gallery were all so Irish that I felt I didn't stand a chance.

The judge was not bad, I thought. He had a strong suntan and seemed fair-minded, though he got suddenly impatient and sighed heavily after he asked me how I pleaded.

'I'm innocent,' I said.

'I asked you if you plead guilty or not guilty?'

Barrington then announced that I was pleading not guilty and told me to repeat that out loud.

The Garda officers gave evidence of receiving an anonymous phone call from a male with a foreign accent, after which they found the victim lying in the street. They also gave evidence of arresting me after being positively identified by the witness. The electrician was there with his goatee beard and he put on a pair of steel-framed glasses to look a bit more intellectual. When he got his chance in the witness box, he said he was frightened even now, seeing me in court. He confirmed that he had picked me out in a line-up and that there was no doubt in his mind that it was my boot that kicked him repeatedly in the head. He claimed that he drank very little due to a potential diabetes problem and that he was a family man, not the type who sought trouble. What surprised me most was that his daughter was there in court, corroborating everything her father said when it was her turn in the witness stand. Barrington got a chance to question them, but their memory was flawless. The only thing that he was able to establish was that the victim could not have been on his way home, but the electrician said he only wanted to stretch his legs a little.

Most of the time, I kept glancing at Kevin and Helen, sitting apart from each other as if they had split up. It made me sad for them. Kevin seemed to have no fear of being identified. The electrician must have been so drunk on the night, I thought, that he could make no connection with Kevin, even though he sat behind him in the public gallery. It happens sometimes that you have great difficulty recognising people, like a shopkeeper you know well who leaves you tormenting yourself when you see him out of context.

I was distracted throughout the whole proceedings, thinking about Helen and Kevin. For their sake alone, I was hoping that I would not be convicted.

I remembered seeing her coming into a bar one night to meet him. She had been caught in a shower and was soaked to the skin. Her hair stuck down on her forehead. She came up behind him and put her hands over his eyes, winking at me, then allowing her cold red fingers to be prised apart slowly. When he turned around to embrace her, she sneaked a freezing hand underneath his shirt so he jumped. She brought the rain inside with her, on her face, on her red cheeks. She wiped a drop from her nose with her sleeve and shook the water out of her hair. She looked to me like she had lived her life outdoors, in caravans maybe. She had a husky voice that night, and drank a hot rum. Other men were looking at her all the time and this may have been a disadvantage, as though she wished that she was more ordinary and attracted less attention.

I could see that she felt sorry for me. She looked over with such an expression of regret, trying hard to apologise with a tiny smile.

The main prosecution argument hinged on one particular witness, an elderly man who happened to pass by at the time of the attack. He was relaxed and seemed better with words than any of the legal people. He was delighted to take the stand and had to be restrained from giving excessive evidence which was not directly related to the case. He explained that he had been walking his greyhound dog on the night in question and had witnessed the attack.

When it came to Barrington's turn to cross-examine the witness, he asked about the state of the victim after the alleged attack.

'He was within an inch of his life,' the witness testified.

'Would you mind telling the court why you didn't call for help?' Barrington asked.

'I don't know,' the witness answered. 'I should have done that, you're right, but you know, you don't always follow your own best advice. Sometimes you do what is most instinctive, like, the first thing that comes to mind, that is. Which was to go to help the man left lying on the ground.'

'It didn't occur to you to call an ambulance?'

'In hindsight, looking back, it took a while to sink in.'

'You say he was within an inch of his life, but you then decided to leave the scene. Is that right?'

'I was scared,' the witness responded. 'There was blood all over him. I was afraid they would come back and do the same to me.'

The witness told the court that it was only the following day when he read about the incident in the paper that he realised he had a duty to help with the investigation. He had already identified me to the court as the main instigator, the man who led the attack. He said he was not very good with names, but he never forgot a face. And the main distinguishing feature in this case was my unmistakable face.

The prosecution were winning hands down. I thought it was over, though Barrington persisted with roundabout questions about what the greyhound man worked at.

'I'm retired,' he said.

'What was your employment before you retired?'

'Electrical contractor.'

Barrington then began to take a personal interest in greyhound racing, as though he was the kind of person who would place a bet every now and again, in moderation.

'What's the name of your dog?' he asked.

'Slasher.'

'Slasher. That's a very good name for a greyhound.'

There was a short burst of laughter around the courtroom. Even the Garda officers present chuckled as much as they could without sounding false. Barrington asked him why he took his dog for a walk at night, and so far away from home. But that seemed like a stupid question, because you had to do that in order to train a dog for racing purposes.

'Has he won any races for you?' Barrington asked.

'Not yet,' the witness answered. 'But he's come second and third a few times, at Shelbourne Park, like.'

Then Barrington produced a list from his briefcase and walked over to the greyhound owner.

'Would you do me a favour,' he said. 'Could you point out the name of your greyhound on this list?'

For the first time, the greyhound owner stalled.

'He's not registered or anything, like.'

'If he's not registered with the coursing club,' Barrington said, 'then how come he's run track races?'

'He's a pet. They make great pets, you know.'

'So it's not true that you have a greyhound by the name of Slasher?' Barrington asked.

'Not exactly.'

'Are you trying to make a fool of us?'

'No way.'

'You're lying to the court, aren't you?'

'Well, maybe I exaggerated a bit,' the greyhound man said.

Barrington said he had no further questions. He told me there would be no need for me to give evidence at this point and I was glad not to have to stand in the witness box and speak in front of all those people. Barrington then had a quiet discussion with the judge and the prosecution, after which the greyhound man withdrew his testimony.

The judge gave his verdict, saying that there was an enormous difference between lying and not telling the truth, but, on balance, the prosecution evidence was no longer credible and he dismissed the case.

Simple as that. Everybody started packing their documents away and I was more surprised than anyone else, because it ended so quickly.

There was an expression of unconcealed triumph in Kevin's eyes, though he kept the celebrations till later.

'Good man,' he said to me, and then he shook hands with Barrington.

Helen didn't share his triumph. She seemed more relieved than anything. Much like me. It took time to absorb the fact that the decision had come down so easily on my side, like the toss of a coin. If it wasn't for the logo of the harp on the wall, it might have felt more like being in a betting office. There was something so arbitrary about the truth, about luck, about the narrow odds between winning and losing.

The electrician and his family were standing together at the door of the court in great shock, unable to look at each other. The electrician's wife put her arm around her husband, in tears, because she believed every word of what he had said in court and must have thought it was a travesty that I could get away with such a crime. I didn't feel good. It was not possible to shake hands over something like this in the same way that you do after a boxing match. The consequences of this failed trial were still coming my way. The electrician was staring at me with great hatred in his eyes, silently saying to himself that this was not over yet by any means. The look on his face told me that I would be hearing from him again soon.

13

What an impression that made on me. The freedom of being out there on the sea. The boat drifting and the waves slapping underneath. The reflection of the sunlight blinding us and the water full of illuminated particles. The coastline slipping further and further away with the tide, everything forgotten, left behind on the shore.

We yelped each time the mackerel started biting. I could feel the tug, like an electric current running along the line. That weightless tremor in my fingers as they swam upwards, swirling to the surface.

Talk about mackerel crowded seas. Kevin said they were practically ejaculating into the boat. More and more of them, jumping out of the water with striped black-and-green backs, like spinal X-rays. Their silver bellies flapping inside the boat. Mackerel scales all over my hands and my clothes, even my hair. Plastic bags full of trembling fish when we arrived back on land.

Our friendship had transformed itself into an undying bond. We went everywhere together. I knew everything about him and he knew everything there was to know about me. We got drunk together and ended up in places where neither of us had ever been before. So much so that at the tail end of a drunken night after fishing he once forgot himself al-together. He turned to me and stuck his tongue deep down into my mouth, just like the electrician's daughter had done, but then withdrew again immediately. 'What the fuck am I doing?' He laughed. This wasn't like him, he was quick to point out. It was just an experiment. A joke. Never to be repeated. Because this was a purely male friendship, not to be confused with sexual heat.

It even got to the point where I was in on his deception with Helen. I was there when he started cheating on her. A high-wire act in which he arrived around at my place at night with a woman called Eleanor, pretending to Helen that he was staying overnight with his mother.

I wanted to tell him about the letter that Bridie had shown me, how he would end up losing Helen if he was not careful, then he would regret it for the rest of his life.

Eleanor was the kind of person who laughed at everything he said. Her body did all the talking. She wore tracksuit bottoms with the word 'Pink' written in large capital letters on her backside, and when she walked along the street, the letters moved, so readable and so illegible at the same time. It powered his imagination. It gave him a new story. And the greater the storyteller, the better the lover, isn't that so?

Why did Eleanor not have a place of her own where they could hide away without dragging me into it as a witness? I wondered. Next time I met Helen by his side again, I felt so transparent. She could read the truth in my eyes like a hand-written letter.

'Is he sampling?' she asked me, while Kevin was up at the bar getting drinks.

I pretended not to understand, which was my right as a newcomer, to play innocent and underdeveloped.

'He's screwing somebody, isn't he?'

The question left me no room to escape. Even for an outsider who had no business getting involved in their private matters, she had me cornered. He was too good a storyteller to get caught. But my silence was like a full admission. She didn't need to hear any more.

I had only just been acquitted and now I began to feel more guilty than ever.

I continued working on the big job on the floor, coming and going like a member of the family. One day, while I was on my way to the building supplier's I walked along the main street in Dún Laoghaire and I ran into Rita. She was coming towards me, carrying shopping bags. Just when I was getting ready to greet her and ask her if she needed a hand with the bags, she turned away and looked into a shop window. She must have seen me coming. All I could do was pass her by and carry on as though I hadn't seen her. She wanted privacy, I thought. Or maybe she had discovered something about me and didn't want to be seen talking to me in public, because she stood staring with great interest into the window of the men's dress-hire shop.

It was only when I collected the materials I needed from the building supplier's and got back to the house that I found out why she didn't want to talk to me in public. Spread out across the kitchen table was a report on the suffering inflicted on people even years later by the war which had gone on in my country when I was growing up.

I didn't read it through all the way. I was too busy putting down a damp-proof course which had never been thought of when they were building these houses. But I couldn't avoid the questions turned up by the newspaper article. The full story of these victims had not yet been told.

I felt that I had been found out.

Later on, when she made a cup of tea, there was nothing said about us passing each other by on the street. And maybe that was the way things were done here, I thought. They often had no formal language for public places. Such as in supermarkets where people avoided each other as though they were invisible. Even the people at the checkout were unable to say hello, so you were quite entitled to walk around all day as if nobody could see you.

'Did you know there were all these Bosnian refugees living here in Dublin?' she asked me.

'Yes, I heard that,' I said.

She pointed to the article in the paper, left open on the table. There was no escape from the accusation in her eyes.

'They're still looking for the bodies,' she said. 'They were buried in one mass grave at first and then dug up again and hidden in other places in order to conceal the crime. They're using DNA to identify them, but it will take years. They've now found the remains of one body in as much as four different sites.'

I glanced at the paper once more. There were pictures of some of the Bosnian women who had been given refuge here after the massacre of Srebreniça. Faded photographs of family members who had been killed by the Serbian army while the peace-keeping troops could do nothing to save them. There was a photograph of a boy who survived only because he was hidden under the seat of a bus by his mother, otherwise he would have been killed like his father and all the other men. He had grown up in Dublin, not much younger than myself, living in the same city as me.

'You should read it,' she said. 'I'll leave it out for you.'

I felt like a war criminal. I crept away back to work, but

my heart wasn't in it. I cleared up for the day and went home. I didn't take the newspaper with me after all and maybe she didn't expect me to either.

Later on, Kevin called to collect me, announcing that we were going down to the Shannon for the weekend to stay with friends who owned a big boat on the river. I told him I would give it a miss, but he was adamant and would not accept my excuses. I would meet all his friends and integrate with lots of women.

Helen was with him again this time. They must have patched things up between them, because he kept shouting the word '*suas*' which is the Irish for up. Helen was wearing a pleated skirt and a woollen cardigan with twenty or thirty small buttons. The light reflected off her bare knees.

Heading out of the city, he drove so fast that he skidded on a roundabout and lost control of the wheel. The car spun around one hundred and eighty degrees and ended up on the grass. There was a smell of burning tyres coming up through the floor and we arrived at a semi-graceful stop, leaving two large streaks cut into the landscaped central island.

It was nothing really. But the force of being suddenly motionless threw me back to the accident in which my parents had died. I felt I had moved no further ahead in time from that day, still sitting in the back seat with the dead bodies of my mother and father in the front and the enormous wedding cake mashed against the back of my father's seat. I could feel the hollow silence, the absence of answers coming back from them. Only the trickle of blood emerging from my father's head and running into his ear and dripping down on the back of the seat, almost the same colour as the flowers we had brought with us in the boot. There was also the sound of a motorbike driving away in the distance. And the sound of the insects buzzing. I could remember the heat building up in the car and the inability to move, as though I was for ever trapped inside my dead family. It was clear to me that I was alive, but I was not quite sure if that's what I wanted. Waiting and waiting for the sound of the ambulance coming from far away, through the valleys, closer and closer but never seeming to reach us, until they finally arrived and I was taken out first because I was the only survivor. Brought back from the dead, you might say, with the face of a paramedic standing outside and his hands in green gloves reaching in to feel my pulse, asking me if I was conscious.

'Hey,' Kevin shouted. Then he laughed and put his foot down again, driving away as if nothing had happened, defying his luck. He was thinking only how much he was alive while I was thinking only that I should be dead.

'Fuck,' was all Helen said.

We made it down to Carrick-on-Shannon by nightfall. We spent the evening on the boat and I was introduced to all their friends, but there was something strange about this gathering that made me feel very much apart. I had nothing to say to them. I was perhaps still dazed by the newspaper article about Bosnian survivors I had read earlier in the day. I was unfit to integrate. I couldn't get drunk. I couldn't laugh. I didn't even find anything they were saying in the least bit funny and perhaps I was trying too hard.

The owner of the cruise boat kept accusing one of the women of letting her dog hump his dog. They continued for a while with dog jokes and I told myself to lighten up. But I could not pay attention and whenever they laughed I thought they were laughing at me. They even repeated some of the jokes out of courtesy, with me as a pupil receiving special attention.

They got drunk and drugged up. They kept shouting '*suas*' and '*suas* again'. They held a spontaneous competition in which everyone had to pitch a movie idea to a Hollywood producer. They did this with great enthusiasm and somebody started off by making up a story of an exploding dog. A woman arrives at the airport and her dog suddenly explodes and there are bits of the animal all over the place. Police and scientists in white suits rush in to cordon off the area and after a full investigation they discover it's a new disease. People start exploding all over the city.

Kevin jumped in next with an idea about a boy going on a school trip to the megalithic site at Newgrange where he falls on the ground and gets a splinter in his arm which goes septic. Then the Stone Age people come back from the past and kidnap him, so he has to be rescued.

Most of the pitches were about people chasing each other and people being rescued. Helen had an idea about a woman who goes insane because her husband is cheating on her. She leaves her family and turns into a mad environmentalist crusader, causing all kinds of reckless damage to property and protesting all over the world until her husband finally sees her on TV and has to rescue her in the middle of winter, out in Siberia, where she is just about to get killed by the illegal-logging mafia.

There was silence all around when she finished, because people were thinking it was not very far from the truth.

When it came to my turn I had nothing much to offer. I began to make up a story in my head about a car crash in which a family is killed on the way to a wedding, all except for one survivor. It felt so obvious. I was unable to invent anything. I only had real facts to play with. I could do nothing but imagine the same accident all over again, going through the same arrangement of occupants and objects inside the car once more. My father's head against the window. My mother's head hanging to one side. And the cake, the big wedding cake mashed against the seat in front of me.

Then it came to me once again that this was no fiction. For the first time, I realised that the car was actually on its side. The impact of the crash must have flipped it over, because I could suddenly recall the cake beside my head. Why had I never worked this out before? And why had nobody told me? Perhaps they did, but there was so much for me to remember and so much to forget, that I had retained nothing of these details. Only now, by trying to re-imagine it and place it into fiction, could I see it clearly for the first time. My mother strapped in by her seat belt with her arm hanging down. The sound of the back wheel spinning, which I had mistaken for insects buzzing and birds squeaking. It could not have been the front wheel, because that would have remained in gear, but the back wheel continued freewheeling for a little while afterwards until it slowly came to a stop or just became inaudible. It was a late revelation, so long after the event itself was placed behind me. The car was definitely on its side. Why else would I have seen the paramedic above me, with the blue sky behind him and his arm reaching down towards me?

They waited for me to tell them my movie, but I was unable to find a place to begin.

14

The following day, in the afternoon, Helen asked if anyone wanted to walk around the town of Carrick. Her father had grown up there and she was interested in having a look at the house where he lived. Kevin decided to stay on the boat because he had done the tour of her 'roots' once before. So she asked me to go with her instead.

As we walked into the town, she told me that her parents had emigrated. They had moved to Canada when she was around twelve, though she had been sent back to attend boarding school in Dublin. She told me that her father was a doctor and that he had died from cancer some time ago. He was a quiet person who got more fun out of listening to others than talking himself. Her brothers and sisters were living in Canada and her mother was over there, too, living in a small town in Ontario where her father once had a practice.

It seemed to matter to her that I should know all this. It was an affectionate thing to do, I thought, to include me, to fill me in on her family biography, standing in front of the house where her father once came out the door and went to school every day. She said it was a pity it had been turned into offices and she could never get herself to go inside.

The light came seeping up the street from the river. We walked to the end of the town, uphill towards a hospital. The dampness was spreading across the fields all around the town.

We turned from the road into the hospital on the left. Cars were driving in and out, so it seemed that we had come at the time of a shift change. Nurses arriving and leaving. The hospital buildings were grey and dark, made of stone, with a series of new block-built extensions attached. Overall, the place appeared unwelcoming, tall and imposing over the surrounding landscape, with high chimney stacks and crows perched on top. It made me feel small. Perhaps bringing back memories of some frightening architectural features in my own country.

Helen buttoned up her cardigan as she walked. Around by the back of the hospital, a woman wearing white gloves and a white shower cap over her head came out to deposit a sack in a bin. Two elderly nuns made their way into a chapel built at the rear. There was a sign on the wall pointing to 'The Workhouse'. We followed a path down the hill along the high perimeter wall made of the same grey stone, away from the hospital. About halfway down, there were three steel cauldrons. Large, rusty-brown vessels, like enormous upturned bells. One of them had handles, the others didn't. There was a V shape cut into the rim so the contents could be poured out and one of them even had a long spout low down.

There was a plaque giving information about the soup kitchens, which we read together in silence. It spoke about the great famine in Ireland during the 1840s. We stood by the cauldrons where they once distributed soup to those who promised to convert their religion.

'My family survived,' she said.

I touched one of the cauldrons and it rocked a little, making a hollow, rumbling sound. It seemed so recent, as though they had just been left there and not moved since the time of the disaster.

'They took up farms that had been left abandoned. They gathered up smallholdings and became prosperous land-owners themselves.'

We walked down the path to the graveyard where many of the dead from the workhouse were buried in a mass grave. Beyond the perimeter wall, there was a row of newly built houses, backing on to this memorial site. We sat down on a small wall in the hollow, with the grey buildings towering above us.

She told me a story from her childhood, before the family went to live in Canada. They had a workman who came to the house to do the garden. His name was Traolach, which is the Irish for Terence. They used to give him his dinner and a bit of money. He had lived most of his life in institutions. He was an orphan, sent by social workers who wanted to integrate him into society, but he would never be his own man and always needed to be looked after.

'He used to go around muttering in his own world,' she said. 'You'd hear him shouting and squaring up to things.'

As children they laughed and watched him from a distance. The spade stuck in the ground while he walked back and forth in his wellingtons, stopping to make a speech with his arms folded. 'I'm trying to help you, but you're not helping yourself, are you?' She could remember him coming into the house once and saying, 'You can't bring a horse to the water and not let him drink.'

'Something must have happened to him as a child, because he was very unhappy.'

She told me how her mother used to collect the left-over food and give it to him on a big plate. She would recycle everything from the dinner table. All the bits of roast beef or chicken that were left behind by the family. Her mother covered it all up in a lake of thin gravy to make it look better, with plenty of potatoes and cabbage. Then she would call Traolach inside and they would watch him eat the whole thing up with a ferocious appetite, saying thank you and 'God bless you' again and again.

'I'd love to meet him now,' she said. 'If he was still alive today, I'd go and find him and give him an almighty big slap-up dinner somewhere nice. I swear, I'd bring him into Patrick Guilbaud's and let him have anything he wanted off the menu.'

On the way back into the town we got talking about Kevin. I was afraid she might start interrogating me, but instead she began to discuss the problems with the Concannon family, with Ellis and the absent father.

She told me the story of the drowned woman, and because I was bound to secrecy on this, I had to pretend it was all new to me. Her version was more heartbreaking. Perhaps she told it from the woman's point of view, how the words of the priest must have terrified the pregnant girl, how the people must have turned to look at her as she was being denounced.

'If there is no man here in this parish fit enough to marry her,' was the way she said it, 'then the best she can do is to drown herself.'

Did she get that wrong? Or was she trying to make it seem less cruel, by putting in the word 'marry' instead of 'drown'? I clearly remembered Kevin saying it this way. 'If the men are not fit enough to drown her, then perhaps she would have the decency to drown herself.' His version was more like evidence in court. Or was it possible that the people in the church that morning got it wrong and misread what the priest had said, turning it into a clear instruction to kill or drown the woman? Murder instead of marriage?

In the end, it all came to the same thing. Incitement. She was expelled into the sea.

'Only Kevin's father knows the real story,' she said.

I wanted to tell her about the letters which he had sent home, but I couldn't do that.

'Have you been to the Aran Islands?' I asked her.

'I get the impression he doesn't really want me to go,' she said. 'I've offered to help him find out a little more, but he wouldn't like that. He went to visit an old aunt on his father's side who was in hospital in Galway once. She could remember the whole thing happening when she was a small girl, but I don't know if he got much information out of her because he didn't talk much about it afterwards.'

Later on, we met up with Kevin and it felt a bit awkward, as if Helen and myself had some kind of secret between us. At dinner with all the others that evening, she made sure we didn't sit near each other.

'Most embarrassing moment,' one of the women announced at one point after the main course, when everyone was drunk. She wanted us all to tell a bad thing about ourselves, some revelation, something we did or said that was really sick or insane.

She got the ball rolling with a story about her five-year-old son coming into the bedroom one morning, picking up a squishy condom that was left under the bed and asking, 'What's this, Mammy? Is it chewing gum?' There was long silence. Some of them laughed a little out of politeness, but most of us didn't know where to look. Helen was staring down at her plate. The woman who had started the idea seemed genuinely embarrassed and then she insisted on everybody else taking their turn. Kevin helped her out with a funny story about himself in Australia, when he was living in an apartment block in Melbourne and found himself sleepwalking one night, fully naked. He went down in the lift and started knocking on different doors because he couldn't find his own apartment, and then he finally woke up when a big sweaty man came out in a vest, with tattoos all over his arms and a beer can in his hand, asking what the fuck he was looking for.

The conversation broke off into a debate about confession and absolution. The owner of the cruise boat said priests had become obsolete in Ireland, replaced by phone-in radio programmes. The whole country had become one big confessional at this stage, everyone getting it off their chest, divulging all the secrets they could think of.

'Do you get absolution on the radio?' Helen asked.

'Of course. Why not?' Kevin said. 'The public gives you absolution. The whole idea is to confess and seek forgiveness, so your sins can be cleared, am I right?'

'That's shite you're talking.'

Kevin should have come out and said that he had been sleeping with another woman called Eleanor. I should have said that my father was in the secret police in Belgrade and brought terrible crimes home with him to put under his pillow. But it was not the place for any of this to be said. Our sins remained on the statute books and it was hard to know if you could ever get absolution for things you inherited.

After dinner we went out looking for a quiet bar,

somewhere that was not too packed and where you could still talk. It was hard to find a place that was not like a night club. The town was buzzing. People hanging around outside pubs. People walking in the middle of the street in front of cars. Somebody getting sick outside a shoe shop. There were lots of hen parties in Carrick that weekend. Girls dressed in red skirts and fishnet stockings, laughing so much they had trouble walking on their high heels and had to hold on to the wall. A group of nuns came walking past the church, talking and shrieking and one shouted to the other, 'You're always the last, Mary,' as they disappeared in the door of a bar with music blasting out from inside.

15

There was a man standing at the gate. It was early afternoon. I was busy, carrying concrete blocks inside, but I saw him stalling for a moment on the pavement. The first thing that came to mind was the worst. His appearance might have something to do with the court case, some retribution still to come. The payback.

I continued what I was doing, because the cement was already mixed and I had no time to waste. I barely noticed him in the corner of my eye. A man in his late fifties. I took in his shape and his height, along with the haze over the sea and the taste of salt and seaweed drifting up the street which always reminded me of liquorice, somehow. Or iodine. Or cough medicine, for a sore throat. There was a light inshore breeze leaning against the hedges, rattling the blades of a palm tree at the corner house at the top of the street, getting ready for a duel.

What did he want?

He stood right outside the gate, watching me. The gate was closed, at the bottom of the chequered path. Beautiful, the way they designed it diagonally in black and terracotta tiles like a chessboard, with a matching terracotta border separating the path from the flowerbeds. I heard his footsteps coming to a stop, the click of leather on the pavement announcing his presence.

I carried the concrete block up the granite steps into the house. There was lots of granite all over the place around here. Granite slabs. Granite walls. Granite buildings. Granite monuments. Two impressive granite piers reaching out into the bay with a granite lighthouse at each end. From the upstairs windows you could just about see where they mined the rock to build the piers. I'm told that they engineered a funicular railway to carry the rocks down along special laneways while they were building. The metals, they call them, and the weight of the granite coming down would pull the empty cart up. Everybody knows that.

Can I help you? I wanted to say to him, because that's what they say whenever you go into a shop. Are you OK? Can I help you? Are you looking for something?

There was nobody else in the house at the time but me. He didn't appear to have any intention of coming inside, doing nothing apart from stopping to look at the house, maybe checking the number to make sure. Is he lost? I wondered. Is he from the tax authorities? Is he just stopping to get a good look at me with a concrete block in my hands? Or does he really have something to do with the legal matters which I hoped were now behind me?

Then I realised that there was something familiar about his face. I made the connection between this man and the unopened letters in the bedroom. Yes, I said, almost aloud. Even though there was not a single picture of this man in the house, I knew him because I had held his letters in my hand. I recognised him. The collar turned up. The hunch in the shoulders. The short forehead. The long hair gone white. The hint of a smile crossing his face, saying good afternoon but not in words.

It was his father. Of course. The man who 'fucked off' and left them. How could I have missed it? It suddenly became so obvious to me that I felt like running out, shouting the answer the way a contestant would on a quiz show. You're the man who sent all the letters, even as recently as last year. You're the man from Furbo in Connemara. You're the man who knows all about the drowned woman. You're the man who gave his children their stony cheekbones, their sandy hair and brown eyes, their left-leaning smiles.

I heard once that the people of Connemara had a lot of Spanish blood in them.

Why didn't he come inside? Here I was, stepping out through the hall door once more to carry in the last block, getting ready to talk to him, but he was gone again. Later, he came back up the street on the far side, carrying the tang of liquorice with him. As he reached the top of the street, he turned away from the palm tree with the leatherette leaves, vanishing into the centre of the town, maybe never to come again, now that he had seen the house where his letters were sent and went unanswered.

That evening, I met him in the town. He approached me directly this time. He waited for me to finish my drink. When I was ready to leave, he stood at the door, not barring my way but stepping up and making his presence unavoidable.

'I see you're doing a bit of work for the Concannons,' he said.

There was a melody in his accent that was unfamiliar to me.

'You're a friend of Kevin's,' he said. 'I've seen you drinking with him.'

I smiled out of courtesy.

'I'm his father,' he said. 'Johnny. Johnny Concannon.'

He opened the door for me and shook my hand. He looked

around to make sure he was not being overheard. He took out a packet of cigarettes, non-tipped, but then changed his mind and decided not to smoke, returning the packet to his pocket.

'I don't want to delay you,' he said. 'But could I ask you something?'

'Of course.'

'I want to ask you to do me a favour. Would you be able to give him something for me? A gift, like? For his birthday.'

He hesitated, then smiled. I had time enough to look into his eyes. He was only around twenty-five years older than Kevin. An identical version of Kevin from the future, but different inside, different memories, different songs, different stories.

'You don't want to give it to him yourself?' I asked.

He shook his head.

'It's a long story.'

My guess was that he had only just come back home and that he wanted to surprise them all. Starting with his son, whom he had not seen since childhood, more or less. The long-lost father, making up for long-lost time.

'I'd be very grateful to you.'

He asked me to accompany him to where he was living. Just around the corner. He apologised again for taking me out of my way. We stopped at a terraced house where he asked me to wait while he disappeared, down the steps into the basement. It was a large three-storey building of the same style as the one I was working on, only less well maintained. The paint was peeling off the façade and I told myself it would take years to restore this one. You'd have to strip the place down to a shell probably. There were torn curtains hanging in one of the windows. The hall door was left open, with two buggies inside and a bicycle. And beside the door, a double line of names and chromatic bells, like a button accordion. Some of the former tenants' names wiped out and new names from all over the world attached with sticky tape.

When he came out he handed me a small package, neatly wrapped in mauve-and-black paper.

'Fair play to you,' he said.

'You're sure you don't want to give it to him yourself?' I asked once more, because I didn't feel entirely qualified to represent him in front of the family.

'You'd be doing me a great favour,' he repeated, smiling.

What a touching mission this was, stepping into the shoes of a returning emigrant trying to make contact with his own son. I understood exactly how he must have felt, not knowing where to fit in, trying to catch up overnight with all the stories of the children growing up which he had missed over the years.

I carried the gift with me as I walked by the harbour, thinking how he must have left, right here, as a young man in his twenties, when things were so different. Kevin had told me about him coming up on the train from Galway and making his way out to Dún Laoghaire to get the boat. He would have had time to kill, looking into shop windows, walking along the seafront, looking at the yacht clubs. He would have passed by the monument to King George erected on a base of four enormous granite orbs, one of which was blown off by the IRA and later replaced. Past the big cannon at the base of the pier. He would have heard the trains going through the tunnel. He would have seen the arrows pointing towards Holyhead, across the Irish Sea, as though it was only down the street. He would have seen the sign announcing the time of the next sailing.

He would have walked as far as the People's Park and sat down on one of the blue benches. He would have seen the neatly kept flowerbeds. He might have walked in a slow circle around the octagonal bandstand and come back again. He would have leaned on the blue railings and stared out over the water, looking with excitement and impatience into his own future. Smoking a cigarette which he didn't really want. Grieving as much as anything, because leaving was like bereavement, losing all your friends overnight. In the old days, they used to hold a wake for the person going away, as if they were already dead.

He would have heard the boat claxon going off. He would have seen the passengers gathering at the Carlisle pier and also those who were saying goodbye, grouping together by the wall to watch the ship going out. He would have passed people who were crying, young women trying to smile as they turned around to wave. Women with infectious tears hidden in their handkerchiefs.

I've stood there and imagined them all leaving. Johnny Concannon in the crowd.

He would have moved with the general flow up along the wooden floor of the pier, hearing the shipping staff calling for passengers to have their tickets ready. He would have seen the sign for 'Passengers Only', both in English and also in his own language. *Paisinéirí amháin.* When it was his turn to cross the gangplank, he would have seen the gap between the pier and the boat and caught sight of the water below. He would have heard the squeak of the boat pressing against the rubber fenders. And just at the entrance to the boat, he would have read the sign 'Mind Your Head' because the door was low and tall men had to bow their heads going in.

And once he was on the boat, he was surrounded by talking and laughter and smoke and people trying to find a place to sit down and store their luggage safely. Families. Clusters of friends. Women banded into groups from their own parts of the country, settling down in corners as though they were going to be on that boat for the rest of their lives. Some of them dressed in mini-skirts and styles already picked up from abroad. Others still wearing the clothes that their mothers would have chosen. Young girls no more than seventeen with handkerchiefs still in their hands, looking at the men at the bar in the hope that they would cheer things up. Some of the men wore open collars and had cigarettes hanging from their lips, looking indestructible. Some of them were drunk and staggering on their feet before the boat had even left. Some of them had Elvis haircuts and some of them had long hair and colourful hippy clothes and somebody must have had a guitar.

He would have noticed the throb of the engines, shuddering through the metal. A knocking, grinding noise as the boat drifted away from the pier. Ropes splashing into the water and dripping as they were gathered up and coiled on deck. He would have heard the door of the boat being pulled shut with a loud bang. He might have gone up on deck to see all the people waving from the shore.

All the sadness left behind. In the walls. On the pavements. In the blue benches. Stored in the granite like the warmth of the day still radiating after the sun had gone down.

He would have inhaled diesel fumes. He would have watched the lighthouse going by so close he could almost put his hand out to touch it. He would have felt the first lurch of the boat on the tide and seen the gulls hovering after them and thought they were tied with strings. He would have watched the land receding slowly, reduced to the size of a postcard. To the size of a postage stamp. To the size of a single line of farewell, neatly written along the horizon before the land dropped out of sight.

16

So there I was, carrying a father's gift to his son in my bag.

I arranged to meet Kevin in order to hand it over, wondering why they had not run into each other already in such a small world. How could he possibly miss meeting his own father? You could hardly walk down the street without being spotted.

I had been chosen to bring them together. It was a great mission, something to be done with tact and discretion. It was clearly not possible to give it to him in some bar like a packet of peanuts. 'Here, this is from your dad.' That would be the wrong thing to do, because you'd only have everybody asking him what was inside and enquiring into his private family business.

I waited for a better moment, later, on the way to a party.

'Kevin, I have this thing to give you.'

But he was concentrating on something else entirely, walking fast, planning the next part of the evening.

'Vid,' he said to me. 'This place we're going to. I want you to slip in first. Check it out. Have to make sure she's not there.'

'Who?'

'Helen.'

So then I became involved in a more uncomfortable mission, going into a house undercover and searching through the guests to make sure that Helen was not present. He could not afford to see her face to face.

'Wouldn't be good, right now. Emotionally.'

He called it the Helen-check. I went in, searching through the faces, staring women in the eyes as if I wanted something from them, eliminating them in a kind of identity parade. Some of them were quite hostile, silently asking me what the fuck I was looking for. I smiled back awkwardly at them, muttering 'I thought you were somebody else', but they didn't like being mistaken for another woman. I kept wanting to see Helen all the time. There was nobody I wished to see more than Helen, but she was nowhere around. I even waited to make sure she was not hiding in the bathroom.

Back out on the street, I gave Kevin the all-clear and picked up my bag with the gift from his dad, still un-given and unopened, because he was too busy to receive it and was already pulling me inside. It was even less appropriate to hand it over while he was talking and dancing and chatting up women and getting so stoned and drunk that he eventually fell down between two sofas and had to be woken up and resuscitated with more beer so he could walk home. He had not scored, as he put it himself, but he didn't see it as a failure because he was only concerned with getting out of his head from now on.

On the way home, he leaned on my shoulder, still talking. He wanted to go back to my place, because it was not possible for him to go back to Helen so late in the night. We walked along a row of small red-brick houses, designed in such a way that the hall door led straight into the living room and the occupants could hear every word that people said on the street, all the voices going by entering right into the house. He stopped for a piss and I was sure the people inside could hear it in their sleep, cascading against the wall and spreading in a frothy delta across the pavement.

There was no better moment than this, I thought. I waited till he was finished and took out the gift. I understood the magnitude of the moment, what it meant to him and to his family, what it meant to me to belong to this reunion.

'I've got something for you,' I said, handing it to him at last.

'Aw. Thanks.'

'No. You'll see. Just open it.'

He took off the wrapping paper and found a shiny red box inside, a case that would normally contain an item of jewellery, with velvet interiors like a coffin and a lovely click when the lid shuts down. For half a second it looked as though I had given him an engagement ring.

'What the fuck is this?'

'It's from your dad,' I said, smiling.

He looked shocked. I thought it was the weight of feeling pressing down on him. But his eyes began to narrow and his frown tightened into a fist. He took in a deep breath through his nose and looked away. Then he dropped the box out of his hands and as I looked down, his arm came swinging towards me so fast that I had no time to escape the blow.

It was the first time I really noticed that he was left-handed. I had seen him holding a pen in his left hand, writing upside down from the top of the page to make sure he could see what he was doing. But the left-handed punch came as a complete surprise. I was totally un-ready for it. I had miscalculated all the signals once again.

It was anger, not reconciliation. Not the great welcome

home I had expected him to give his father at the end of all this absence. Not the open door, back from oblivion. He kicked the gift across the street and I heard the object inside skitter away with a dull clang, some kind of ancient coin. The black-and-mauve wrapping paper glided out of his hand like a tropical bird coming to land on the street behind him.

I staggered back against the window of one of the houses. My bag had a hand-planer inside which I had bought from somebody that evening. It dug into the small of my back and rang against the bars which had been erected outside the window like a prison to keep intruders out. My head hit one of the bars, though I felt nothing at the time, only the shape of his knuckles imprinted on the side of my face.

'You fucking Serbian cunt,' he shouted.

'Why?'

'I thought you were my friend,' he said. 'I've done everything for you and this is how you repay me.'

'What's wrong?' I said. 'What did I do?'

The anger in his face was familiar to me. I had seen it before, but had always thought of him as my protector, on the same side. I could not understand what my transgression was.

'Never, ever, interfere with my family. I fucking warned you about that.'

'This is no offence,' I pleaded.

'I thought I could trust you,' he shouted.

'I was trying to help. It's from your dad, Kevin.'

My words came in a stammer, out of breath. His words came in a spin, a power drill going into masonry.

'Well, let me tell you this, you little Balkan creep. We don't need your help. How dare you even think you can start intervening, Mister Fix-it, Euro-fuck? Go home and fix your own bloody country.'

He was crying. Or did I just imagine that? He stared at me for a moment with his chin quivering, then walked away, not even turning back.

How could I have got it so wrong? How could I have become so intoxicated with my fantasy role as mediator? And how quickly I had turned from being his best friend into the most hated person on earth.

I felt the warmth of my own blood going down the back of my shirt. The collar was sticking to my neck. There was an old woman looking at me through the window. She pulled back the curtains and then jumped away once she realised that I was looking in at her, with blood on my face and hands, a horror scene unfolding right in front of her own house.

'Are you all right, son?' she mimed from behind the safety of the glass and the metal bars.

I nodded and she went away, but the curtain continued moving and I knew she was still watching, turning me into a victim.

The weight in my bag became more apparent to me now. Along with my anger. The impact of his fist had introduced a strange, dizzy kind of energy into my body, releasing a stored rage of my own, like a shout escaping from inside my head.

How could I allow this to happen? Was I not entitled to stand up for myself? I wanted to get even and thought of running after him, swinging the bag and giving him a blow on the head from behind. Pinning him face down on the street with my knee on his back, taking out the newly bought plane, which they swore to me was not stolen goods, and hitting him with it again and again. Opening up his skull, shaving off the top of his head without stopping until his mind came lifting out in a bright mess of colour and violence.

This is how he repaid me for taking his place in court. This is how I will repay him for his betrayal. It was the moment of vertigo. At school, we read a book by a Czech writer that explained how it was not the fear of falling but the voice of emptiness calling you. It's the same feeling that you get when you hold a newborn infant in your hands. The same feeling you get every time you look at the spinning blade of an electric saw. It's the fear of doing exactly what you tell yourself not to.

I went over to pick up the red jewellery box. I hardly understood what I was doing. The item inside turned out to be a medal of some sort. I placed it back into the box, folding the wrapping paper neatly around it once more. It was only later that I found out the significance of this gift, after I showed it to the experts in the local bar some days later and they explained to me that it was an All-Ireland hurling medal.

'Galway colours, that wrapping paper.'

His father had been a great hurling player who played for Galway before he left the country. This was a precious medal. Years later I met a woman who had lived for some time in a place called Hammersmith in London and found one of those medals under the floorboards when she was doing up the house. It was like an archaeological treasure.

For Kevin's father to part with it would have been like a chieftain handing on his spear or his favourite feather for safe-keeping into the future. A moment of immortality. This medal contained all the feelings, all the pride, all the cheering as he stepped up to the winning stand to receive it, still out of breath from the game and the excitement.

I felt the full blow of rejection as I examined the medal in my hand. The weight of it and the sudden loss of friendship keeping me under. I hid the medal away on top of the wardrobe in my bedroom and tried to forget about it, but it continued glowing in the dark along with something in me that was not welcome any longer.

That was it. I refused to work for them any more. To hell with them all, I said to myself. They can put the floor back themselves.

The following day I spent walking instead. All that friendship was worthless currency now and I knew exactly how his father must have felt. I understood how hard it was for him to return and meet people from his own family. All the guilt he must have felt over leaving them. All the songs begging him to come back. All the friendships he left behind and had to remake abroad. All those difficulties with language and accents, as though his own words sounded like a translation. I knew what it was like, mishearing things. Misreading people's thoughts. Looking over your shoulder to see who was listening before you allowed yourself to speak.

He must have come home expecting more than this. He must have been hoping for a foothold and felt instead that he was more of an exile here on his own doorstep than he had been anywhere abroad. There is no such thing as returning, I thought, only going further away.

17

He's going to regret this, I kept saying to myself. He's going to stand there one evening looking at the sun going down and feel the moment of remorse. He's going to say that friendship means more to him than anything else in the world. He's going to look for me and he's going to look for his father.

I had withdrawn my labour indefinitely and maybe that's what brought him around. I went missing and his mother must have been asking if the job had been abandoned now with a big hole in the middle of the house.

It was easy for him to make it up to me. He did it with great exaggeration. He turned it into an oversized gesture which was funny and serious at the same time. He came to find me and went down on one knee. Up there on the hill overlooking the bay where he brought me fishing after winning the court case. I was walking along in my own emptiness, feeling a bit like one of the seagulls gliding on the updraught over the coast. The sea below me, looking like the texture of boiling milk from that height, bubbling at the edges on the beach.

There he was, kneeling on the path with his head down. At first I thought it was somebody doing up his shoelaces.

Only when I got closer did I recognise him, genuflecting like a courtier in front of the Pope, with his hooded jacket around his shoulders and his hand stretched out towards me.

Well, what can you say to that? It was audacious and original, so that's what counts. Full of imagination. The big smile. The eyes slanted in supplication, so innocent. He bowed his head right down low as I approached, waiting for me to shake his hand and tell him to get up for Jesus sake and stop acting the clown because it was impossible for me to hold on to my anger under these circumstances. He stood up and embraced me with his head down, colliding against my chest. Walkers passing us by with their dogs sniffing around our legs must have thought we were lovers. Then he moved back, leaving two hands resting firmly on my shoulders, looking straight into my eyes. His breath was mint and coffee.

'I've been to hell and back over this, Vid.'

He drew me over to the bench with one arm left around my shoulder.

'Are you on the level?' I asked.

'I swear.'

'You're not arsing me?'

'Listen, Vid. I don't deserve your friendship after what I've done. But I'm here to apologise. I'm going to make this up to you a million times over. Even if it takes me a lifetime, my friend.'

What can you do? I felt like a complete sucker, getting my shoelaces tied together. It occurred to me that I was a bit like the character of Gulliver, more internally out of scale though, tied down with all these promises of friendship. Maybe this was the way things were done here, I thought. You make a friend, you hit your friend, then you shake hands and achieve a closer, superior grade of friendship than ever

131

before. He made it epic. I could hear the optimism in his voice and didn't want to be excluded from it.

It had nothing to do with work. I could have gone back to the sites. I could have done more security work at the pharmacy any time. I could have gone into business with Darius. People were coming up and asking me to fit them in, so I could even have set up my own workshop, if I wanted to. It was not just the money. I was not an opportunist, here to make a quick stack and fuck off again. It was the friendship, the family, the idea of belonging that mattered to me. To be honest, I didn't have the guts to see it any other way. I couldn't afford the bitterness. I couldn't afford to be alone.

'Come on,' he said. 'We're going to a wedding. Belfast.'

He was that confident. Within half an hour we had gone to my place to collect some clothes and were driving north. No looking back.

'What about your mother?'

'I told her you were on secondment.'

That was another disadvantage, having to ask him to explain everything, not being able to check out his words before I accepted them.

'You know something, Vid,' he said to me in the car. 'That's what I like about you. You've got no guile.'

'What do you mean?'

'No guile. You're so conspicuous. Conscientious, honest to a fault.'

I had to translate those words back into my own language to see what exactly my deficiencies were. It was obviously time for me to pick up some of this guile, but where do you get lessons for that?

'You're so genuine,' he said. 'You have such a forgiving

nature. I swear, I'm not going to let anyone take advantage of that.'

He was a master apologiser. And the world was full of forgivers, queuing up to shake hands with him. Ready to believe anything he said. I've seen him doing it so often, with women especially. His hand on his heart, holding out a bunch of damaged flowers from some petrol station. Bashed-up yellow lilies that smelled more like a funeral. Women throwing their arms around him when they should have been turning away. Listening to his twisted-soul explanations when they should have held their hands up over their ears and screamed.

A handshake will cost you nothing, so they say. The history of this country was not unlike my own, full of handshakes and refused handshakes.

On the way up, he told me the whole story of the troubles in Northern Ireland. He divided it up for me in a simple way, like a football match between Catholics and Protestants, Republicans on the one side and Loyalists on the other, with the British government as the referee making a right mess of it and giving bogus penalties to one side until the peace process finally came about. It was all about supremacy and looking down on other people, he said, marching through streets in triumph over the losers. He said it was free market capitalism which brought an end to religious and political disputes and allowed people to walk away and go shopping instead.

The best way for me to make any sense of it was to compare it to my own life. I could not afford to have enemies. I was an immigrant and I had no right to be angry. I didn't want to be left on the outside. I needed the endorsement of his friendship and was ready to take peace at any price.

The landscape up north had the same green fields, as far

as I could see. Same cattle with black and white patches, chewing the same grass. The road signs were different, missing the translation in the old language. He took me on a quick tour of Belfast city to see the famous murals painted on the gable walls of houses. Pictures of Bobby Sands on the Republican side and King Billy on the Loyalist side. Flags and emblems borrowed from conflict zones elsewhere. Palestinian flags on the Catholic side and Israeli flags on the Protestant side, as though they were still fighting the same war by proxy, far away in another part of the world.

I thought of the gift from his father which I had hidden on top of my wardrobe. A lump of enriched metal inside the jewellery case. He didn't know that I still had it, so I asked him about his father and what I should do if I ran into him again. He became reflective once more. The same fist-like frown. The same intake of breath. The delay. The blink. I realised that I was just one knockout punch away. I could feel my back teeth loosening in their sockets. Ready to flinch and get my head down.

'Let's be clear about this, Vid. My father doesn't exist. Do you follow me? I don't want to go over all the stuff that my mother had to endure. He is nothing to us.'

We arrived at the hotel and saw the wedding guests gathered outside. There was a strong breeze and the women had to hold on to their hats and their hair and their dresses. Lots of cleavage and goose pimples and bra straps. The young men were hunched on the periphery, lighting cigarettes out of the wind. There was a man holding up a video camera in the air, recording everything that moved, even the flowers without petals blown sideways inside the window boxes. There was a door banging at the entrance and the flags on the lawn in front of the hotel were flapping so much, they were almost rigid as cardboard in the gale. The Irish flag and the European flag and the American flag, for some reason, to make sure everyone felt included.

The bride stepped out of the limousine and embraced an obese teenager with enormous affection. She looked in my direction for a moment, perhaps wondering if she knew me. She had bags under her eyes, probably from all the excitement and not sleeping very well coming up to the wedding, possibly wishing she was just a guest like everyone else.

The only person Kevin knew was Eleanor. He told her how much fun I could be once I had a few drinks in me. He wanted me to say something, for God's sake, because people were wondering what was going on inside my head.

'You look a bit like a spy when you don't speak.'

But there was no need for me to talk. The woman beside me at the dinner table did all the talking, telling me about all the concerts she had ever been to. Bon Jovi. Britney Spears, twice in America. Bruce Springsteen in Dublin was by far the best value for money because he played for three hours. She told me that she and her husband went dancing a lot lately and that was the cheapest way of getting out of the house these days.

Everybody said the food was out of this world. The waitress kept putting her hand on my shoulder and offering me extra helpings. Her bosom crashed into the back of my head a few times while she was lifting plates from the table.

They had different customs here. For example, they didn't toss coins in the air for good luck and they didn't barter for the bride with an envelope full of money handed over to her family. Instead they made lots of speeches, full of family information that was lost on me. Jokes and embarrassing stories about the bride and groom when they were children.

The only thing that made sense was when the father of the bride talked about people who were absent, in America, in Australia, and somebody who had lost his life in the fight for freedom. Then he sang a song, totally unaccompanied, that made everyone cry, including the woman beside me.

It's a beautiful noise.

I was already drunk by the time the dancing started. Eleanor and Kevin brought me outside to smoke some weed. From then on I was not even in the same country as anyone else and Kevin handed me the key to a room. In the corridor I met the woman who had sat beside me at the table.

'I'm buckled,' she said, holding on to a radiator for support.

I passed out as soon as I got to the room. A while later I heard somebody banging on the door. The light came on, blinding me, though I hardly even woke up. I felt sea-sick. The bed was rocking and I tried not to give in to the swirling in my head.

The spotlight was shining in through the curtains from the lawn at the front of the hotel and when I opened my eyes, I saw him on top of Eleanor. They were right beside me on the bed, rocking back and forth. The bed was squeaking and the headboard was knocking against the wall. She was so close that I inhaled her perfume. I could hear her breath in my ear and her long hair swiped across my face.

I had been turned into a voyeur, trying to remain still and not let them know that I was awake, listening to Eleanor's voice accelerating beside me. Tiny, restrained screeches, like the call of a seabird along the coast. He exhaled up towards the ceiling and fell off. I got an elbow in the ribs which I couldn't complain about because it was not intentional. Maybe I was becoming a participant at last.

18

I was kind of expecting this to happen. The place was too small to think you could get away with it for ever. Talk about six degrees of separation. Six hundred degrees is what I needed.

Who did I run into in the supermarket, doing his late-night shopping with his wife? You have it. The electrician. The man with the broken hip. The man who was beaten up and left for dead in the street. Here he was, right in front of me, leaning on his trolley, doing just fine. The picture of health, as Kevin would say.

He seemed to be a long way off his beaten track and I wondered if he had moved house out to Dún Laoghaire. This was a real cause for concern, because we would never see the end of him in that case.

I hardly recognised him at first. I must have passed him by numerous times, brushing up quite close, thinking he was familiar to me but not acknowledging it consciously. Because everybody is invisible to each other in a supermarket, isn't that so? You have the right to complete anonymity. You don't see anything apart from the items on the shelves. You could even pass by your own mother, as the saying goes.

I had a basket of groceries in my hand, intending to do

my own cooking from now on. They'd have you living your whole life on sandwiches and take-away food in this country if you were not careful.

The electrician then came face to face with me in the deep-freeze section. My instinct was to half smile at him out of politeness, mistaking him perhaps for a former boss on one of the building sites. But that was the wrong thing to do. He didn't smile back. Maybe he was trying to maintain his shopper's anonymity, and maybe it was still the anger from losing the court case, because he didn't look very pleased to see me.

I had to check a second time to make sure that it really was him. He had the goatee beard, though his face seemed rounder. He had a strong suntan and wore a football shirt and a baseball cap, more undercover. In fact, I might have passed them by if it wasn't for his wife standing there beside him, glaring at me with a jumbo frozen pizza in her hand. She elbowed him, drawing his attention to me.

'Well, look who it is,' he said.

I tried to walk past them as if the supermarket was still a polite and safe environment where everybody was more or less equal. But there was too much history between us. I could see the anger rising in her eyes. The audacity of me appearing in the same shopping centre as them, after all that happened. He had the same grimace on his face that I remembered from the court hearing, as though he had something bad in his mouth, as though he had just bitten on a lemon seed.

What was I meant to say? I tried to pretend I was looking for a particular type of rare frozen vegetable. I avoided glancing into their trolley, which is something I like doing out of curiosity, just to match the items people buy with their faces.

The trolley was blocking my way. He would not let me pass, pushing me back along the side of the deep-freeze unit. When I tried to escape to the other side, he moved over as well, forcing me to reverse in such a way that nobody would really have noticed anything strange. Other shoppers might have thought I was backing away out of courtesy, or at the most that we knew each other well and were playing a little game.

'I'll pull your fucking eyes out,' he said in a growl. 'You think you got away with this? Well, just you wait, my friend.'

I almost fell backwards at that point and had to leave my shopping basket balanced on top of their groceries.

'Leave it, Larry,' she said, holding him back. 'He's not worth it.'

There was no point in me trying to win, so I abandoned the idea of shopping and tried to get out of his sight as fast as possible. As I fled back along the aisle, he picked up a jar out of his trolley and flung it after me. Even though he missed, I could hear the jar glancing off the freezer unit and smashing on the floor with the contents spreading out in a sort of star-shaped, big bang design. Tikka masala possibly. Not something from my basket, anyway.

'Scum,' he shouted after me.

What amazed me was that the staff and the shoppers didn't seem to think there was anything out of the ordinary about this. Everybody just carried on with what they were doing, the music ever-present around them, a song by a man who seemed to have trouble remembering whether or not he had recently told his girlfriend that he loved her. Everyone was looking for deals, two for the price of one, twenty per cent extra and twenty per cent off. By the time I passed by the checkout empty-handed,

I heard an announcement being made over the system. 'Staff call. Spillage. Aisle six, please.'

I couldn't help worrying about this chance meeting. I was in a heap over it, you might say, unable to sleep. You could never tell what was coming around the corner, and I felt it was best to stay out of supermarkets. Stick to paninis and kebabs and fish and chips. There was no point in worrying Kevin about it either, so I didn't mention it to anyone, hoping it would all go away again.

In the meantime, Kevin had extended the job at the house. I was getting more and more involved in the Concannon household. The joists were down, ready to take the floorboards. Then they realised what a terrible state the casement window was in and asked me to replace the entire downstairs frame. The wood had gone completely rotten over the years with all the salt air coming up from the sea and I agreed with them that it could not wait any longer. It was an emergency at this point.

It was a job I needed Darius for, because he had the workshop with the equipment to make up such a complex frame. A PVC frame would be out of character. So we got to work and ripped out the old casement window downstairs, placing massive sheets of plastic and plywood across the opening, shutting off the interior in darkness.

Darius is a pretty decent guy. Always good humoured and funny. He kept talking to the wood while he worked, holding an ongoing conversation with each piece of timber while he shaped it. Whenever things fit, he used sexual analogies, suggesting that he was getting into bed with the wood. Even worse when the thing didn't fit and it brought out all the curses that he'd heard on building sites over the years since he'd arrived.

140

He complained about not getting paid for his work. He hated chasing people for money and said it felt too much like begging. It often took him more time to get paid than it did to do the job itself, and maybe he was using the wrong expressions, like 'I suppose there's no chance of a cheque, is there?' He envied me for having so many friends here. Now and again he reminded me of the offer of going into business together, which was not a bad idea in principle, except that I was no better than him at asking for money.

'I'm a no-good hustler,' he said.

'Me too.'

'But you're well in,' he said.

'I'm well out, you mean.'

'The Concannons,' he said. 'You're well in with the Concannons, aren't you? You have Irish friends. Me, I still get drunk in Russian.'

He was a good bit older than me, but he hung out mostly with other non-nationals from Eastern Europe. He told me that he had been a conscript in the Russian army and you would not believe how hard that was to endure. Very little food. Freezing barracks. Away from home. Endless beatings and pointless cruelty. He said recruits were always committing suicide and he often thought of doing the same. One day a comrade shot himself in the head, leaving a splatter on the walls of the barracks, everybody throwing up in their beds as they woke up covered in blood and the gun danced across the floor on its stock end, away out of the dead man's hand.

'War might have been better,' he said. 'This was just like going to jail for a few years of hard labour.'

What I began to notice most at the house was that Ellis was ripping loose from the family. She had got through her exams somehow and finished school, celebrating for a while, stalling before deciding on what she was going to do with her life, determined to play her own luck for the time being. Her older sister Jane had already gone to look for accommodation in Limerick. She fulfilled every expectation that her mother had for her. I never got to talk to her very much, but you could see that she was going to achieve things that her mother and father could only dream of. And Ellis was bent on going in the opposite direction, as though there was a rule that no two sisters from the same family could ever reach the same level of success.

I could see that Ellis needed to break free and conduct a few essential experiments out in the open world. She should have gone travelling all over the globe, couch surfing, going to festivals, all those things her brother did. But she stuck around instead. I saw her once on the street, outside a night club in the town centre. She lifted up her T-shirt and flashed her breasts towards some people across the street. The women on the far side did the same, baring their breasts back, like some kind of fertility display. Or was it a prelude to war?

Ellis recognised me and called my name, though she seemed completely out of her head. She introduced me to her boyfriend, Diller. He seemed like a nice-enough guy to me, though he didn't say much, apart from asking who the fuck I was. Then she put her arm around him and told him that I was all right and there was nothing to worry about.

What I noticed more than anything else was that she was learning how to spit and that she had also changed her accent. It was far more difficult to understand her on the street and maybe she wanted to belong to the real people, closer to danger, away from the protection of her family.

In the meantime, I had started working on renovating a small boat in my spare time. I suppose it was the closest I would ever get to boat-building.

I also had an absurd wish to restore the Concannon family to what it once was or might have been. I had fantasies of the family reunited. I was worried about Ellis because she seemed to have run away from home.

'I saw Ellis the other day,' I said to her mother, quite casually.

'She's none of your business,' Rita said.

'Excuse me,' I said. 'I didn't mean to be nosey.'

I was mistaken again, lured into a false sense of security. I thought we had got to know each other well enough for me to enquire about her daughter at least. In fact, I had been given the impression that being nosey was a good thing. Was this not how you made people feel welcome and happy about themselves? Making them feel at home by showing concern and letting them know that we all have our own troubles.

Maybe she was still bitter at me for not confessing my own secrets. But later on she gave me a smile, like a refund.

'I'm sorry,' she said, bringing me a mug of tea to make up for it. 'It was not my intention to get angry with you, Vid. It's just that Ellis is intent on destroying her life very rapidly right now.'

'Fair enough,' I said.

'She's doing drugs, isn't she?'

'I wouldn't know about that,' I said.

'I'm afraid,' she said, almost to herself, 'you can't save somebody that doesn't want to be saved. It's like somebody drowning with the lifeboat on its way.'

I wanted to help them in some way, but there was nothing I could think of suggesting. And why would anyone want to stop Ellis from cutting loose? It was just the speed of her happiness that worried me, that's all.

19

While I was waiting for Darius to make up the casement window frame, I had a lot of spare time on my hands to restore the boat I was working on. The floor was on hold until the new window was in. So I also had time to slip in a small job for the old woman next door to the Concannons. Her name was Rosie. She was over ninety and I wondered what was the point in putting up shelves for her. It was more about being a hired listener, while she gave me all kinds of valuable information about the Concannons. I could have done the job in an hour, but it went on indefinitely and I didn't even ask to get paid.

There was a picture of Michael Collins on her mantelpiece which I first mistook to have been her husband.

'He was in the army? Your husband?'

'I'm not married,' she said, looking at me as if I was stupid.

'I'm sorry.'

'Michael Collins,' she said. 'The freedom fighter.'

She told me that she had gone to his funeral as a girl and there were thousands of people at it. She took out a box of newspaper cuttings gone brown with time and began telling me about his life. He was the great revolutionary hero, the Irish Che Guevara. Kevin later told me that Che Guevara was Irish and that he once visited Ireland. He landed at Shannon airport and took one look around and said: 'get me out of here' in Spanish, because he would not stand a chance with the place already full of revolutionaries.

Rosie asked me to hide the suitcase with the Michael Collins cuttings in the attic for her. She complained about the crime rate and how much things had changed over a lifetime. She had a dog named Rusty who looked like a dingo with large triangular ears pointing upwards and said he had come all the way from Australia and walked straight off the ferry up to her house. She told me that this part of the city by the harbour was called Kingstown when she was born. All the piers and the granite monuments were built by the British. They were great builders, she had to admit, and there was nothing like it going up since then, only Tesco. She said the people who built the shopping centre were town killers because all the small shops had been shut down since they arrived. She once owned a sweet shop herself, years ago. Now the town was mostly vacant and semi-derelict with every second shop closed down. The public swimming baths had also been closed for thirty years and she tried to explain to me how little respect Irish people had for public property.

I had seen some of the old photos of Dún Laoghaire in black and white. Times when people were dressed in old-fashioned clothes and everybody seemed to be waiting for things to happen. Photos of shops with neat displays of goods in the shape of pyramids. Boxes of tea and biscuits and sweets. Drapes in the windows and flower baskets hanging outside and skinny shop assistants in their bow ties and long dresses standing beside the entrance. These were the photographs that Rosie came from, in a time when you could trust people to give things back that were lost.

She was worried for young people now.

'Ellis,' she said. 'She's the one I'd be concerned about.'

It turned out that Rosie was not just a neighbour but a great family friend. She had known the children since they were very small and had often been asked to baby sit. They came freely in and out of her house every day after school to play snakes and ladders and throw the ball for the dog.

'Very sensitive child,' Rosie said. 'The youngest.'

Maybe I should have been more courageous. But what could I do to save anyone? I was a carpenter, not a lifeboat man.

'She always missed her father,' Rosie told me.

I thought of the All-Ireland hurling medal which I still had in my possession.

'She was the most affectionate child I ever met. Always throwing her arms around me. You really felt close to her, much more than the others.'

'What about her father?' I asked.

'London,' she said. 'Tried to move back in with them once, but that was a disaster.'

'He's back now,' I said.

'So I believe.'

Then she explained the trouble to me and why he was not welcome into the family any more.

'She had to get the guards for him one night. The children spent the night here with me, for their own safety.'

There must have been some love between them, I thought, if they had three children together. How did things go wrong? Maybe the answer lay in the letters.

'Will you keep an eye out for her?' Rosie said.

'Ellis?'

'She's the sweetest thing. I'd hate to think of anything happening to her.'

'Don't worry,' I said. 'Her brother will look after her.'

'Kevin? You must be joking. He's mad. Stone mad. I wouldn't even ask him to look after Rusty.'

She said he was just like his own father. 'Very charming. Very playful and very generous. But you never know what he really wants from you.'

Then she started telling me about one afternoon, when the girls were young, when Ellis was only nine.

'I used to take them swimming. You couldn't bring Kevin because he always had to be in charge. You had no free will with him around, even when he was a boy. He'd come into the house here and tell me what to do. Very polite and friendly. He's a good boy, but I could never decide anything for myself when he was around.'

She told me how she brought the girls down to the sea to do some fishing on the rocks. 'Crabs and stingrays, that kind of thing.' She went with two other women from the neighbourhood and their children as well. They got ice cream and minerals, as she called them, with straws. She described buying the green nets on bamboo sticks. The shops all had them hanging by the door. Lots of fishing tackle and buckets and spades. Swimming rings. Goggles. Plastic sunglasses.

The tide was out, she told me. She had decided they were going to look for starfish. There were two of them, petrified on her mantelpiece. It was rare enough to find one. You needed to go out a long way, she explained, when the tide had ebbed fully and left the land far behind. Even then you had to be very lucky.

She wanted them to find something they would never forget. A starfish memory to keep all their lives.

They were wading in the shallow waters, dresses held up, hunched over, looking under rocks and bits of seaweed. They saw crabs running sideways for cover. They saw little darting fish around their feet. Translucent shrimps staring up, waving their tentacles. They saw their own reflection and their own crooked legs, refracted through the water, but no starfish. It was a long afternoon with the bells of the church ringing out from the land and Rosie had gone out further than any of the others when she suddenly came across a starfish lying on the sandy bottom.

'I've got one,' she called to the others and they came running.

She reached her hand down into the water to pick it up. But then she discovered that it was not a starfish she was holding at all, but the hand of a young man. His dead body was submerged, hidden underneath the seaweed. Only when she pulled at the starfish did his face come up towards her in the water, all ghostly and white, with his black hair waving and his eyes closed as though he was asleep on his back and dreaming underwater with his arms out. His shoes and socks were missing. He had gone barefooted. His chest was bare and the buttons of his shirt had burst open in the struggle of drowning. What she had believed to be a starfish was in actual fact the cold, white, outstretched fingers of a man in his early twenties who had drowned himself by jumping off the pier at Dún Laoghaire harbour one night and was being delivered back. She held the boy's hand, ready to dance together across the floor of the sea.

By then the children were running over towards her, splashing through low water with great excitement. She dropped the starfish and turned around, waving them away.

'It's nothing,' she shouted. 'Go back.'

She could not let them see what she had found. Instead, she ushered them away towards the shore in a great hurry and the children must have been wondering why the search for starfish on a beautiful afternoon had come to such a sudden end. They must have sensed something was wrong. What explanation could she have given them? She had to make sure they saw nothing of this. She sent them home quickly, while she went in search of help. The tide was already turned and coming in to take back the land it had lost. She warned some of the adults along the seafront to keep people away and not let anyone near the spot where the body was.

How could she have explained it to the children, that people sometimes do this kind of thing to themselves because they're so out of their minds with loneliness they don't know who to ask for help? Was there something about drowned people, some dark inspiration that lured the rest of us to come and join them under the sea until we were all holding hands like starfish meeting? If only the boy could have talked to somebody, he might not have ended things in that way, so suddenly, so brutally, with such violence against his own family.

She found two Garda officers and told them about her discovery. They rushed to the spot where the tide had already begun to rise, lifting the seaweed and waving it around gently. The policemen both waded out in their uniforms to the spot where the dead boy was now beginning to drift away again.

She felt most sorry for the younger Garda. He was not much older than the boy who had drowned himself. And there he was, having to pull his body out of the water and carry him like a brother in towards the land.

'I knew the family,' she said. 'He left a note to his mother saying "I love you all".'

All afternoon, parents were hurrying their children home, promising soft ice-cream cones, anything that would keep them away from the waterfront. There were small groups of people standing along the rusted blue railing, keeping a kind of vigil, looking at the body of the young man lying on the cold concrete with a coloured bathing towel over his face. They were whispering the name of the deceased. They were saying that he had left his shoes and socks neatly placed on the pier as if he was only going to bed. They were waiting for the ambulance to come and take him away, saying he was a nice boy and nobody would have expected this.

'Do you think she knew?' Rosie asked me. 'Ellis. Do you think she might have suspected something? Do you think that's the reason she doesn't come to talk to me any more?'

20

One day I got a call from Helen saying she wanted to meet me, privately. She would not tell me what it was about, but I think I had a fair idea. I knew she was going to cross-examine me again about Kevin's side-stepping. Talk about sampling, he was trying out every woman he met, going nationwide, as he put it. All women, apart from those who were not interested in him, and those he said were not worth going after anyway. He even had a night or two with my ex-girlfriend Liuda, so he told me himself. Maybe I should have been more angry about it than I let on. He shook my hand and congratulated me for finding her, telling me that she was quite a specialist in the sack. Which was fair enough, I suppose, only now I had to go and meet Helen in the city to answer all her questions.

'We need to talk,' she said, a bit like somebody calling you about a serious medical condition.

I was in the building supplier's when I took the call. I stood beside the wood preservatives, trying to hear her voice over the sound of the saw in the yard. I could see the guy from South Ossetia with goggles and headphones on, cutting planks of deal. In fact, the man who imported Liuda from Moldova was also there at the time and I got the impression that he was keeping his eye on me because he thought I should be buying his hardwood mouldings instead of getting them made up at half the price with Darius.

Helen made it clear that it was very urgent, so I dropped everything and decided to come back later for the stuff I needed.

I love being in the building supplier's because of all the talking. They keep asking you questions. How's it going? Are you up to much yourself? Keeping busy? What's the gizmo? When I asked one of the men behind the counter what a gizmo was, he answered me in a Russian accent for a laugh and told me they didn't stock them any more, but I could try the charity shops for a secondhand one. I was only asking because you tend to hear about things in there, new inventions like hammer-fixings and washered masonry nails which I had never seen before and which are very handy for pinning up a plastering mesh. Anything that didn't require pre-drilling was always very welcome and I suppose we're all waiting for the day that somebody invents timber that cuts itself to size. The plumbers sometimes pass around blurred pictures on their mobile phones, telling me that they are new flotation devices for cisterns though they look to me more like body parts because I haven't a clue about plumbing.

One of the guys at the desk once insisted on rolling up his trouser leg and showing me a big scar across his knee. He had fallen from a bridge and landed in a shopping trolley in the canal. He had been trying to shock-impress his girlfriend one night, but he picked the wrong bridge, one without a ledge on the far side to catch him and stop his fall. He knocked on the kneecap. All plastic, he told me. There was a pin inside that went off every time he passed through a security check at the airport. The doctors said they could remove it, but he was fond of it now and wanted to keep it.

You could say that the building supplier's was as good a place to meet people as any pub.

'No bother,' they all kept saying.

I knew they were only joking most of the time. You just had to watch out for when they were serious. Some of them said I was all right. Some of them said I was not the worst. Some said there was nothing wrong with me and some said I was the nicest person on earth, which is not really such a compliment because you don't want to be a walk-over, all conspicuous, with no guile.

There was one guy behind the desk who kept asking me if I ever laid eyes on the man with the beard, what's his name, Radovan Karadžić? The man who committed all the war crimes for Yugoslavia.

In general, the questions were not actually intended as serious enquiries, only as a way of recording your attendance in a roll call, you might say. I enjoyed standing in the line with other men because it made me feel part of the action. You were served by numbers. You picked up a number and waited to be called so you could order your requirements. It's an old-fashioned system, I know, but the people in the trade still preferred it because they got the stuff at more competitive prices than they did from other mainstream hardware stores. They talked and cracked a few jokes and complained about their work and had a quick chat with Jenny at the cash desk while they were paying or signing the docket. So it was not entirely about getting timber and plumbing needs but also a place where people kept an eye on each other. They would go there to be seen. If you had not been seen there lately, then you had dropped out of sight and become forgotten. They'd be asking if you vanished off the face of the earth. What happened to you? Did you fall off a ladder?

You had to make sure that you were seen and remembered in this country. There were all kinds of tricks to let people know you were alive and well and not forgotten. Talking and telling stories and asking questions. Doing each other favours, that kind of thing.

And making noise in the street at night.

For example, I was on my way home through the centre of Dún Laoghaire one night and I heard a group of women screeching. They were wearing high heels and tea-towel dresses, clustering around one particular young woman in white hot pants, with the orbs showing. At the other end of the street there was a man with a big chest and strong arms and a tattoo around his neck being held back by a number of other lads. They staggered against the wall with the cash machine and the big lad kept shouting: 'I just want to talk to her.' The other lads holding him back, for some reason, pulled his shirt off in the process. When he finally freed himself and ran down the street bare-chested, the women fled, screaming even louder. He failed to catch the woman in white hot pants he so badly wanted to talk to, because she darted away in her bare feet with her shoes in her hands for protection. So he then kicked the telephone box and let out an almighty roar. But it was just a bit of street soap, acted out in public. In the end, they fell into each other's arms and you could see them with their heads together in the back seat of the taxi as it spun around up the street and the town centre returned to normal.

There was a security camera mounted on the corner of the bank, recording all this on a small screen. A man in uniform, probably not from here originally either, watching this drama for a living, with his take-away dinner on his lap.

It's quite possible that I went into the building supplier's a bit more often than I needed to, going back again unnecessarily for items that I should have got the last time round. A drill bit. A blade. An extra tin of filler. And maybe it was a way of making sure I was seen, letting people know that I existed.

I met Helen in a café in the city. There was darkness around her eyes from crying. She told me that Kevin was refusing to meet her. He was not even picking up her messages or answering her emails. He was the walking-away type, but she didn't want to believe it. For all his great storytelling abilities, he seemed to have no idea how to write a person out of his life, other than disappearing and never looking back.

'Is he serious about this other woman?' she asked, refusing to mention her name.

'You mean Eleanor?'

'Yes.'

'I don't think so, really,' I said. I didn't have the heart to tell her that he had already moved on to others long ago.

You've heard this story a million times. It's pretty universal, though every country has its own guidelines for deceit and betrayal. The only problem was that I ended up doing the walking away on his behalf. I became his envoy, more or less.

'Are there others?' she asked.

'Other women, you mean?'

'Don't pretend you don't know, Vid.'

'A few,' I admitted.

'Why the fuck does nobody say anything?'

She said this with a bitterness in her voice that was not

really in her character. There was a seagull calling outside, somewhere up on the rooftops, almost laughing by the sound of it. Making the café seem strangely out of place, more like Dursey Island.

'Jesus fucking Christ. You're covering for him, isn't that so? He's your best friend and you can't betray him. You watch him cheating and you say nothing. You go right along with it. You back him up all the way. You tell his lies for him. Because you have this loyalty pact between you which means more than anything else in the world. It's like the fucking Masonic lodge, the two of you.'

'I thought it was better for you not to know,' I said, but that was really cheap.

'You see, you're lying for him right now.'

'Helen,' I said, trying to make her feel better, 'this is nothing. The sampling will stop soon.'

'Just listen to yourself,' she said with a desperate laugh. 'You think I can just forget all this and pretend it never happened?'

I was getting totally mixed up, guessing, muttering, trying to fight his corner for him and getting nowhere.

'He's made a mistake, Helen. You're still the only one for him, I'm absolutely sure of that.'

'You're just living in his pocket,' she said.

She was crying now. She tried to hide it by looking away into the street. I could see men coming into the café, frightened by her tears, standing back with shock-waves of self-doubt on their faces.

'What am I doing, Vid?' she said, wiping her eyes with her sleeve and turning towards me, trying to smile again. 'It's not your fault, is it?'

'I hope you get back together,' I said.

'That's kind, Vid. Thanks.'

All it took was a small conversation like this to bring out a spate of forgiveness in her. I tried to cheer her up and changed the subject. I told her about the men in the building supplier's. There was a funny guy there who kept saying 'use your head' whenever anyone was lifting something heavy like a sack of cement. There was a guy from a company called Accurate Plumbing who whistled the same ABBA song every day and I heard one of the other men saying that there was an old Irish proverb which says: Beware of the man with only one tune.

I managed to get a smile out of her, but I think it was only out of politeness, making up for the interrogation she put me through.

Trying to stay optimistic, I told her about the small wooden boat that I had begun to renovate in my spare time.

'I met this old man in the boatyard down at the harbour and he said I could have the use of his boat if I was prepared to restore it.'

'I hope he's not having you on,' she said.

I ignored these doubts and told her I couldn't wait to get out fishing again. No better place to be in the summer, with no cars around you, only the sound of the water under the boat and the odd seagull looking down to see if you had caught anything.

'If you want, I can take you out,' I said. 'Soon as it's sea-worthy.'

I meant both of them, of course. I was full of hope, expecting their arguments to end any day, just like the muscle man and the girl in white hot pants.

'Nothing standing in the way of us going fishing,' she said.

I wondered what exactly she meant by that because she

asked me to accompany her back to her apartment where all his stuff had been piled into boxes. Socks, underpants, shirts. A leather pilot jacket from the Second World War, given to him by his uncle. His books. A bashed-up guitar with a white soundboard which he had brought with him on a trip around Australia and which was signed by all the people he had met along the way. Hill walking boots. Some computer equipment, leads and things that should have been thrown out long ago. Pictures of them together which had been worth printing out. One particular immortal photo of the two of them out in the open, on a cliff somewhere over-looking the sea, probably taken on delay setting. Him with his arms around her, smiling over her shoulder, with one hand inside her trousers. She no longer cared, or told herself not to care. It was all being thrown out now. Erased, along with all the messages on her phone.

She ordered a taxi for me, pre-paid. She helped to carry the boxes out. She embraced me and said goodbye.

'Thanks for doing this, Vid.'

She spun away so I could not see what she was saying with her eyes. By the time the taxi drove off, she had already gone inside again, out of sight.

21

What would you have done? With the medal, I mean. I couldn't just hold on to the thing for ever. I couldn't leave his father thinking that I had not bothered to hand it over, or that I had kept it for myself, because he was still waiting. What alternative did I have? I had a duty to return it or bring some kind of answer back to him.

I thought of posting it. I thought of leaving it lying around in Kevin's new apartment, the place he was meant to move into with Helen. I thought of putting it in with all the family artefacts in the Concannon house for Rita to find. In the end, I decided to bring it back. What took me so long was the knowledge that I was breaking a promise. Even before I got the red box down with the medal inside it, I knew that I had gone into a forbidden zone.

My problem was not having the language skills to stop things being straightforward, black and white. I was playing the duplicitous game of being myself.

They told me that he had a job as a caretaker in one of the yacht clubs. He sat there every night, surveying a set of screens watching boats in a yard, occasionally looking out through the window or walking around to see the same view with his own eyes. It's a job I could have done very well.

I tracked him down in his basement apartment on a Sunday afternoon. There was a light on and music playing. Traditional music. He coughed as he opened the door. Upstairs, there were people shouting. The main hall door banged. I heard coins falling in the street and somebody cursing in a language I could not understand.

Strictly speaking, I should have handed him back the box with the medal at the door and left again. But he asked me inside and I didn't have the heart to refuse. Of course, I also have to admit that I was very curious and wanted to know more about him, about the letters he sent home, about the story of the drowned woman.

Johnny Concannon was unshaven, with his shirt collar open. He hastily cleared a newspaper off the table and turned the music down. His clothes smelled of smoke. There was a hint of soup in the air also, and mildew. Everything he had owned in his life was here in this underground room where it was always night, it seemed. A single bed with a steel frame, an old Formica breakfast table, two steel chairs with white stars on the upholstery, some books stacked on the floor, his radio on the window sill. There was a small hand-sink on the wall and an electric kettle on a dresser beside it, along with a mirror and some shaving gear. The toilet must have been out in the back, or upstairs, or maybe in the local pub even. Clustered together on the table, there was a loaf of sliced bread and a dented, metal teapot, a bag of sugar, a packet of teabags and a carton of milk. There was also a CD player with a stack of his favourites including Jimi Hendrix and Bob Dylan and Neil Young.

Again, I could see the similarity with Kevin, but the expression was less manipulated. His expectations seemed so much more curtailed. He had remained frugal. He asked me to sit down and offered me a cup of tea. And while he was filling the kettle, I looked around and saw the photograph of himself and Rita on the wall. They looked very young, just married, perhaps. Both of them smiling.

'Would you like a drink instead?' he asked. 'A drop of whisky?'

'No thanks,' I said. 'Tea would be great.'

He offered me a Twix, but I shook my head and told him I didn't eat chocolate or toffee. I watched him pour the tea and remembered what Darius had said about different security zones in Irish families that you passed through with each cup of tea.

Without anything else to say, I produced the box with the medal from my bag. I didn't give it into his hand. Instead, I placed it on the table like a piece of neutral information which spoke for itself and still left a degree of ambiguity, maybe a bit of hope.

'He wouldn't accept it from me,' I said.

'I see.'

He looked at it, but didn't touch it. It contained too much rejection.

'That's the end of it, so,' he said. 'Thanks for trying.'

He smiled. But I could see the self-doubt in his eyes. He had begun to grasp the impossible. All he wanted was some acknowledgement, some illusion of being welcome, at least from his own son. Entire lives were propped up on illusions like that – half a story, a mere suggestion, a line of optimism in the language.

I asked him how long he had been away in England. He had left in his twenties, he said, not because he had to, but just following the music which all came from England then.

'It was the thing to do in those days,' he said. 'Get out.'

He had a good job in a bar in Galway and could have become manager eventually. But there was something missing, some feeling that the floor was not solid underneath his life and that everyone around him was disappearing.

'My friends were all gone,' he said. 'I thought my life was over if I stayed in Ireland. Then I met Rita in London and we got married and started a family. But things didn't work out.'

Perhaps I was the only neutral listener he could find to accept his explanation. I didn't feel entitled to this information, but I could not just walk away as if it didn't interest me.

'I should have made more of an effort,' he said, nodding at the picture on the wall. 'But she didn't make it easy for me.'

He had done reasonably well over there. He wasn't one of those people who worked on building sites, looking at concrete pouring like porridge into the foundations. His lungs would never have stood up to that kind of work. Instead, he worked in the bars and managed to get a franchise on a pub where a lot of Irish people drank. He did great business. But with Rita working as a teacher, they never saw each other much. And then she decided to move back because she didn't want her children growing up in England with a man who was drinking so hard all the time.

'She never wanted me to go back with her,' he said.

He looked at the space between his shoes for a while. He asked me if I had anything against him smoking a cigarette. He said he had smoked since he was fifteen and it was the only thing that stopped him coughing. It got the immune system working, he explained, though it was probably time to go back to rolling his own.

'She closed the door,' he said. 'I came back here for a while to live with her at the house, but she hated me being there. She had such a way of putting me down. I know I did wrong, but some of the things she said were worse than a fist in the teeth.'

What struck me was how different it might have been if he had stayed here with the family. Even his appearance and his health would have been better. The hunch in his shoulders corresponded to the luck in life. He should have been far more confident, more certain of his place in the world. He should have owned a car and played golf, should have gone on foreign holidays with his wife and children and looked quite different. His life had given him a hardened, outdoor look, as though he had not lived in comfort, as though he had walked a lot and waited for buses in the rain instead of driving.

After she left with the children, he gave up running pubs and became a caretaker. He managed apartment blocks in various parts of London over the years. He tried his luck in America for a while, and in South Africa, then Canada where most of his older brothers had gone. He wanted to become rich like them and win his family back that way, by arriving home loaded. But it never worked. Instead he always came back to London. Another job as caretaker, not even as flash or as well paid as the earlier ones, but still a good job with a nice basement apartment which was warm, not like this one here.

He was like a person who had arrived here for the first time. He could hardly recognise the place. Worse than that were the small corners of familiarity which made him feel this country was more hostile than any other place in the world. The landmarks left unchanged must have made it clear how quickly his life had gone by and how impossible it was to change anything that happened back then.

He told me how his mother had gone to see him in London before she died. At this point he broke into his own language, as though he could only talk about her in his mother tongue, a bit like me being able to remember certain things only in Serbo-Croat. Speaking in Irish, then translating for me instantaneously, he told me that she came to visit him because he and his brothers in Canada were so reluctant to go home. He gave her his bed and slept on the couch and in the morning she had died in her sleep. Maybe she planned it that way, peacefully, in the company of her youngest son.

He was trying to hide his feelings from me, saying only that there was nothing left for him in Connemara apart from the empty house and his memories of growing up with his seven brothers, the oldest of whom he only met for the first time abroad, after he emigrated himself.

He asked me if I missed home and if I was thinking of going back. Maybe there was something in my eyes that revealed how similar we were, in between places, neither here nor there.

'You know, I've felt loneliness many times in my life,' he said, 'but the worst loneliness comes from what you've done yourself.'

It was too hard for him to talk about. Going back over things that he did at my age, when he hardly understood what was going on his own head. Best not to remember anything, to move on and never look back.

'I'm barred,' he said. 'I'm not allowed anywhere near the house, or the children.'

He checked my eyes to see if I would disown him now that he had revealed the worst.

'Believe me, Vid. You don't want to hear it all. I've spent my whole life regretting just one moment of madness.'

He asked me how the work was going at the house and I told him they were already talking about putting in a new kitchen.

'Looks like I'm there for good now,' I joked. I had all but taken his place, walking in and out of the family home from which he had been expelled.

'How are they all?' he asked.

'They're very well,' I said with great enthusiasm. I listed off what they were all doing like a great expert on the family. Jane away doing biochemistry. Kevin with his law practice.

'Ellis,' I said. 'She's flapping her wings a bit. But that's only what you would expect, she has to let go a little.'

'And Rita,' he asked, 'is she happy?'

I told him about her battle with cancer and assured him that she was doing fine, still teaching and getting involved in bits of charity work on the side and just hoping that her cancer didn't come back.

'She kept all your letters,' I found myself saying in a burst of sheer good will, and maybe I was trying to open a door for him to come back. I didn't have the heart to tell him they were all unread.

Instead we got on to the subject of the drowned woman and he told me the story all over again in his own words, the exact same way that I had heard it from Kevin. At times Johnny broke into Irish again and translated for me, as though speaking in Irish was the only way the memory could be trusted.

He confirmed the same details, how exactly she was denounced from the altar. The way he had heard it from his mother. The priest had put it up to the men in the congregation to drown her. Because every man in the whole of Connemara was under suspicion while she was walking around with a baby in her belly and no husband by her side. And if they were not men enough to do that and clear their own names, so the story went, she should have the decency to drown herself.

He spoke as though it all happened very recently and there was no separation in time, only the distance of a few generations back.

He told me how her body was said to have been washed up on the island in a place called *Pointe*, in a spot which was later called after her, but not by name. He described to me how the men must have found her. They used to go walking along the coast looking for items of salvage brought in by the tide.

'Shore-ranging,' he called it.

The person who found her must have seen nothing more than a bundle of clothes, perhaps, discoloured by the saltwater and the sun. Only the barking of the dog drawing attention to the shape of a human corpse and the creatures that may have already made the discovery before them. The man would have made the sign of the cross instantaneously. He would have touched nothing and would have called his dog back. He would have examined the body from a safe distance and walked around it in a circle and spoken his thoughts out loud, ending each sentence with half a prayer. He would have seen the bruised feet and the long hair lain across the grey rocks and the damage done to her skin by sealife and birds while in the water. He would have known that she was carrying a child by the swollen belly. He would have wondered what the women would be saying about this and what advice they would have to give on what to do with the body and who it might belong to.

Once the news was passed on around the island, people would have been asked to keep away. Women and children would not have been allowed to see the tragedy with their own eyes because there was enough of it around, enough drowning of their own to witness this one as well. The body would have been left there, secured with rocks, perhaps, until it was decided what to do with it. There was no policeman on the island at the time and not for a long time after that either. So there would have been no police investigation and no formal identification of the body.

News of her disappearance from Furbo would most probably have reached the island by then, so perhaps her identity was already known to them as the young woman who had been denounced by the church. The men on the island would have had no option but to go to their own priest for guidance in the matter. The priest in charge of the islands would have known that this was the woman who had brought scandal to the coast of Connemara. And because she was with child and unmarried, she could not be given a place of burial in consecrated ground.

He had never been out to the islands himself and didn't know where she was buried. There were some stories going around that she was brought to the edge of the cemetery and buried outside the walls, unrecognised by the church. There were stories that she lay in that spot outside the walls for many years until the cemetery was enlarged. The perimeter walls were extended and she may have found her way back in after a long time alone, slipping inside quietly, included at last.

'It's just a rumour, I think,' he said. 'I'm not so sure that's true. It's impossible to verify, in any case, because there would have been no headstone erected with her name on it.'

He said people may have got her story mixed up with somebody else, because it was not uncommon for people to be excluded back then, even unborn babies which were not baptised, buried alone in unmarked graveyards by the sea. There was an English sailor washed up on a different island, on Clare Island, during the Second World War. A man whose body was buried outside the Catholic graveyard and given a headstone but then became included later when they steered the stone wall around his grave. He had even heard of a graveyard in Belfast where there was a wall built underground to keep the dead apart.

'What was her name?'

'Máire,' he said. 'Máire Concannon.'

'Was she drowned or did she do it herself?'

He looked away, unable to answer that question. He appeared not to be in the same room any longer.

There were a million phrases for letting people know that you were leaving. It was the hardest thing of all to learn, getting up and saying that you were on your way. I coughed a bit and stood up and said it was time to go, but he didn't hear that. Trains could have come and gone through the room without him noticing. Then finally he looked at me.

'You're going,' he said.

I gave him my number. I told him that if there was anything I could help him with, he could call me any time. I suppose I was trying to stop him from disappearing again. I fumbled with gestures and made all kinds of promises which nobody would have expected me to carry out.

His handshake was very firm, lasting a long time. It seemed to ask me why I was leaving so soon and would I not stay and go for a drink with him. It was asking me to believe him, to trust him, to speak well of him. A handshake of ten verses.

The longest handshake that I can remember, holding on for well over half a minute, maybe a full minute, maybe even a lot longer, turning me into a child in his presence. I didn't pull away. His hand contained the entire journey of his life, on ships and trains, through airports and cities and bars, all the places that he had worked in. All the names of people he met. All the stories and memories, the laughs and triumphs and failures and injustices. A handshake full of things that I still wanted to know but had not thought of asking at the time. A handshake that remained imprinted on my hand long after I had walked back down the street. Days later. Weeks later. I still felt the strong grip of his hand around mine as though he would never let go.

22

I suppose this was the real trespassing. Going against all the rules of friendship and privacy and confidentiality.

I told Rita that I had to go back to Belgrade for a funeral. I said I had managed to get a cheap flight and would be back before she knew it. The work was suspended to some degree, in any case. I was still waiting for Darius to deliver the frame for the casement window, I made sure to explain, so it was a very good time for a funeral.

'You'll have the house to yourself for a few days,' I said, which was not a particularly good thing to say.

The same story went out to Kevin. It was all a complete lie, of course. I had no intention of going to a funeral back in my country. I was starting to get the hang of making things up and going on detours with my words.

'You're not doing a runner now, are you?' she said, looking at me as though I was one of her pupils in class.

'No way.'

'I've heard that some people are just dropping everything and going home.'

'I swear to God, not me,' I said. 'I wouldn't let you down like that, Mrs Rita.'

I gave her the exact time that I would be back. I had even

learned off a bogus travel itinerary, with return flight times, in case they asked. She was waiting for me to confess what I was really up to. But I kept my nerve and didn't reveal a thing, not even the fact that I had met her husband and that he was asking about her and that he still had the picture of their wedding day on the wall of his basement apartment, not far from here.

'Don't forget to bring me back a tin toy,' she said.

My way of looking at this was not so much that I was breaking the rules of privacy but still trying to get the family back together, in my own way.

On the bus to Galway I felt I was being watched and that everyone knew what I was up to. I must have had the look of urgency in my eyes, needing to find out things.

I got to Furbo early in the afternoon. *Na Forbacha* it's called in Irish, a wild rocky coastline with lots of stone walls and crooked fields and some cottages still in existence. You can see how the people tried to make the best of it by compiling as many rocks as possible on to the walls so there would be some space on the land for things to grow and feed a cow. There was little to sustain the people back in the old days apart from their language and their stories, living on a strip of rock between the bog and the sea. I saw some of the small fishing boats they called Currachs. Black canvas rowing boats with pointed oars that were no longer in use very much because they were as light as a paper boat on the water and were the cause of too many fishermen being lost by drowning.

Riding to the sea, they called it.

The place must have changed quite a bit in recent times. There is a big hotel situated right on the shore now which seems to have come from a different country and been dropped on the landscape, looking more like an institution with the usual three flags flapping in the forecourt and a thousand bedrooms and a piano that plays by itself in the dining room. There are some wooden shelters erected on the shore for the guests to sit and look out across the Atlantic towards the islands. It's no wonder they would build a hotel here in this place, because the guests got the spectacular view all to themselves.

What was the view worth in times of hardship? you had to ask yourself. Because I was from somewhere else, I had the ability to censor the big hotel from the map. The only thing that didn't change was the sea and the waves still pounding with the same rhythm after all this time. I thought of how things must have been here when life was still in the hands of luck and faith and when there was no such thing as jam and peanut butter and biscuits in the shops, when the people here must have been subjugated by forms of power that was not unlike the way things were in my own country.

What would it have been like for a young woman to become pregnant? An unmarried mother, denounced as unfit to live among her own people. She had become a stranger overnight. Her residence permit had run out, you might say. Faced with deportation, only in her case she was forced out into the sea. She had lost her rights and had become an alien in a place where she had grown up thinking of as home.

Looking out across the bay, the Aran Islands appeared to me like whales with grey rounded backs coming up out of the water. I was probably not the first person to think of this, but it felt to me like an original way of describing them because it was my first time seeing them. Whatever way the light falls, they keep moving a little, dipping and coming up again. They say the distances before you in these parts can hurt your eyes, and that's true. The islands are an illusion, out of reach. The coastline at my feet was real, with a gentle slope down to the shore. I could see how easy it was to get carried away across to the islands by the tides. I found lots of places along the shore where you could easily walk out into the tide in desperation and disappear.

I walked along the beach at Furbo and thought of myself shore-ranging, looking at items washed in on the tide. Bits of saturated wood. Logs. Bottles. Plastic containers full of sand. A trainer filled with a sand foot. Submerged trousers. Shells. Seaweed. A gull feather. The skeleton of a sheep, with some wool still attached. Bits of fishing gear. Blue and green nets, half buried. A crushed lobster pot. Rusted metals. Buckets. Bins. Bicycle wheels. A car tyre. The remains of a suitcase. A Spanish milk carton and a red interdental brush, items that were probably tossed overboard by fishermen or by sailors on those enormous cargo ships. All the bits and pieces that are returned eventually by the force of the waves.

I was sorry I had not asked Johnny Concannon more questions, such as where he had lived and was his house still standing?

There was little that could be verified about the drowned woman. No police report. No inquest. No eye-witness evidence. No death certificate, most likely, under the circumstance. Only her name, which would have been known locally as Máire Conceannain, though probably registered in the parish records as Mary Concannon.

I walked up to the church in Furbo and knocked on the glass porch of the small parochial residence. An old priest came out with his collar undone. He brought me inside, into a small office off the hallway. It was hard for me to explain what I was looking for, a foreign national asking about a young pregnant woman who was ordered by his predecessor to go and drown herself.

'I'm only a visiting priest myself,' he said.

He explained that he was standing in while the parish priest was on holidays. He was not from the area, so he had not heard of any pregnant woman being drowned. He didn't seem to think there was anything unusual about a person with my accent investigating these matters. He also explained to me that there was no church in existence in Furbo until quite recently.

The nearest church at the time of Máire Concannon's life would have been in Barna. That was some kilometres away, but still accessible on foot. On occasion, the priest from Barna would have come to say Mass in the school in Furbo on feast days, perhaps, for the old people mostly who could not make the journey. But that would have been quite rare and most of them would have walked it into Barna and back on Sunday mornings, unless they had a bicycle or a cart pulled by a donkey or a pony and trap, which was also an exception. He could remember when only the odd priest and the doctor owned a car around Connemara.

If I was looking for the parish records, he added, then I would have to go back into Rahoon in Galway. All births and deaths and marriages would have been entered into the records at Rahoon, which had by now become part of Galway city.

I walked as far as Barna because I wanted to know how long the trip would have taken for a woman carrying a child. The church in Barna was new. The old one had been knocked down and rebuilt. Inside, I spoke to a woman who had not heard of any drowned woman either, but who was able to show me a photograph of the old church in the parish magazine on sale in the porch. It was a stark kind of building with high windows and a square bell tower, one of many around the country, so I believe. The woman even pointed at the small, overgrown ruin of an earlier church on the far side of the road, a further century back. The modern church seemed out of context with the landscape and the events which had taken place there. It was hard for me to get any idea of what it might have been like to hear the words of the priest denouncing a pregnant girl from the pulpit. But as I came out of the church, I felt the cutting wind coming in from the sea where she had been told to drown herself.

Most of the town in Barna was like a new shopping centre. It could have been any suburb in a city, except that you couldn't avoid being reminded that this was Connemara by the landscape and by the sight of the blue sea by your side at all times. Also, the people. You could never forget where you were when you talked to the people in the shops, because they wanted to know where you were from and what brought you here, hoping that you might get into a conversation when you only asked for a bottle of plain water.

I walked down as far as the small fishing harbour. There was a row of houses along the way, one of them with white lichen spots all over the façade and the last one ending the terrace had become a fish restaurant. Some lobster pots were stacked up on the pier and I saw a few of the old black canvas boats lying upside down like the shells of giant mussels which had come from the bottom of the sea.

The church at Rahoon in Galway was more like a cathedral. You got the impression that the congregation was enormous at one point and how it grew so big that the parish was divided up into more and more sections with new churches being built in small places like Furbo and beyond, but which now had very little followers left apart from the old people.

Right beside the church at Rahoon is the Presentation Convent where the parish records are kept. I went up to the door of the convent, which was streak-painted in brown, like many doors belonging to religious orders in Ireland, a particular coating of paint that sends the shivers down some people's spines whenever they pass by, so I'm told. I met with a nun by the name of Sister Consuelo. She seemed to think there was something odd about me and asked me if I had sought permission from the parish priest to investigate the records. I told her I hadn't. I gave the name of Johnny Concannon and said he was unable to make the journey from Dublin himself and asked me to step in and enquire about the records on his behalf as a favour.

She told me that I could not consult the records personally. She asked for my name and when she repeated it in her accent, it sounded more like Vitch. She said she would be glad to help me and offered to look up the name of Mary Concannon, within the approximate bands of time that I outlined. She said it was a very common name around Connemara and there might be a lot of them, so I might as well do something useful with myself in the meantime, such as walking into the city or by the Corrib river.

I went into a few shops and accidentally came across a tin toy for Rita. I was delighted with myself because my alibi was complete. A robot man, painted red. The woman in the shop set it in motion so he walked across the counter in a stiff stride with his arms moving. I bought it and she placed it into the box for me. There was a sticker on the box saying this was not a toy and not suitable for children.

By the time I got back to the convent, I discovered that Sister Consuelo had been looking up only the death records for some reason, so I had to explain to her again that there would not have been any death certificate. In the eyes of the church and the state alike, she was possibly still alive or had emigrated and died in a foreign place.

By then it was too late for her to do any more for me and I had to come back the following day at noon, which ruled out doing a trip to the islands. The weather had turned bad overnight, in any case, with a serious storm coming up, so I would have to keep that part of the journey for another time.

Next morning, Sister Consuelo dug out a list of possibilities, all identical female babies named Mary Concannon and born in Furbo, in and around the turn of the twentieth century or after. She explained to me that the district of Furbo contained as many as twelve smaller sub-divisions or townlands with names like Ballynahown, Seercin, Derryoughter, Trusky East, Polleney, Ballard and Rough Furbo, all within a stone's throw of each other and all divided into strips, more or less, from the bog to the sea.

The list of names was written out in neat, frail handwriting. For some reason, Sister Consuelo had included the name of Julia Conncannon who had died aged eighteen and was buried in Barna, 1922. What happened to her, she didn't know. Perhaps it was hard to accept the story of a pregnant woman being drowned and she gave me the option of supplanting it with another, more legitimate, tragedy.

I thanked her and took the list with me. Later, I looked at the names and the date of birth in each case. It was impossible to say for certain which one it was. Not even Johnny Concannon could do that because the names went back so far, beyond human memory.

I thought of the church in Barna with the high windows. I thought of the echo that might bounce back from the walls, even when the church was packed. The sudden emptiness, the sudden weakness in her stomach when she heard her name being announced from the pulpit in front of her people. She would have known it was coming. She would have heard the rumours drifting behind her and would not have been surprised by the words of the priest, only the severity of the judgment, asking her to have the decency to drown herself and the child.

How must she have felt, leaving the church that day, turning back home under the gaze of all the men and women outside? All the neighbours and friends whom she knew by name but who now saw her as a complete stranger. What about her family, her mother and her sisters, what would they have felt, seeing her walking away alone? Her legs hardly able to carry her weight. The sickness in her stomach throwing up what little she had eaten and carried by the wind against the stone walls. Her coat hiding the bulge in her belly, denying herself and her future offspring, despising the sound of her own name and wishing that she and her child would become invisible. Her head spinning, wondering if she still had a place that could be called home. Her face white and already lifeless with panic as she walked back along the road with the clang of the priest's words echoing in her head like a sentence of execution. How could she ever show her face in the open again?

The big question remained, whether she drowned herself in the end or whether she was drowned by somebody else. Her death was not accidental, that much we can assume with certainty. She was murdered by the words of the priest and by the complicity of the people who failed to stand up for her, including her own family. Can it technically be called suicide, to be let down so badly that you were driven to it?

Who killed her? Was it somebody in the family? Was it the father of the child? I didn't have any answers to bring back with me after the journey, only more questions.

For example, I wanted to know if her pregnancy was the result of an act of love or an act of violence. I wanted to know if she was betrayed, whether somebody took advantage of her and whether she was abused, left to the mercy of the church and the congregation who listened silently as her name was called out. I wanted to know why she didn't run away and escape to London, like so many other women did.

And another thing. At the exact time of drowning, was there a possibility that the foetus might have carried on living even a fraction of a second longer? Are both heartbeats connected as one and therefore expire as one? Or does the foetus die alone, like the mother?

23

Ellis was nowhere to be found. She had disappeared, emigrated to the land of dreams and drugs. I began to think of myself as an agent, given the self-appointed task of rescuing her. I searched for her in places where I had seen her once or twice before, out of her head, sitting on benches with her friends. Down near the harbour in the evening sun, overlooking the bowling green where the old people in white suits quietly play and you hear the clack every now and again of bowls colliding. Next to the hollow with the stagnant pond and the floating beer cans instead of water lilies.

Down at the harbour, I stopped in front of the Carlisle pier which had been replaced by a new terminal for the super ferry to take all the cars and container traffic. The old pier abandoned, like a grey, derelict arm sticking out.

The doors through which so many people passed over decades had been boarded up. The windows left open, with pigeons flying in and out. The entrance area in front of the building had been given over to parking spaces. The ticket office had become a yacht sales agency. The curved railway tracks running right up the quay to the boat had been levelled over and the space was being used to store large, expensive yachts in winter. The familiar roof of the station was still there, a triangular front piece made of blue boards, with an oval cut out and a short spire on top. Everything crumbling and fading. Some of the signs pointing the way to the trains for the city were still there, but nobody arrived here and nobody left from here any more. Nobody leaned on the granite wall to wave goodbye or wait for anyone to come back.

You could see how the pier was built on stilts, with a tunnel allowing fishermen in small boats to pass underneath. You could imagine how the terminal building itself was once considered modern and how the passengers coming through would have been impressed by the size of the halls and the bold, rounded design.

There was a man I got talking to in the pub who was a ticket collector on the Carlisle pier for years. He remembered it well in thriving times, with thousands of people emigrating every week. He remembered, out of compassion, allowing people on board to say goodbye. He told me you had to be immune to the tears, because otherwise you'd only soak up all that sadness over the years, which he probably did without knowing it. He described boisterous people getting on drunk. 'Half seas', they used to call it. He told me about scouts who came over to Ireland on behalf of building contractors in Britain looking for workers, putting tags on men's coats so they could be easily identified and directed to various sites as soon as they arrived in London or Manchester or Northampton. Girls on the main street in Dublin approached and told of great jobs waiting for them in London, given tickets and identification tags so they could go straight across and work. He told me about the stories of the Irish drinking and fighting among themselves over there and the rough conditions, with men having to sleep together in the same bed and saying the rosary to be safe. The pub was the only place where they could be warm and feel at home.

More recently, he said, the people who went away were more educated and did well for themselves, even highly talented young lads running the place over there.

For a long time, nobody knew what to do with the Carlisle pier. At one point, the authorities held an architectural competition for an extravagant new building. The shortlist included a design by the famous New York architect, Daniel Libeskind, which was meant to incorporate a museum on emigration. An impressive design, like the prow of a ship, heading straight out towards the harbour mouth. It didn't win the competition. But the winning project was never built either. For a long time it was just left as a derelict monument to emigration. And in the end, the only plan they came up with was to flatten it all and have a car park.

Alongside the pier were all the other monuments and landmarks going back in time. Like the cast-iron fountain for Queen Victoria. The yacht club with the mast and yard arm erected on solid ground. The anchor from the HMS *Leinster*, which was sunk by a German torpedo with the loss of many lives, recovered from the sea floor and exhibited to remember those terrible days when bodies were brought ashore here. The granite bollards with the blue chains strung between them and the weal marks in the trees next to them from generations of children passing by swinging the chains against the trunks. The buoy into which you donate coins for the lifeboat. Some of the black-and-white pictures show women in long flowing dresses and parasols standing by the bandstand on the pier. Horse-drawn cabbies waiting for passengers to disembark from the old steamer ships.

And the sheds. Along the sea road, there's a row of wooden sheds, painted blue and white. They could be seen in many of the old photographs, designed in a time of courtesy when there was an abundance of time. For people sheltering from the rain, before all the traffic on the road. Places where you could sit and watch the mail boat coming and going. The yachts and small sailing vessels like clothes on the line. The sun shining in one part of the bay and the curtains of grey rain lashing down in another. And when the sun came out again and the steam rose from the pavements and the granite rocks, you could step out and carry on walking.

At one point, the sheds became popular with emigrants coming up from the country who had no money to spend on accommodation or taking afternoon tea in the hotels. Later, the sheds were used by homeless people, even though they were too cold at night. You could see, by the shape of the trees on the seafront, how strong the winds can be around here, turning the branches into rigid manes blown inland.

The wind did some funny things to the trees and there was no reason to believe it didn't do the same to the people.

Later still the sheds were taken over by cider gangs and the druggies, as they were called, leaving needles behind them. They were desecrated over time, even partially burned down. Then it was decided to restore them with great care and I would have loved the job myself. Only now they've been closed up with steel bars to prevent anyone from sitting there and looking out at the rain.

Ellis had lost her foothold and I went around asking people about her. I spoke to a guy who owned lots of snakes and reptiles and kept hundreds of mice for food in a cage at the back of his house. His cat got in one day and let all the mice out. He stood in the street with a snake coming out of his shirt that looked like a tattoo only that it began to move as he talked. He knew Ellis. The girl with black leggings and a little tartan jacket with lots of colours in her hair. The girl in her own world, with earphones inside her hood. He told me that she had not been seen for a while but that she was with a guy called Diller and he was in charge of looking after her.

It didn't fill me with confidence.

The druggies are the real exiles now. They have as much time on their hands as the people in black-and-white photographs. They speak in a slow, swollen language. I'd often see them on the main street, sitting on the low wall outside the church, drinking coffee. Concentrating hard on opening a sachet of sugar. Terribly thin, most of them. They had their own dialect and their own routines, collecting their medication. They seemed to be full of kindness and full of advice, helping one another out. You could see why it would feel good to belong to that group, meeting up in the mornings and putting their arms around each other like real friends, asking how things were going and if they had slept well. They did things for each other, giving away sleeping tablets and other prescription medicines, lending a bit of money for a few cigarettes. Ghostly shapes in hoods and tracksuits who never needed much food any more, only sleep. They were like a separate ethnic group, living at the heart of the community, but with their own customs and rituals, free from having to own anything, sharing everything around them. I saw one young woman squatting down near the cash machine one day with her jeans around her ankles, looking up in astonishment as though she had forgotten to lock the bathroom door. One of the bank staff came out and said 'Welcome to Dún Laoghaire.'

Kevin told me it was a management issue, like everywhere else in the developed world. The epic contradictions of democracy, he called it. He had even seen a man standing outside the door of the church with his trousers down and everything hanging out for all to see, injecting a needle into his penis.

Ellis turned up at home again one day, but not for long. Working away, preparing for the casement window, I heard a noise upstairs and thought it was Rita. But it could not be her, because it sounded more like an intruder, searching for something, marching up and down the rooms, throwing things around.

After a while, she came running down the stairs. I tried to stop her and talk to her, but she was in too much of a hurry.

'He works in the yacht club at night,' I said to her. 'He's the caretaker and you just have to knock on the glass and he'll come out.'

She had accusation in her eyes, ready to cry, or maybe only waiting for the next hit. I wanted to hold on to her and explain things, but she disappeared again, leaving me alone in the house once more.

While I was in the kitchen getting a drink of water, I noticed a bad smell when I ran the tap, so I went upstairs and ran the tap in the bathroom as well, to see what was wrong. As I passed along the landing, I saw what Ellis had been up to.

The letters. She'd opened all the letters which her father had sent home. The entire bundle all over the floor.

I caught sight of the horrible black ash doors which were open and had the urge to tear them out again.

The boxes had been removed. Things left all over the place.

Letters scattered everywhere. It made me feel I had become involved in some transgression. I stepped back into the bathroom and watched the water running, wondering if it looked a little brown, afraid to taste it.

I thought of going into the bedroom and quickly clearing up the mess that Ellis made, but it was better that I did nothing.

Moments later the hall door closed and it was Rita. She was happy with the tin robot man I brought back for her, though I was not sure she believed it came from Belgrade. She seemed to have become quite suspicious in general.

I'm a slow reader of social situations. It took me ages to work out the implications of my presence upstairs. But I knew it felt wrong. The letters scattered all over the bedroom and Mrs Concannon calling from the hallway.

'Vid. Are you there?'

I was trapped. She was going to ask what business I had being upstairs. I was going to get expelled from the family in disgrace. I was going to be like her husband, barred from ever coming near the place. Not only that, but Kevin was going to kick the shit out of me. They would call me a treacherous foreigner, an intruder with no respect for privacy. No matter how I tried to explain this, it would look like a great breach of trust.

'Vid,' she called again.

I remained silent. I moved around in the bathroom and switched on the bath taps as well. The boards creaked. I had plans for de-creaking the whole house one day because they were so bad in some places. They might as well have been screaming down to her, he's upstairs, Mrs Concannon, reading all your letters.

I heard her coming up the stairs.

'Is that you, Vid?'

'Oh yes, Mrs Rita. Mrs Concannon.'

I left the taps running and stepped out to meet her on the landing. Her eyes stared through me, beyond me. She looked into the bedroom and saw the ransack of her life scattered on the floor.

'The water,' I managed to say. 'Don't drink the water.'

'Who did this?'

I pretended not to have seen anything, but the letters had finally released their words.

'Was Ellis here?'

'Just a few minutes ago,' I answered. 'You didn't see her?'

Standing in the door of the bathroom, there was a moment where I thought her suspicion might turn to openness. I wondered if she might begin to confide in me. She was going to sit down and tell me the whole story, why they broke up and what was wrong with the family and why they never talked about their father. Why they never spoke about the drowned woman in Furbo. I could see us going over the whole thing calmly. Sorting out the world and becoming the best of friends. She would send me out to gather her family around her. It was not that she had to have her husband back into her bed or listen to him murdering Dylan songs all night with his Connemara accent. All she had to do was talk to him and let him live on the edge of the family. It didn't mean she had to surrender. She was not going to lose anything. Nobody was going to think badly of her for showing kindness.

I waited, but she said nothing. She held everything to herself, hard as hammers. There was a new sharpness in her eyes. An anger that made her look a bit masculine once more. Her lips tightened. She wanted to strike something, somebody, anybody.

'I better take a look in the attic,' I said.

She stared ahead, hardly hearing what I said.

'The storage tank. In the attic.'

Moments later, I came up with the ladder and erected it against the banisters. By then she had gone into the room, hastily clearing all those things back into the wardrobe, trying at the same time not to look at them too closely and see her past in front of her. I ran back down to get a rope to make sure the ladder didn't slide back on the carpet. She came out to watch me going up, lifting away the stained-glass skylight. I climbed into the attic and made my way over to the tank and sure enough, I was right.

'Pigeon.'

'Oh my God,' she said.

I went back down for a plastic bag and some cleaning materials, the strongest disinfectant I could find. I took the opportunity to run all the taps and flush each of the toilets in the house. Then I went back up into the attic until the whole house reeked of detergent.

She waited for me on the landing. Her anger seemed to have given in to defeat. Things were falling apart on her. She wanted to know how the hell a pigeon would get in under the roof. I told her I found a hole under the slates, though I had already fixed it. But it might be no harm to have the roof checked out at some point because there was no adequate insulation either.

'The roof,' she said. 'Is it that bad?'

I could hear the vulnerability in her voice now. Behind that steely, schoolteacher tone, there was so much she didn't understand.

By then, so I gathered, Ellis had already run off with the money which was contained in the letters. She had met her father in the street and he had told her that he had sent her a gift each time. Each letter had a short note to her, the youngest, with a bit of money. She had never received it. Now the letters were torn open, the money extracted in one large withdrawal. There was not even enough time to read the little note he had sent her, asking how she was getting on, with his address on the top and the money attached with a paper clip. Already, Ellis was spending the contents of these unanswered letters on substances that would help her forget everything.

'Nothing to worry about, Mrs Concannon.'

I told her the roof was grand and would do for a while longer. I didn't want to appear as though I was scouting for more work.

'Not immediately,' I reassured her. 'Down the line a bit.'

When I came down the ladder she was still full of suspicion and wanted to take a look inside the plastic bag, just to see the evidence for herself. The contents would confirm my honesty and prove that I did not read through the letters left lying all over her room.

Her head snapped back with the smell. The dead bird inside looked like a black sponge, almost gone completely liquid, not much more than a thin ribcage, with curled-up claws and dripping wings. The life of a bird decomposing in front of her eyes, slowly converting into gas. Its substance turning back into energy, evaporating into new life forms crawling out of its open beak.

I told her I had cleaned out the tank thoroughly, but advised her not to drink the water for a few days. I told her to boil everything before using it. Then I went down to dispose of the dead carcass in the skip.

24

I was never really given much time to be lonely up to then. It's only when I got the phone call telling me that they were going to kill me that I began to feel I was on my own. I had fooled myself into believing I was at home here. But my presence was full of doubt after that. I drank doubt-tea. I ate doubt-sandwiches. I felt doubt-doorknobs in my hand and walked on doubt-floorboards. Everything I touched was invalid and full of self-questioning, even the screwdriver became unsure of which way to turn.

'We'll take you out of your misery,' they said to me.

Which I thought was quite funny initially. I tried to take it in the right spirit, as a joke, but I was laughing before the punchline came with a second phone call, just to make sure that there was no misunderstanding.

'You're fucking dead,' the voice confirmed, among other things that I didn't quite get. 'Say goodbye to your mates.'

It couldn't be clearer than that. They were giving away the ending.

This was the big day. Darius and myself were putting in the new casement window. One of those days when an entire week seems to pass in a matter of hours. It started so well, with me and Darius stopping off at the petrol station for one of those breakfast rolls and coffee. His van loaded up with the frame, everything neatly labelled so there would be no confusion. The two of us eager to get stuck in because we knew this could only be done inside a one-day turnaround.

'No rain please,' Darius said to me.

We arrived at the Concannon house and looked up at the boarded opening, everything ahead of us. At seven in the evening that same day, we would stand there and admire the new frame in place. Glass and all. We would look back over the various stages of the job and wonder how we got it all done. A series of stacked-up miracles. All the hold-ups, the re-measuring, the making sure. Moments when it all seemed too good to be true, when things went far too smoothly and you became suspicious or even careless and over confident. Followed by tricky, unforeseen snags that took for ever. Moments where you utterly underestimated the measure of time and how long the small things take. An hour fitting up one corner, chiselling away a few milli-metres of concrete, so that we started thinking the whole thing was actually going to take a week. Moments where wood and stone and plaster refused to co-operate, leaving the two of us looking at each other and wondering what to do next. We were obliged to obey the rules laid out by the materials. We had to be creative to get around them. We had to cheat a little and adjust the flaws with dressing. We cursed and complained, affectionately. We asked ourselves why the hell we took on this job in the first place and why we had not taken up something simple like delivering pizza instead. But we carried on, sticking to it solution by solution, until we could see the end in sight.

'Keep her lit,' I said, but Darius didn't understand that

phrase. 'It means keep the fire going or keep the joint passing around. But it really means keep it up, that sort of thing.'

I told him I had heard it down the country once or twice and he repeated the expression again and again, absorbing it into his general talk. 'Keep her lit, you little whore, don't do this to me.'

Darius was a brilliant craftsman. His accuracy, his confidence, his perfection. We worked like a team of interchangeable limbs. He knew what my hands were doing as though they were his own. I trusted the holding pressure of his grip on the frame. I saw the tight strain in his arms, on his face. His smoky breath right beside me while I marked the fixing and drilled the holes – the old-fashioned way. They constantly came up with new fixing agents, such as quick-drying cement, with no drilling required. But we did it by the conventional rules, with screws bolted right into the walls. And all through the day, Darius had a way of demonstrating things with physical gestures, swinging his hips like an exotic dancer as he told me to make sure it was not going to move. In other words, we didn't want this whole frame doing a lap-dance one night when the wind came up.

'We are a right pair,' he said to me.

'Yes, we are. A right pair, all right.'

'Vid and Darius.'

Things were beginning to fall into place.

Darius sometimes appeared to think the wood was on the same evolutionary level as us humans. And maybe he was right. Wood was female. Screws were male, because the bastards sometimes refused to co-operate. He spoke as if this was a full day spent in bed with a woman with the curtains drawn, shifting her around in different positions. 'Get your arse up here.' He held up the side panel to the opening in the wall, then took it down again, saying she needed to lose a bit of weight. He got the electric planer to shave a few millimetres off the top corner. Blonde, girlish ringlets falling to the ground, carried around the front garden on a breath of wind.

'Come on, sweetheart. Head first.'

I couldn't help laughing and wondered what Rita would have to say about this if she heard it. Women are not timber. I almost preferred it when Darius switched to Russian for his most obscene fantasies. It was all part of the noise of work that, when things were going well, his analogies turned pornographic, far-fetched, full of desires which could never be satisfied by wood alone.

He'd told me that his wife left him because of his obsession with things being put away in the right place. She accused him of tidying everything before she even got a chance to make a mess. She felt smothered. She said it felt like living with a ghost. He joked about it now, but you could see how it would be hard to live with his kind of perfection. Right and left socks. Herbs in alphabetical order. You should have seen his workshop, everything labelled and tagged and numbered. All the blades in ascending order. Shadows marked out along the wall for all the different hand tools. A million small drawers with screws and dowels and washers. He once dragged me around five different DIY stores looking for a particular brass, round-head screw when he already had dozens of flat-head screws of the same gauge which would have done perfectly well, and after all that trouble it had to be countersunk in any case and couldn't be seen.

Quite possibly people would say the same about me. While Kevin was briefly living in my place, he left things lying around, reassuring me with his presence. But since he moved into a new apartment, I had to practise some disorder to give myself the illusion of not being alone.

Halfway through the job, Mrs Concannon returned home and we had to stop to let her admire the work. We answered half a dozen questions politely, without trying to rush her, explaining all the precautions we were taking to make sure the window was anchored securely against the wind.

'Better let you get on with it, so,' she said finally.

'Keep her lit,' Darius said.

'What's that?' she asked, a bit irritated.

'Keep her lit. You know. Keep up the good work,' I explained.

She smiled awkwardly, more like a silent sniff, then went down the hallway into the kitchen to read the paper. I told Darius not to start laughing immediately because that would make it look like we were mocking her.

And then the phone call came telling me that I was already dead and should not even be bothering with any of this work, unless I was concerned about my posthumous reputation for finishing things.

'One of your girlfriends?' Darius asked.

'I wish it was.'

We laughed, but there was a crash in my smile. And just to increase the doubt, the sun was blocked out for a moment, casting a shadow across the house. The sea went all goose pimples. Then the street flared up again at the flick of a switch.

I felt alone. For the first time, I wanted to go home, even if that was no longer a place where I belonged. It was more a wish to return to my childhood, before I understood much about the world. I focused on the best moment I could remember. My mother baking. The smell of cake just out of the oven and the way she talked to me, explaining every-thing she was doing. I remembered her slicing through the cake sideways, twice, in order to make three layers. Two into three, she said, and I always remained confused by that mathe-matical equation which came out in a beautiful tiered coffee cake in the end. My father too. There were great moments to remember with him, when he taught me woodwork. He was so patient with me, showing me how to do dovetailing and how to bore for dowels and how to measure everything again, one last time, before you went beyond the point of no return. We built kitchen cupboards one summer, to store all the jam and the preserves my mother made.

But even these memories were not enough to make me feel at home. In fact, I felt all the more vulnerable, thinking of the past. It was like descending the stairs backwards and not knowing what I might find when I turned around at the bottom. I was unable to protect myself from my own memory. Not confident enough to be alone.

We carried on working. I was glad to hear the dry sex of Darius's ongoing fantasies. But even this distraction could not hide the premonition I now had. I could no longer delude myself into thinking that I was making progress here. All the faces in the courtroom came back to haunt me, the hatred in the eyes of the electrician when I was discharged. The rage in his expression when we ran into each other in the supermarket. My acquittal meant nothing. All that guilt was still there, coming after me like delayed justice.

I imagined what it must be like to disappear without leaving any trace behind. I began to feel guilty about all those people who left no trace behind in my own country. Unmarked graves, a thousand miles away. Places where bodies were buried anonymously. People standing by them years later as they were being excavated, waiting to identify clothes and shoes and watches hanging around limp dead wrists. Women holding scarves up to their faces, forearms across their noses, hands up to their eyes. DNA was perhaps the only trace left by which they could be recognised.

If it wasn't for the threatening phone calls, I might have wished the day would carry on indefinitely. I was disappointed when it came to an end as we put the double glazing panels in. We pulled the windows up and down, trying to find something wrong, something that still needed to be adjusted. I clapped Darius on the back and told him he was a genius, I could not have done this job with anyone else.

We needed to get drunk together and walk back over all the details of the day in our heads. The work had turned us into fellow achievers. We needed to grab some food and celebrate. Conquer the work and leave it behind, let it slide away with a few pints. All that talk about women and wood. The VIP lounge of our own jokes.

But that was not possible because there was another phone call. This time from Kevin. He had left messages which I ignored, thinking they were further threats. I didn't want to hear any more announcements about my own premature leaving.

'In private,' Kevin said.

Reluctantly, I told Darius that we would go for a drink another night, which was not the same and would never have that immediate buzz and brotherhood of getting drunk at the end of the work day. You might as well tell a child you're going to postpone Christmas till St Patrick's Day.

'It's OK,' Darius said with a smile. But I could see his disappointment. He got into his van and drove away with the most important part of the day gone missing, as though, once again, he hadn't been paid. I felt angry with myself for letting him down. I could imagine him in the local chipper, forking tasteless fish and chips alone, with nobody to share his appetite. Off to drink in solitude.

'You did a great job,' Kevin said, but his admiration seemed out of context. Like switching from one movie to another midway.

I washed and got some of the sawdust out of my hair. As we left the house, I took a last look at the casement window.

'I got this call today,' I told him. 'Like, a death threat of some sort.'

He smiled.

'It's only a joke,' he said, playing it down.

I told him that my days were numbered and that they were going to take me out of my misery.

'Sounds a bit washy to me,' he said.

'They told me I was fucking dead.'

'Empty threats,' he assured me. 'Pay no attention to that kind of stuff. Trust me. I've heard it all before. Wait till something happens before you worry about things like that.'

He had other things on his mind. He took me to the nearest bar, though I constantly felt I was washing down the dust with the wrong person. Kevin drank fast. He drank to get to a destination, not for the journey. It was not a celebration but more like a gathering rage.

'Where does he live?'

'Who?'

'My father.'

He wanted me to give him the address. I looked at my watch and wondered if his father was already at the yacht club for the night.

'He might still be at home,' I said.

He left the car behind. We walked along the street together and though I was leading the way, he still gave the impression of walking ahead of me. We arrived at the house with the shabby façade and I pointed down the granite steps.

My optimism was beginning to return, thinking this could be the great reconciliation happening in front of my eyes at last.

I remembered his father's handshake. The trace of his life left on my hand. All the things I had been able to verify since then by going to Furbo and seeing the place where he grew up. The homecoming sound of wind through the walls. Rain making its way slowly ashore at walking pace. And the sweet smell of turf in the air. Even the taste of creamy black pints in the pubs was like drinking liquid turf smoke.

I tried to convince myself that Kevin was finally coming around, that he would allow his heart to speak instead of his head, that he would shake his father's hand and be gripped by the imprint of his friendship.

25

There was no handshake. The face-to-face meeting between father and son was so brief, it might as well not have happened at all. Not much more than five minutes.

'Kevin,' his father said, surprised.

He invited us to come inside but the gesture was not taken up. Kevin stood back, well out of human reach, swept his sandy hair back and spoke in a businesslike tone.

'Where is she?'

He seemed to have no way of addressing his father. Not Dad, or Pa, or Johnny or anything.

'Ellis, you mean?'

'I need to talk to my sister.'

'She's in trouble, isn't she?' his father said.

'What do you mean?'

'With drugs. She has an addiction, isn't that so?'

'Is she living here with you?' Kevin asked.

'No,' his father replied. 'But I'd like to help her, if that's possible.'

'You stay away from her,' Kevin said, with strong emotion rising in his voice.

'I've got a right to see my daughter, she's of age now.'

'I'm warning you to stay away from my sister. I will do anything within my power to protect her.'

At least they were talking now. Brown eyes looking into brown eyes, reflecting each other in the family mirror. Their strong faces were so alike, distinguished only by the Connemara accent reverberating in his father's voice. Their foreheads the same. Same paper-clip frown between the eyes. Though his father seemed like the younger of the two, more like a boy, despite his white hair. Kevin more parental, more prosperous and secure, staring back with authority at the failures of his father's generation.

There was nothing I could do to mediate, so I stood back on the granite steps, trying not to take sides.

His father carried a paralysis with him, in his laughter, in the cynicism and lack of opportunity of his time. He came from a time when people mistrusted success, when they laughed at enterprise, when they could not even trust friendship because emigration spread so fast, like contamination. Every friend he had was like a trapdoor opening up underneath his feet, bound to go away. All that leaving over the years must have changed the way people here thought about friendship, making it more needy and intense, more urgent, more temporary. Something that could be left behind overnight. Something portable that could be taken away in a story and remembered long after.

Kevin stood looking at his father without any compassion. Even the surroundings seemed to offer no hope – the bad light, the snivelling summer dampness, the green moss on the steps. He saw his father only as a bum, a dreamer, unable to take what was available in the world. The only foothold he had was in his songs and stories. A life measured out in vagrant years of aimless conversations repeated over and over in bars, not completely unlike Kevin himself, but without the same level of success and self-confidence.

'What do you want from us?' Kevin demanded. He spoke like a lawyer.

'I want to make it up to you,' his father said.

'Bit late now, don't you think?'

'She never even opened my letters. She never even passed on any messages to you. My own children.'

'After what you did?' Kevin shouted. 'I saw it myself.'

'She closed the door on me, Kevin. I know I did wrong and I've been in hell all my life over it. I only want to make up for it some way.'

'The courts have dealt with all this,' Kevin said.

'I've begged her forgiveness but she won't even talk to me.'

'There is no forgiveness for what you did, in front of your own children.'

Kevin was already turning away in disgust.

'I'm not asking for anything, Kevin.'

'So.'

'I just want to apologise to you and Jane and Ellis for what you saw. For me being away. For me not being a father. That's all I can say.'

'Fair enough,' Kevin said. 'Now I'm advising you to keep away from my mother. And keep away from Ellis.'

It was hard to listen to these words. He gave his father no room to come out of his banishment. He turned and came up the granite steps past me. I was blocking his way and stood aside.

'He's a good worker you've got there, Kevin.'

His father was left standing alone at the door. What could I do? I felt lousy, walking away down the street after his son.

'He's a great friend,' I heard him shout after us. 'Don't lose him.'

That was it, more or less. There was no further talk about his father. Kevin brought me into the city and we drank until we remembered nothing.

I was tired, but the alcohol gave me the energy to forget. We ended up in a night club. I didn't want to go, but I could not desert my friend at this point. I stuck by him. He met some people he knew from college, including a woman called Samantha. 'How could you screw a woman with a name like that?' he said to me. But after an hour of dancing around to music that sounded like a mobile phone, he ended up changing his mind and disappeared with Samantha after all. Then I made my way home on my own.

In the middle of the night I got another call.

'He tried to burn my mother out.'

His father? An arson attack? The words suggested the high-end of the scale, close to catastrophe.

I got down there as fast as I could. Kevin was already there, pacing up and down with helpless fury in his eyes. His fly was undone. Black tideline marks on his lips. Waiting to get a hold of the person who did this so he could demonstrate exactly how much he loved his mother.

'Have to get security cameras installed,' he said.

The Garda officers tried to calm everybody down. They spoke to Mrs Concannon as she stood on the granite steps in her dressing gown, inhaling the bitter fumes of scorched wood after the fire had already been put out. They referred to the people who carried out the attack as 'right little gurriers'. It was a way of minimising the event in their own minds. Classifying it in terms of severity and police priority. In their estimation, it was a random incident, a drug-fuelled piece of irresponsible madness carried out by passing thugs who picked an easy target. The blue light was flashing across her face, turning her eyes black and her complexion white as a mask. They asked if she knew of any reason for people trying to set fire to her house and she could not think of anything. Bad and all as it looked, they assured her, it was a Saturday night, after all. If somebody was really trying to burn down the house, they would have done it properly, not by setting fire to a wheelie bin outside the front door. It was the work of amateurs, in other words. They were taking the matter very seriously indeed, but still hoping that it was nothing more than a prank.

Rosie from next door came out in her coat and slippers, saying that she had heard young people coming up from the seafront. She invited Mrs Concannon in for some tea and tried to make her feel better by saying it was a far cry from what went on in Northern Ireland.

Placed in perspective, the damage was slight. Nothing like the damage done inside the family.

The attackers had carried the green wheelie bin up the steps and leaned it against the door, igniting the contents, mostly paper and cardboard, adding vodka and Red Bull, perhaps. It was hard to imagine they went to the trouble of getting petrol. The bin itself had melted comically out of shape, reduced to a squat tub on wheels with volcanic, bulging layers. The front door was scorched, but intact. As expected, there was more water damage in the hallway than anything else. The main problem was the glass side panel. It had burst in the heat. Frosted stained glass that was over a hundred years old and almost impossible to replace.

I cut some pieces of plywood and sealed the broken panel shut from both sides for the time being. The door needed nothing. The scorch marks, in the shape of Africa, could easily be dealt with by the painters who were going to do the new window frame anyway, so the timing was not that bad. Why didn't they set fire to the skip instead, with all the old wood inside? I wondered. It would have been less trouble and far more spectacular.

Kevin stood leafing through various explanations. He slowly realised that it was not his father who had done this. Instead, his eyes were on me, connecting it back to the death threat I had received. The combination exploded in his imagination.

'It's them, isn't it?'

'Who?'

'Scumbags. That electrician you got in with.'

Next day, I started getting things back in order. I got rid of the bin. I installed a dehumidifier in the hallway to reduce the dampness and was already working on putting down the floorboards again. I even tracked down a stained-glass designer who still had a few panes of that particular glass left, so I was able replace the side panel. I later found out that the glass panel had been broken before. Once it was replaced, you would hardly think anything had happened.

But something had changed utterly. I could see it by the way they were looking at me and speaking to me. The scorch marks left on the front door. The new glass panel. The lingering smell of burned wood in the hallway. I had brought all this with me. I had introduced it into the country like an air-borne disease, spreading to the Concannon family.

26

There is no such thing as closure, is there? Only opening.

Ellis had become obsessed with unlocking her father's absence. She could not stop herself from going on the adventure of blame and self-destruction, narrowing everything down to the missing parts of her life. She was like a child who has only just discovered the power of the light switch, looking around the room in amazement at the genius of her own invention.

'This is my genetic inheritance we're talking about,' I heard her screaming at her mother.

'Well, follow your inheritance,' her mother snapped back. 'If that's what you want, go and be like your father.'

'I just need to know what made me the way I am.'

I felt sorry for her mother. Only me left in the house, hammering nails down into the floorboards with all the noise I could possibly make, trying to pretend I didn't know what was going on.

Ellis didn't want to meet her father any more either. She only wanted to understand the cause of her own behaviour. Why she was destined to go downhill, sending the blame back along the family line. She matched herself up to the genetic trademarks of her father, a man she hardly even recognised when he stopped her in the street. He was the explanation for everything in her life that was outside her control. All the ingredients of her identity, her talents as well as her deficiencies. All those emotional detours and addiction problems. Lack of initiative. Shoplifting adventures. Criminal damage to public property. Why she once flirted with self-starvation.

She underestimated her own capabilities. The effect that she could have on people with her smile. A smile she inherited from her father, beginning at the corner of her mouth, then spreading to one side, right up into the eyes and spinning around her face like a flint-wheel toy.

She was living her life in spite of her mother rather than for her own good. Moving out of the family home into a crazy, free-fall scene with Diller. A dodgy apartment that was more like a landfill site, if my sources were correct, with the smell of refuse coming from the kitchen. And the ever-present drugs. The plastic, re-sealable pouch of tabs, the hand-mirror and the rolled-up bank note on the sofa.

Johnny Concannon was the only person who could supply an explanation for any of this. I visited him again one afternoon. We sat down and he took his time going over things, walking through his thoughts, as crooked and erratic as the stone walls and the landscape he grew up with. But in spite of his absence all those years, he seemed to have a father's obsession with family details. A paternal talent for remembering important events regarding his own children. The disaster which led to him being expelled from the family.

He told me how he had come back to Dublin to make a go of it, rejoining his wife and three children with every intention of being a real father. After Rita had inherited the house, he tried to make things work and carried out some renovation work himself. He had so much energy then, doing things to make people happy. He got a job and they seemed to get on very well as a family. He loved telling stories and the children believed everything.

But there was always some imbalance, because Rita was a schoolteacher and the family home was owned by her. Even if it was dilapidated, her name was on the deeds, and no matter how much he worked on improving it, he didn't feel it could ever belong to him. He admitted that he drank too much and that he squandered everything, until he felt more of an employee in the house, like myself.

He told me how things ended. He had bought the children a dog. A grown puppy, tearing up everything he could find. Utterly un-trainable because of all the affection he received, from Ellis in particular. He could recall the summer they went to a seaside campsite on the south coast. Rita tied the dog to the rear bumper of the car, so as to keep him from getting at the food and puncturing the children's beach ball with his teeth. And there he was, Johnny Concannon, happily driving off in search of a bottle of wine, with the children screaming and running after the car. He waved back at them with his bare arm out the window, not realising that he was dragging this unfortunate pet dog off to such a brutal and spectacular death before their eyes.

Rita didn't make things easy for him. She called him a waster, a dog killer. They returned early from the camping trip and he went out to get drunk, trying to forget about the dog he had buried on the beach with a plastic spade and bucket, crying to himself like a small boy. By the time he got home that night she had already packed his things into a suitcase, everything, including the All-Ireland hurling medal. She said she wanted him out of the house.

'I don't know what came over me,' he said. 'I saw my suit-case standing outside the door. I broke the glass and forced my way inside. She started telling me to fuck off back to England, as if that was my country.'

He punched her and she fell back, holding her mouth. The children were standing on the stairs, clinging on to the banisters as he left.

'They'll never forget that, will they?'

'Children forget all kinds of things,' I said, trying to help him out.

But I was wrong. Your childhood is like a dog tied to the bumper of the car coming after you, all the way into your adult life.

'I threw it away,' he said. 'I have no family now.'

Then he decided to give me his All-Ireland medal, because there was nobody else who would accept it.

'I would like you to have it,' he said.

'But this is not correct,' I said. 'I wouldn't be the right person for it.'

'Of course you are,' he said, getting up. 'You are the only person I have in mind for it now.'

He took out the red box with the gift wrapping still around it and gave it to me. I tried to refuse it politely, but he insisted, telling me again about the day that he had won it.

He had the need to gather some kind of imaginary family around him. He talked to me about his mother and father. The names of his brothers. The countries they emigrated to and what they were doing, how many were married and how many children and grandchildren they had. He gave me the whole family tree, spreading out into the future across the world, in case I was ever in a foreign country, he said, and needed somebody to call on.

I told him about my trip down to Furbo. I described the new hotel and the pagodas on the shore and the piano playing on its own in the dining room. I told him what little I had managed to dig out about Máire Concannon and he began to fill in the gaps, telling me what he knew.

'Over the years the tide brought in more and more rumours after her,' Johnny said. 'Like the truth, I suppose, coming and going all the time.'

Some people referred to it as a crime. Others referred to it as a tragedy. Others still as a scandal. But whether it was suicide or homicide, double homicide at that, was almost impossible to answer.

For such a case to be established in court, you needed more concrete evidence than rumours expanding and contracting with the tide. Some said she suffered from what was called melancholia. What gave her melancholia was not known, other than what was said about her by the priest and the insecurity of her circumstances after that. The priest who denounced her from the altar may have been an accessory to the crime, having suggested drowning, voluntary or involuntary. But he was no longer alive to answer the charges.

Perhaps she was trying to save up enough money for the fare to London, Johnny suggested, and didn't manage to get it in time before the moral curfew fell. Melancholia was possibly the convenient way of saying that she was in fear of her life and had nowhere to turn. She had lost the protection of the community, driven out of the parish, driven off the map and into the sea.

'Are you religious?' he asked me.

'No.'

'That's good,' he said. 'Because sometimes I wonder if this was an Irish re-make of the Blessed Virgin Mary story. When there was no father to be found, the story was written back-wards with great flair.'

One of the rumours making the distance of time was that she was seen walking out into the waves, close to where the big new hotel stands. Possibly on the beach or one of the shallow sandy places among the rocks where the water would have slowly risen around her dress all the way up to her chest until she fell beyond her depth and disappeared. Her frame of mind would have been frail. She would have seen even less hope in the land behind her than in the sea ahead of her. It was also possible that she might have walked to Barna and plunged from the wall of the small harbour there. If so, she would only have had her own thoughts for company as she passed by the grey house, speckled all over with white discs of lichen, like the face of an old woman staring at her and saying nothing.

Perhaps she spoke out loud to the baby inside her belly as she walked, and people hearing her going by would have thought she had gone mad.

Why did nobody stop her? What about her sisters, her mother, would they not have tried to hold her back? She could have been overpowered. They could have changed her mind. But if they had done so, they would have become accomplices, breaking the word of the Lord, as it was known. So it had to be assumed that nobody went to her assistance, if that was how it happened.

Further rumours alleged an even darker ending in which she may have been taken out by boat against her will. It was said by some that she had been seen on the water in the company of some men, family members, brothers, uncles, local men, her own father perhaps, even the priest himself, who knows? All the suspects in this case, you might say, including the man whose child she was carrying and who for some reason or other could not marry her to make things right in the eyes of the church. All the paternity suspects who were so terrified by the consequence of birth that they might have been driven by any means to silence her.

Was she about to reveal the identity of the father? Was that why she was drowned?

Another question. This may not have led to any particular conclusion in a criminal investigation either. It would not have closed the file, so to speak, but it might have helped to explain something inside my own head.

'Why was her body not claimed by the family?'

'You have to understand the times,' Johnny said. 'And the geography. Often they used to bury the bodies where they landed. There might have been heavy seas preventing the family from going over at the time. It was not unusual for people from the islands to be buried, for example, on the mainland, if that's where they were found.'

'They never went out to find the grave or put a headstone on it?'

'They would not have had the money to do that,' he said. 'I don't think so, anyway.'

'No identification mark of any sort?'

'Nothing apart from the place being named after her,' he said. 'Where her body was discovered.'

That was the only inscription, the location on Inishmore known to the people there as *Bean Bháite*, drowned woman.

There was no evidence of grief. Her mother and her sisters would not have been allowed to express it in the open, not in any ritual passage. No funeral. No wake. Even when the fine weather came back, nobody would have been permitted to go out and find her grave. Nobody would have gone to the island to say a prayer or lay down some flowers and wonder if it was a boy or a girl.

At this point, Johnny told me about a lament in the Irish language which talks of drowning. He spoke some of the words and translated them. He explained how the drowning in the song was first compared to a wedding, with horses and people gathered in the street. But then it turns into a funeral. The drowned person was normally brought ashore and placed on a wooden board. '*Ar chlár*' was the term for it. Laid out on a board. Maybe even a door taken off the hinges. From there, the body would be carried home to the house where a bed was made up for it to lie in. The mourning would then begin and the wake would go on through the night and not for one minute would the body be left alone. The song speaks of how the drowned man's bed was never as well made as this before.

Máire Concannon would first have been laid out on a board, down at the shore, just above the tide line. She would not have been brought to any house or laid in any bed. There would have been no grief and no wake and no singing.

Johnny then began to sing the song.

Tá do shúile ag na péiste,
S'tá do bhéilín ag na portáin,
S'tá do dhá láimhín gheala ghléigeal
Faoi léirsmacht na mbradán.

The maggots have got your eyes,
And the crabs have got your mouth,
And your fair white hands
Are in the salmon's domain.

27

The ending came quite abruptly. I was not expecting it so soon, with so little advance warning. I thought I was right in with the family, rock solid, until Kevin brought me for a drink one night after work and gave me notice to quit.

'Listen, Vid,' he said. 'I think it's probably best to wrap up as soon as possible.'

'Wrap up?'

'The work,' he said. 'Finish the job.'

'Finish the job?'

'It's my mother,' he said. 'She needs a break from all this building and shit.'

'You don't want me to do the kitchen?'

'Not now.'

'No bother,' I said.

'We're worried about Ellis, as you know.'

'Of course.'

'We've nothing against you, Vid,' he said. 'It's just dragging on a bit, that's all. My mother needs to get the house back to herself.'

'No bother,' I said.

'And stop saying "no bother", will you? Sounds really fucking stupid with your accent.'

This was the first instalment of the farewell. He tried to assure me that it did not reflect in any way on my character, only that the fire at the house made his mother very nervous. He blamed the scumbags and said he would have to put in an alarm system.

As if to illustrate the point, a fight broke out in the bar we were in. At the other end, there was somebody laughing and accusing another man of being a drug dealer. Nothing more than that. People were constantly saying things about each other here that had no basis in fact. Just for the fun of it, they would call somebody a knacker or a wanker without any proof whatsoever. But this time, the accusation was taken seriously. There wasn't even time for a fight to develop. The alleged drug dealer just walked away, leaving the other man standing at the bar with pieces of glass sticking out of his neck, still laughing for a moment until it gradually sank in what had happened. It was mostly by reading the reaction of the people around him that he knew something was wrong. People moving their drinks away to other tables. Empty space opening up as the blood began spilling on to the floor in bright dribbles. By the look on his face he seemed to be asking himself what made him so ugly and friendless all of a sudden. He held his hands up, like parentheses around his neck, afraid to touch himself or the bubbling fountain below his chin. Falling back into the abandoned tables and letting out a restrained, mechanical scream.

The ambulance came to take the man away. The bar was cleaned up and some Garda officers arrived to take statements, though nobody could remember seeing anything.

Kevin explained to me that the lines between good and evil had become blurred. You could no longer trust your instincts. Things were getting worse than ever before, spreading into all corners of the world evenly. Every city had its mafia and its Third World and its safe people who could not be touched. He was a lawyer and he dealt with all levels of society. The city was the greatest place on earth but it was also a dump and a war zone, depending on your entry level.

'Don't worry,' he said. 'Nothing is going to change. You're still my friend, my VBF. No question about that. It's only that we need to be careful. These scumbags are not going to go away.'

Two days later, Darius's workshop was burned down with all the wood and equipment inside. I went over to see it and stood there in the ruins of the smouldering building. Everything still had his signature neatness to it, even in total destruction. The tools still hanging on the walls in their designated spaces. Saws and hammers and chisels, grade by grade, blackened and warped by the heat. The fire must have had a great time with all those cans of lubricant and French polish. The electric saws were worthless. All the routers and mitre equipment, not even a tape measure to be salvaged.

Fire officers carried out an investigation on the spot, but the source of the fire could not be established. Darius never smoked on the premises and he never left sawdust lying around. He always cleaned out the machines and made sure to unplug the equipment before he left. On the evening before the fire he had taken some recently finished work out of his van and placed it into the workshop to be safe. All destroyed now.

There were no electrical faults to be detected and no visible signs of a break-in or arson either. It could have been accidental, if I didn't know better.

Black drops of water were still dripping from the sunken roof beams. Darius showed me individual pieces of equipment, like an inventory, telling me where he had bought them and for what price. It had taken years to accumulate such a collection of hand tools and the value would never be replaced with an insurance claim. Then he laughed, an exhilarated, desperate sort of laugh that was closer to tears as he picked up two screwdrivers which had fused together by the handles at a ninety-degree angle.

'I'm sorry about this,' I said, because I knew it was my fault.

'It's all right,' he said, trying to put a brave face on it. There are so many different ways of saying the word all right here, anything on a scale from brilliant to mediocre to utter resignation and helplessness.

He kicked a few things around, a piece of hand-turned timber that seemed to be covered in treacle, too sad and mutilated even to be thought of as female any more. He was trying not to cry, holding it in like a man. I put my hand on his shoulder, knowing that I was the importer of misfortune, bringing nothing but trouble with me.

They had mistaken Darius for me, but I didn't have the heart to tell him. I felt like a scumbag, withholding this information. I told myself that I was doing him a favour, trying not to alarm him with thoughts of xenophobia.

But it was not fair to him. It was only right to tell him about the threatening phone call I had received. About the original confrontation and the court case and the arson attack on the Concannon house. When he heard this, he was so disheartened that he walked away from me in disgust. He could not even get himself to speak to me. All our achievements had turned to nothing. How could I expect him to work with me again? The news had possibly persuaded him that there was no point in rebuilding his business, that it was better to leave the country and go home.

Of course it was totally understandable that the Concannon family wanted their privacy back at this point. Kevin kept urging me to hurry up and get out of there as fast as possible.

'Don't hover,' he warned, and I knew exactly what he meant. He had once told me that his mother said that to the waiter in a restaurant.

What took me a while to realise was that this was also the end of friendship. Not much more than a week later, I was out of the house for good. I worked from morning to night getting the place finished, from black to black, as Johnny Concannon would say in his own language. Rita went to stay in the Royal Marine Hotel, overlooking the harbour, while the small plastering jobs were given time to dry. Then it was the floor sanders and the painters.

There was a happy kind of sadness associated with finishing up. I sat drinking tea and talking with some of the other workers, knowing that I was only an employee like them. The painter told me that he was an illegitimate child, as the term went long ago. He had grown up in a Protestant orphanage and only recently discovered who his mother was. They had to set up secret meetings so as not to upset her new family. He went to visit her twice a month in Kilkenny where they sat together for an hour or two in the café, undercover. He would tell her about his work and she would tell him about her children, his half brothers and sisters whom he would never meet. Until it was time to leave, each of them back to their own lives.

When we were all finished, I got the painter to help me replace the furniture. The house was ready for living again. For a while, it had belonged to me and I would always remember the sounds and shadows, the hollow places, the creaks, the fragile, tragic air. Shouts left on the stairs. Doors slammed. The emptiness without a father. I would never forget this family.

It was great to look out through the new casement window one last time and catch that slice of blue sea in the corner of my eye. It went right into my deepest memory drawer, with all the other mental souvenirs I had collected, glad to have had the chance of standing here for a quiet moment and call it mine before I left for good. It didn't bother me that the improvements would soon be taken for granted. Made me happy almost that I would be forgotten, like a perfect carpenter, disappearing without a trace, returning the home intact to its rightful owners.

I saw the sunlight bouncing off the floor. I smelled the last remaining hint of gloss paint. What a nice job, I thought, straight from a property magazine. I would never forget the joy in Mrs Concannon's eyes, thanking me sincerely, right from the heart.

'You're the best worker we've ever had in this house,' she said with some emotion in her voice. 'Dependable and honest as the day is long.'

Then she reminded me to give back the hall door key.

That was it. I got very well paid. More than expected. I brought the money that Darius was owed but he hardly even wanted to take it from me. And there was no way that he would go with me for a drink to celebrate the job, like we were meant to, because all that sense of achievement and camaraderie was in ruins now.

I went for a drink alone and made my way home that night on foot. I walked the long way round, by the harbour, along the seafront, still hoping that the friendship with Kevin would soon be reinstated, once everything had died down again.

From time to time, I looked around, just to make sure that I was not being followed.

I passed by the old people's home where I had worked and where Nurse Bridie would be looking after sleepless patients, joking with them to make them calm down. I stood looking up at the windows, hoping to see her and maybe get a wave, but then I realised that, under the streetlights, she would not recognise me after all this time gone by. I wondered if I should go in to visit her again. I even thought with some fondness of that place which once felt like such a dead end, as though I had become one of the inmates myself. Some of them used to talk to each other without making any sense, as if they were speaking in different languages. It struck me that I had been too impatient to get out of there, afraid of suddenly getting old. I was always rushing to get on with my life. Leaping ahead constantly and only living my life in memory, after it had already gone by, just like Bridie was doing, keeping the letter of dismissal from her boyfriend in her handbag.

Then something happened which taught me a lot about the Concannon family and also about myself and the whole world around me.

I walked on and stopped in a laneway because I was bursting after the beer. As I stood there, out of sight, in total darkness, a car pulled up right at the entrance to the laneway. I could hear the occupants inside the car shouting at each other. A man and a woman, stopping to fight.

'Don't push me,' the man kept repeating. Then I heard her in the front seat beside him, laughing like a schoolgirl, a wild cackle. She seemed to be taunting him and he was waiting for things to get worse.

'You stupid fucking prick,' she said.

'Watch what you're saying, Fuzzy,' he warned.

'I should have listened to my mother. I should never have married you. Look at you. You big, fucking hunk of shite in a pair of trousers. Jesus let me out of here, I want to puke.'

I could only think of Rita and Johnny Concannon. I pictured them arguing inside the car, while the children were staying with Rosie next door.

She was speaking right up to his face, only inches away. He was staring straight ahead through the windscreen, gripping the steering wheel in order to keep his hands under control.

'I'm warning you, Fuzzy.'

'You're a wanker.'

'Fuzzy, stop it.'

'You big Limerick wanker,' she shouted, right into his ear.

I wanted to stop them. I wanted to run out and tell him not to take it seriously. But it was too late, already gone beyond words. His hands left the steering wheel and I heard the crack of her head against the glass. He was holding her neck with one hand and punching her face repeatedly with the other, a free target, with no protection. She didn't even have the time to put up her hands.

'Oh Jesus,' she screamed. 'Oh Jesus.' But that didn't stop him because he no longer believed a word from her mouth. He kept looking for better, more innocent parts of her face that he must have loved and hated in equal measure, until there was nothing left un-punched. 'Oh Jesus, my teeth,' she kept saying, though her words were muffled, gasping as he put his two hands around her throat.

I was such a coward. He was killing her in front of my eyes and I stood there, doing nothing. She went silent and he gripped the steering wheel again as if he was going to strangle that too.

But the car didn't move away. Instead he opened the door and got out. He came around the front with his legs eclipsing the headlights. He walked straight towards me, into the lane. I could see the rage in his eyes, still glowing from the act. His face jaundiced from the streetlight. He looked away towards the car to make sure she didn't move. No other traffic had passed in all this time, no late witnesses walking their dogs, nobody around with a phone camera willing to record the incident. Into the laneway he came, as though he had known of my presence all along and was now going to take it out on me for watching. He stopped just inches away. I stayed still with my back to the granite wall. Then I saw him hunch and begin to piss, right next to me. My impulse was to jump away quickly to avoid the splash, but I remained motionless, like a piece of cast-off timber left leaning against the wall.

The door on the driver's side remained open. I heard a groan, a tiny high-pitched whimper. She's alive, I thought, but in what state? He looked over to check and see how she was doing, maybe thinking that everything was fine and they were level again, made for each other as on their wedding day. He finished, shook himself, bucked once or twice and walked away, back across the headlights, closing the door on the dark side of the car and driving away finally, so I didn't hear what they said to each other next.

28

Nothing. Not a single word or a phone call even. Zero contact. We were already edging into the autumn and I had not heard from him since the job was finished. The closest friends in the history of friendship from the beginning of time, and now, less than nothing. I tried keeping in touch. I contacted him many times to invite him out fishing, but he didn't return my messages. I expected to meet him accidentally on the street, to pass by and wave at least. He must have discovered a new underground map where he could travel without being seen any more.

Only once. There was one occasion where I came across him by chance in a pub where we used to go together, his favourite place. Sitting there at the bar with his new friends and fresh pints in front of them. As I walked towards him with a big smile on my face, he looked around over his shoulder and saw me coming. I waited for him to stand up and put his arm around me and ask me what I was drinking, then introduce me to his pals. But there was something blank in his eyes. He didn't recognise me. Or maybe it was more like being de-recognised. De-friended.

He turned away and elbowed his friends. Spoke to them briskly and then stood up to leave. As if we couldn't be seen in the same pub.

'What have I done?' I asked when he was passing, but he didn't say a word, only walked out with his new friends following.

Three brand-new pints left standing on the counter abandoned. Even the barman found it hard to believe that anyone would walk away from his own drink in disgust like that. He asked whether the pints were gone, but left them on the counter, thinking the men who ordered them were outside smoking. All night, they stood there, a triptych to lost friendship.

You had to understand his position. There was a perfectly good reason for him not being my friend, of course. He had helped me as much as he possibly could, but I was nothing but trouble.

At times I thought people had begun to check me out on the internet and rake up my history. I could feel they were still connecting me with Serbia and all the things that happened there.

I did a small job in the meantime for a woman who wanted shelving done in salvaged wood. She was environmentally aware, as she called it, and would not let me get anything new, not even the brackets. One afternoon we got talking about where I came from and she told me that she had once been to Bosnia during the siege of Sarajevo. The women of that city had sent a message out to women all over the world to come and stand by them. Women from places in Europe and Canada and the USA responded to the call to break the siege. There were buses waiting to take them into the city. She was frightened because they were all marked with bullet holes. Some of them were like colanders on wheels, she told me, with no glass in many of the windows and old blood stains gone brown on the seats. She took the bus which had the least bullet holes, believing that this might make the journey marginally less dangerous. She would never forget travelling along winding mountain roads at night, mostly with no headlights so as to draw as little attention as possible to themselves from snipers who lay in hiding all over the mountains around the city. Sometimes the buses had to stop when the sound of gunfire came close. Sometimes they only crawled along with no light at all, just guessing the road ahead in the dark, making sure they didn't drive over the edge. When they finally arrived, the women of Sarajevo cried out of sheer relief at being reconnected with the world outside. Their visitors had brought gifts of food and baby things and essential medicines. They were asked if any of them wanted to get out of Sarajevo, but they could not desert their families. Then the visiting women went away on the same buses, leaving the women of Sarajevo behind, waving through the blue diesel fumes. She told me that the journey back was even more terrifying because the city was harder to get out of than it was to get in.

Helen was the only person left that I could talk to. We met once or twice, like a lonely hearts club. The dumped and the ditched, was how she put it, talking mainly about Kevin and remembering some of the good times.

The boat I had been working on was in the water by now, floating – for the time being, anyway. My ambitions as a boat builder were beyond my talents. Some things need to be passed on to you and I was still trying to work out what exactly it was that I had inherited. Not boat-building, in any case. Beware of the man who doesn't know his limits. I was sure that was another old Irish proverb.

Helen came down to the harbour to meet me one day. She was wearing a black leather jacket this time, with jeans and runners. The boat wobbled from side to side as she got in and she had to hold on to the gunwale to keep her balance.

'Keep your tongue in the middle of your mouth,' I said and she laughed. But it wasn't my own joke. It was something Kevin had said to me when we went fishing together. I copied things like that from other people, but I couldn't get them to sound right no matter how much I practised. I was always a secondhand man. There was a while when I tried to learn a few jokes off by heart, but they never worked either. Even when I got the punchline correct, there was always something awkward about the way I told it in my accent that was just not funny. Nobody ever laughed. And if they did, it was only out of politeness. It was easier to get them to laugh at me.

I rowed out into the bay. It was a calm evening and still quite warm, but always cooler on the water, so she zipped up her jacket. She looked at me from time to time as I was rowing and she was no fool. She could tell by the way the boat was gliding so easily across the water that it was the tide which carried us and not my rowing. I was impressing nobody. I might as well have put the oars vertically up in the air. She also knew that there was no way I could row back against the current either.

On the way out, we talked about what it was like to live in Belgrade. I had to tell her finally that I hated the music, particularly the turbo-folk that was pumped up during the war. She laughed and said it was probably like some of the freedom ballads that were sung here during the Troubles.

We stopped on the island. I tied the boat to one of the rocks, wedging the rope into a crevice in the granite, giving it enough slack to allow for the tide to ebb. There was nobody around and we sat down on the rocks and talked.

'It's not Dursey Island,' she said. 'But it will have to do.'

She had a funny way of twisting words around and she said I laughed like a collapsing building, detonated from inside with a cloud of dust rising and people looking on in amazement.

It was threatening to rain, just one or two drops. She put her arms around me without any notice and kissed me as if she had been inspired by the idea of rain. Our eyes were closed and I can remember thinking that her lower lip was so much bigger to touch than it was to look at. Her teeth disappeared, so it seemed to me, but it still felt like a big smile breaking across her face. She invited my tongue to step across her lips into her mouth. There was no need for any explanation. A kiss was, in fact, the biggest word ever invented in anyone's mouth that could not be spoken or written down.

'We're not doing this to get back at him?' I asked.

'Absolutely not,' she said, laughing.

I put the unhappiness of my questions aside. We must have known it was coming all the way. We loved each other right from the start, only we could not admit it because the friendship with Kevin stood in the way. And maybe this was the reason for all the trouble in the first place, why he lost control, beating a man half to death in the street. Maybe he saw something in our eyes that night that freaked him out.

She didn't want to look for shelter. She opened her leather jacket, encouraging me to take ownership of the place we were in. We made love together on the island, with the sun going down and a few sporadic drops falling at the same time, making everything more urgent. I was expecting to forget about the entire world, but the opposite happened. As we lay down on the grass, I began to remember things. There was something in this encounter with Helen that opened the door on my memory. The smoothness of her stomach right up against mine. A tiny drop of rain on one of her eyelashes. Her breathing in my ear, much louder than any of the waves exhaling on the rocks close by.

She didn't press me too much for information. She was a good listener, good at uncovering all those things that were hidden under rocks and crawled out of a man's memory.

I told her that my father was in the secret police in Belgrade. He worked under a man by the name of Stanišić who was on trial for war crimes. I explained to her that I was not aware of what exactly my father did in his work. From what I gathered, he was a gifted communicator, involved in extracting information from people in police stations.

'I knew none of this when I was growing up,' I explained to her. 'He was the nicest man on earth. A good father.'

'Tell me about the car crash.'

She left her arm around my shoulder and waited for the story to emerge. I told her about the wedding of my sister, Branka. Long after the war was over, in peace time. The wedding was to take place in the mountains, in a place where her future husband came from and where they were going to settle down because he had taken over an auto-repair workshop that had been abandoned. My father was dressed up in his suit and my mother wore a blue hat and matching blue suit. The wedding cake was in the back seat beside me, special order from one of the best cafés in Belgrade.

The morning of the wedding was hot. The entire village was gathered at the church, waiting. My sister dressed in white. The brass band ready to strike up and begin the great celebrations. I could remember driving through the countryside with a sheet of grease-proof paper over the wedding cake and the sweetness filling the whole car. My father talking, full of excitement because it's not every day that your daughter gets married. The wedding was to take place in an area which had been badly scarred by the war, a place where people had fled their houses. I can remember passing by burned-out homes and not thinking of anything really, because my mother and father didn't say a word about why some parts of the landscape looked so empty without cattle or goats.

Then the car just spun out of control and bounced off a wall on my mother's side. She was killed almost instantly by the impact.

I explained that for a long time I could not actually remember any of this happening, only what they told me afterwards. I must have been knocked out for a while and maybe only now beginning to wake up again.

'I didn't even know at the time that the car flipped over on its side.'

It was only more recently that I began to work these things out for myself. Why the cake was thrown into my lap. Why the windscreen was shattered even before we crashed. And the sound of the motorbike starting up shortly afterwards, driving away into the hills like the sound of a mosquito in my ear. Leaving nothing eventually but the back wheel spinning and the sight of blood collecting in my father's ear.

My father was killed by a single bullet through the left eye. A piece of lead that was reshaped on its passage through his life into a warped grey pebble, buried in a wedding cake that was never cut.

'Somebody got his revenge on him?' Helen asked.

'I'm not so sure,' I said.

'Who else would have killed him?'

'I think it was one of his own people,' I said. 'Maybe he

was beginning to regret some things after the war and was about to reveal secrets.'

'Was he present in Srebreniça?'

'I don't know,' I said. 'All I know is that he transferred to the military at some point.'

'Do you want to find out?'

'I vowed never to go back.'

We got into the boat again. The tide was so strong that I could only row across the sound between the island and the mainland at a bizarre angle, picking a spot that would eventually bring us on course into the mouth of a small harbour. Otherwise the strength of the current would have taken us all the way down the coast, along the rocks where the train glides through the granite tunnel and comes shooting out of the side of the hill and finally descends down to the level of the beach.

'We can go there together, if you like,' she offered, once we stood on the land again.

'What do you mean?'

'Back to Serbia,' she said. 'And Bosnia. I'll go there with you and visit Srebreniça.'

We left the boat there behind us, tied up against the pier. The sun had gone down and the lights were on all around us. As we walked away up the hill, she put a cold hand in under my shirt and I had to start laughing, like an entire department store collapsing into rubble and dust.

29

Ellis was pregnant and didn't know what to do. Helen told me that she had got in contact because she had nobody else to turn to. Her boyfriend Diller had gone missing. Rita had reacted very badly. And Kevin accused her of destroying the family, showing no consideration for the feelings of her mother, who was sick with worry and disappointment.

'I'm afraid for her,' Helen said to me on the phone.

Ellis told Helen that Kevin had shouted at her, telling her that being a single mother was no joke at her age, just out of school. She could expect no help from anyone in the family. He described her future life with his own unique flair. An endless cycle of nappies and unhappiness, sitting in front of the TV without any plan, throwing all her intelligence away. Besides, it was insane to bring a baby into the world in such precarious times, when the place was already vastly overpopulated and in crisis management. A baby was the last thing the world needed right now.

'He's told her to get a termination,' Helen said.

'What do you think?' I asked, because teenage terminations were not unusual where I came from. But then Helen explained that such operations were not permitted here and she would have to travel abroad.

'She needs to be allowed to make up her own mind, without any of this blackmail from her family.'

'Best if you speak to her,' I said.

Helen had a way of allowing people to discover what was in their own minds without saying a word herself. While she was on her way to meet Ellis, I went to visit Johnny at the yacht club. I knocked on the door and he came down to let me in. He was glad to have company for a while and brought me upstairs to where he sat all night looking out through a big glass window at the boats. There were two screens with the same view split up into two sections, one focusing on the boats that were moored along a jetty, the other showing the boats on dry dock. What appeared on screen was also recorded, in case his memory of events was not believed.

Through him, I had got a few small jobs. He had put in a word for me and I was commissioned to build a series of trophy cabinets and also to mount navigation charts on the walls. It was nice work and I liked being there, looking at all the paintings they had of the sea.

There was one painting that I could not get out of my head. It was of a ship in distress. You could barely see the shape of the vessel in the eye of the storm, pitched at an angle, rolling at the mercy of the waves. A flash of lightning had illuminated the scene for a moment and made the ship look so small, like an insect in the palm of somebody's hand. There seemed very little holding it afloat against the force of nature. Only an act of faith keeping it from going down under the towering waves. Standing in front of the painting, you could almost hear the shouts of the sailors over the howl of the wind as they tried to maintain control. Blessing themselves with the lurch of each wave. The lash of salt water folding across them, getting worse. You could sense the tension in the ropes. You could hear the groaning of wood. You could feel the ruthless speed at which objects were pulled out of their hands. The wheel spinning. The rudder whipped about like a barn door. The dark, deep water staring at them all around until there was nothing to hold on to but the rails and the cleats and whatever else was fixed. Their families. Their memories. Their own names. Their loved ones, left back on land, praying for their safe return.

I told Johnny about Ellis. Even though I was not really part of the family any longer, I still cared about them.

'I need to buy her an ice cream,' he said to me, staring out the window at the sea.

'How is that going to help her?' I wondered.

He began talking about a place close by called Teddy's where you could buy soft ice-cream cones. They were meant to be the best in the world. People came from all over in the summer to queue up outside. Even late at night, after dark, which was strange to me because I always thought ice cream was something for children, consumed only by daylight. Even in the middle of winter, at Christmas, when the sea was lashing across the road and there were bits of broken seaweed blown up against the walls of houses like brown lizards, they still queued up for Teddy's soft ice cream.

I could verify that it really was the best ice cream in the world, not because I had travelled to that many places where ice cream was sold, but because I believed what people told me until I heard otherwise. Teddy's was not very far away from the Concannon house, so I tried one for myself and I had to say they were right.

Johnny told me that he bought himself a Teddy's ice cream on the day that he left Dún Laoghaire for the first time to get the boat across to Holyhead. He never forgot the taste of it. There was so much time to kill before the boat left that he found himself passing by Teddy's a number of times before he finally persuaded himself to try one. He joined the queue, even though he was a little embarrassed as a grown man, asking for an ice-cream cone. It was not as though they didn't have ice cream in Connemara, only that he had never had the cone before and the taste of it made him feel like a boy again.

Thirty years had passed and they were still selling the same ice cream now, the very same recipe, and he said it was good that some things had not changed.

'I thought it was a terrible waste of good money at the time,' he said, 'buying such a luxury item for myself.'

He explained that he grew up in a time when any money spent on food seemed wasted. Food was nothing more than a necessity, whereas drink was essential. He wasn't sure how he had inherited this way of thinking, but most of his friends were the same, even though they loved food and were always starving. They were embarrassed to be seen eating and had a store of phrases to deflect from it. I'd eat a nun's arse through a hedge. I could murder a steak. I could murder a sushi, anything at all, including the hand that feeds me. They never respected food, only laughed as if it was the enemy of drink.

He was a thin man who had survived on cigarettes and alcohol. Things had changed with all this talk of celebrity chefs and live competitions on how to stuff a chicken on TV. He regretted not knowing how to cook and care about himself.

'Is it like that where you come from?'

'People drink a lot,' I said, 'and they also love ice cream.'

The location of Teddy's ice-cream shop is unique, wedged

in between the railway and the coast road. Behind the shop is the open shaft where the railway lines run below. Parents coming from the People's Park hold their children up over the wall sometimes to let them look down. When you cross out on to the coast road you cannot possibly pass by Teddy's without noticing it. It's painted blue and has an unusual, triangular shape, the last building squeezed in by the railway and the road. Even though the bathing place opposite has been closed and lying derelict for thirty years, the people still come for ice cream. At one end of Teddy's is the sweet shop itself where they once sold tea and buns. At the other end, the thin end, there is a small blue hatch where the ice cream is served. The person buying the cone stands on the pavement at a far higher level, so that the woman inside the hatch looks up as if she exists in a subterranean world, down with the commuter trains clattering below. You can hardly see her face, only her hand holding up the cone and taking the money. There is a hum from the ice-cream machine whenever it is switched on and she twirls the cone around, creating a smooth spiral with a neat point.

You have a choice of getting a plain cone or one with a bright dash of strawberry juice or a sprinkle of hundreds and thousands or a cone with a chocolate flake stuck into it, called a ninety-nine. Johnny told me that the Italian man who invented the ninety-nine cone died at the age of ninety-nine, precisely. Belfast, he seemed to recall. He had read that in the newspaper and it was a happy coincidence, did I not think so myself?

All through the summer the people lined up for Teddy's ice cream. It seemed like a mad place to have children and adults gathering on such a narrow pavement, having to look right and left as they crossed the road when they could only really keep their eyes on the cone itself. People slowed down once they saw cones being carried and took care not to run anybody over, possibly because they wanted one themselves. You'd see a father crossing the street sometimes, delivering four or five cones to his family sitting in the car, handing them in through the windows to his wife and children before getting back into the driving seat. You'd see the mother saying she didn't want one for herself because she's on a diet, but then she got a little taste of her husband's cone and also a great big lick from each of the children's cones, so she probably ended up with more than you would get in a full cone. Sometimes you saw the mother wiping ice cream off the car seats and off the faces of the children. When the children are very small, the ice cream melts faster than they can eat. It begins to run down the side of the cone and on to their tiny hands and down into their sleeves. I saw a father once taking his child's entire hand into his mouth to clean it and then doing the same with the other. Some children are good at handling cones and they know when to bite off the end and create a hole in the bottom to suck down the ice cream. Couples love cones and they buy them for each other because eating ice cream is something intimate which you need to do in company. Eating alone makes you look a little guilty, which is what Johnny felt, though he could not explain why. And that's possibly why people had children in the first place: so they could have a legitimate excuse for buying ice-cream cones.

Another thing. You sometimes saw a cone on the ground, face down, with the pointed end tragically sticking up and father going back to buy another one just to console the crying child who dropped it. Later on, you'd see a crow with his head leaning to one side, sucking up the white puddle on the pavement with his black beak and flying off with the rest of the cone.

From time to time you heard people say that Teddy's ice cream had changed over the years and that it didn't taste the same any more. They must have changed the recipe or watered it down, they said, which is hard to believe because the queue for Teddy's has never let up in all these years. You could be absolutely sure that the ice cream is every bit as good as before, only that it does not compete with your memory. The taste of the ice cream is never as good as it was in childhood.

'For a Teddy's ice cream,' he had written each time in the letters he sent home. He had included a bit of money for the children. He thought Ellis would have remembered all those accumulated cones when he met her, but then he discovered that the letters were never opened. By the time Ellis got the money she was too old for ice cream and spent it all in one go on drugs.

We heard the lifeboat being called out. Two shots of a cannon in succession, the signal everyone around here associated with trouble out on the sea. Johnny stood up and looked through a pair of binoculars, but there was not much to see and perhaps it was a false alarm, which frequently happened.

I asked him about his house in Furbo. He told me he would love Ellis to have it, but not all the brothers in Canada and the USA were in agreement on whether to sell it or not.

He said it was a great place to be in the summer and if Ellis lived down there she might be very happy, speaking Irish and getting to know the people.

'Do you know something,' he said. 'On the beach at Furbo you would see a lot of sand-hoppers jumping in the summer.

Small insects, maybe a bit like fleas, jumping up and down at your feet for no reason at all.'

'Why do sand-hoppers hop?' I asked him.

'Big question.'

He had been told that they do it because they're happy. He had always believed that explanation. The sun breaks out and they jump around the place in a spontaneous sand-hopper festival. It had nothing to do with procreation or courtship rituals or survival instincts. Nothing to do with who jumped the highest or the longest or most frequently. He said there would be a scientific answer one of these days, like the one for weasels dancing in fields with similar delight at sunset, or so it was thought until they were discovered to have a parasite in the brain. Scientific facts make a fool of us all, he said. He preferred to believe in his own continued sand-hopper survival.

'I've always wanted to say this to Ellis,' he said. 'Will you tell her when you meet her? Tell her they jump because they're happy.'

At that point we heard a helicopter flying overhead, so there was something going on out there on the water. He could not leave his post, so I said I would go and have a look.

'Tell her to come and see me,' he said. 'I'll buy her an ice cream.'

As I walked along the harbour, Helen called to say that Ellis had not turned up to meet her. She had waited for an hour and she was hoping that nothing had happened to her.

I could only make assumptions based on my short time here in this country and what I had been told so far about the place.

I began to run towards the spot where the helicopter was

flying low over the water. Half-running, at least, trying to convince myself to calm down and not worry until something had happened. Premonition man, that's who I was, always waiting for things to end badly.

People were standing by their parked cars, stopping to have a look without turning the music off. I kept running, not as far as Teddy's, but away up along the pier, past the band stand and the brass plaque for the great Irish writer who talked about keeping the darkness under.

It was a calm night. The sea was flat and black. A few night walkers along the pier, looking over the wall at the helicopter hovering some distance away from the lighthouse, outside the harbour walls. The sound of the engine and the blades slicing through the air, coming and going, sometimes louder, sometimes more distant. The lifeboat was there as well, circling around, but the helicopter stayed in the same place, shining a strong searchlight down on to the surface of the water, concentrating on one single area.

Somebody must have reported seeing something in the water. One of those night walkers. The lifeboat moved in wider turns and the helicopter cast the beam on to the stage below for the men to get a better view. There was a small crowd of people gathered around at the top of the pier, watching. I asked what was going on and one of them shrugged. I tried to sound impartial, like a casual bystander, but they must have noticed an edge of concern in my voice.

'Drowning is the worst way to go,' somebody muttered.

I waited for a while until it was over. It was hard to see what was going on, but then the helicopter flew away and the lifeboat returned. There was an ambulance waiting on the shore with a blue light flashing around the Carlisle pier. I was in time to see them transferring a body on a stretcher from the boat to the ambulance. I asked one of the lifeboat men if they had made any identification but he didn't answer me and maybe I had the wrong way of putting that kind of question because everyone else around me seemed to know already without asking. Then there was a glimpse of the face, uncovered for an instant as they lifted the stretcher into the ambulance and the crew taking over confirmed the situation with their own instant checks. A hand slipped out for a moment from under the covering, not very different from the hands of the paramedics in their white plastic gloves, only lifeless.

Her face looked so different in the yellow light, so pale and unrecognisable. But then it came to me that her hair was too short and it could not be Ellis after all. Definitely not a girl. Definitely not Ellis, I virtually said out loud. I heard the Garda speaking about a young male and you cannot imagine how I felt in that moment with my worst fears being proved wrong. I was so elated that I could no longer see the reality of what was in front of me or think of this man's family and their grief.

The silence at the harbour was punctured by the sound of messages on the radio of the Garda motorbike. The officer cleared the way for the ambulance and they were gone quite suddenly with a small yelp of the siren, leaving a number of people behind them, shifting on their feet and moving away reluctantly, coming to terms with what they had seen.

I looked around with something like happiness in my eyes. It was hard for them to understand my frame of mind because I was like a sand-hopper, you might say, unable to keep myself from jumping.

30

One thing was certain, I was bound to meet Kevin again at some point. The world was too small for us not to come face to face one last time. I still held out hope that he would see things in a big-hearted way, blessing myself and Helen with his generosity. Sooner or later, we would all pick up from where we left off, I thought, the greatest comeback in the history of friendship.

The big surprise to me was the circumstances under which we would meet. You could not have foreseen the family reunion coming in such an unlikely and tragic way. It brought the Concannons all back together at last, but not as would have been hoped.

Much of the detail has been kept in the Garda reports. Re-constructed in the early hours of the morning by various officers in uniform and plain clothes. Everything recorded and gone over many times to be certain. By which time, of course, everything had already happened and could no longer be reversed.

My own recollection was not very reliable, so they understandably had to support their evidence by other means. Was it the fear I brought with me to this country or something picked up since I arrived? I had also brought too little

judgement and guile with me to be in a position to influ-
ence the facts in my favour. I had no interest in clearing
my own name any more, so I answered their questions with
too much honesty and neutrality for my own good.

Initially, so I told them, I thought it was the lifeboat men
coming after me. I was happy as a sand-hopper and I imagined that they had some issue with the spring in my step
as I walked away from the drowning tragedy. There were
other indicators which I must have ignored at the time and
which were more relevant to the investigation than I thought
myself, such as the sound of car doors banging.

Only when you're being asked questions in a Garda station
do you begin to realise all the notes you should have been
taking at the time of the incident. You should be taking notes
from morning till night in case you ever get involved in
something. Because you sometimes underestimate the
danger. I should have learned to mistrust my surroundings
a little more. I should have been more aware of footsteps
behind me.

They seemed quite friendly at the beginning. Three of them,
a bit younger than myself. Some signs I should have inter-
preted as unwelcome, but I deliberately eliminated them from
my thoughts, because you had to let things happen before
you started worrying about them, isn't that so? They all wore
hoods over their heads. They were all able to spit without
moving. One of them carried a bottle of coke, holding it in
his fingers by the cap, twirling it as though he didn't care if
it dropped. I was not fooled and knew there was something
stronger added, otherwise he would not have been passing it
around among his friends and not even complaining about
the backwash when he got it back. There was also something
about their faces that was unusual, some icy glaze in their

eyes that reminded me of a husky dog, with gleaming blue gas rings around the black pupils.

They were not night walkers either, nor did they seem to have any pressing need to get anywhere. They seemed to have an abundance of time on their hands. They knew my name, even though they got it slightly wrong and called me Vim. They knew where I was from, which was more important.

'Hey, we just want to ask you something.'

They formed a small tribunal of enquiry around me, while I backed up instinctively against the nearest granite wall for support. Somewhere in the back of my mind I knew that they had come to take me out of my misery, though I didn't let on and carried on being polite because I actually liked the look of them and would not have called them scumbags myself.

They began by reminding me of the situation outside the bar in which the electrician rescued his daughter from me when she was only a young mother with a six-month-old baby.

'You tried to rape her didn't you?'

At this point I laughed involuntarily. I loved the exaggeration and tried to answer in the same spirit.

'Yeah, sure I did.'

One of their heads came flying towards my face. I honestly thought it had detached itself from the neck as it cracked across my left cheek. I only had enough time to turn away so that my nose didn't get the full force of the impact. There was a blinding flash across my eyes, like the headlights of a car coming straight at me.

The head that struck me seemed to reattach itself to the body it belonged to and the urgency of the moment calmed

243

again. I was left holding my broken cheekbone, wondering why they didn't carry on and get it over with, complete the job they had come to do. It turned out that they had supplementary questions to ask me about the exact circumstances around the electrician getting the shit kicked out of him on the street.

'Who was your friend with you that night?'

'Is he Polish?'

I refused to be drawn into this questioning and didn't answer one way or the other. I think I was trained well by Kevin to remain silent at all costs. But saying that I had a bad memory because of a car crash at home was not going to wash with them.

'Just give us his name, that's all, then we'll let you go.'

'We know it wasn't you,' one of them added.

'Was it the other guy you work with? Darius, is that his name?'

'No,' I said immediately. 'It wasn't him.'

'Well who was it then?'

There was no chance of me revealing the name. I was surprised that they hadn't worked it out already for themselves, but it seemed that Kevin may have appeared too much like my employer to be regarded as an accomplice or a friend of mine.

It struck me just how my own father must have conducted his business, extracting information from people in Belgrade when there was none to be had. Perhaps it helped me to deal with this situation, some inherited genius in reverse, pretending that I had nothing to give.

An impatience came over them. A fist came from nowhere and connected with my mouth. I was confused because their hands were in their pockets. Apart from the hand that held the swinging coke bottle, I could not work out which fist was responsible. I even tried to count the amount of fists they had as though there might have been an extra one somewhere that I was not aware of.

'You better give us the name or else you're the end of the line. You get his share of the pain.'

They had done their homework. They said they had heard all about me and my country. They knew where I lived as well.

I put my hand in my pocket to try and speed dial on my phone, but they spotted that trick instantly. They made a joke about phoning a friend and kicked the phone out of my hand. One of them picked it up from the ground and threw it right into the harbour.

Another thing I tried was what I had learned from Rita Concannon and how she dealt with assailants who were after her handbag.

'Johnny!' I shouted. 'Get the guards.'

They looked all around them, but they saw through that one as well and laughed. I knew their fists were getting ready inside their pockets, so there was no option left but to act in my own defence. I selected from a minimal range of tools in my bag and brought out a hammer, which I felt was a better choice than a screwdriver or a chisel. A hammer seemed to suggest less intention to kill. One of them responded instantly by producing a lock-knife, and when I saw this, I instinctively used the hammer to dislodge it. I felt the soft crack of knuckles coming all the way back through the handle of the hammer into my own grip. The knife fell to the ground. The boy who owned the injured hand held it out as though it no longer belonged to him and he would rather not have it any more. It was floating away from him with the extreme

245

lightness of pain. He gave a squeal from his mouth that seemed to describe it quite accurately.

'Sorry,' I said at the same time, because it was not my intention to hurt anyone, only to save myself.

While they were all looking at the broken hand, I managed to make a run for it. They took their time picking up the knife before they came after me.

It was a mistake to defend myself. Because the fear began ringing inside my head. Easier to run away from attackers than it is to run away from your own nightmares. There was also the fear of my own actions. Already, I was re-imagining this moment with violent inspiration, wishing the hammer had connected with a skull or an eye or a set of bright red teeth.

I ran down towards the yacht club where Johnny worked. I should have given myself up and allowed them to take me out of my misery once and for all. But I held on to some instinct of survival. Like a mindless sand-hopper, I ran all the way down past the front of the building, ignoring the main door and deciding not to knock or shout for help at that point. Some supreme intelligence told me not to bring Johnny into this.

What surprised me was the lack of night walkers present that evening. Nobody around to alert the authorities. I turned at one point and threw the hammer at my pursuers, but that only stalled them for an instant and provided them with a further weapon.

Because I had been inside the building with Johnny many times, I also knew where the weak points were in the perimeter fence to the boatyard. With this knowledge, I ran straight to the best place and began to climb. I managed to pull myself up to the top before they reached me. They were left jumping up to try and drag me down. Unable to grab my foot, one of them leaped up with the hammer in his hand. Though it only glanced against the knob of my ankle, it drew a note of extraordinary payback that I could only describe as one hundred per cent, distilled pain. It took a moment before I could draw my foot up over the barbed wire, doing all kinds of further damage to my leg, concentrating on my ankle as though it was some kind of tuning fork that held the note for ever.

I jumped down on the far side and limped away like a xylophone on foot, making things far worse. The only consolation was that I was on the inside and that my improvised plan had a chance of working. I was able to pass in front of the cameras and alert Johnny to the problem. As soon as I appeared on the security screens, he would call for help. I even thought of telling my pursuers this so that they would waste no more time on me. Look, you're going to be recorded on security cameras and be famous all over the country on *Crime Time*.

Coming up to where I understood one of the cameras to be, I shouted and waved my hands. I called for Johnny to get help right away.

There was no reaction from inside. But that didn't matter because it was recorded anyway. I stayed in sight of the cameras as long as I could until they came in across the fence after me. They had found my bag. They also had any amount of implements at their disposal, oars, anchors, chains, lead pulleys, a whole range of imaginative tools which could be converted into perfect objects for extracting pain and death.

I hid behind some of the boats so they had to come looking for me. It also gave Johnny time to act. I thought of bargaining with them so we could all get back to more important things like football and computer games and sex and whatever, but there was no point.

There was no movement in the windows of the yacht club and I began to realise that Johnny was possibly not watching the screens himself. He had his small teapot full of whisky, as always, sitting back and relying on the screens to remember everything by themselves. That was the trouble with security cameras, they were meant to act as a deterrent, but only provided encouragement because it told people that the place was abandoned. It was a breach of trust in the community, asking people to commit their crimes in full view of the law.

They were getting closer and I thought they were equipped with heat sensors to track me down. I picked up a shackle and threw it at the window where Johnny sat. It was one of the skills that might have made me into a marksman in war. The window cracked and I saw Johnny appearing. This gave me the chance to run from my hiding place along a row of boats covered with canvas hoods, right out into open view of the cameras and the first-hand eye-witness of Johnny Concannon. I ran right on to the jetty. Even though I was running into a dead end, there was a comfort in the fact that it was being recorded for later use in evidence.

One of them threw a gaff at my feet, causing me to fall. In fact, I may have voluntarily thrown myself into the water at that point because there was nothing else I could think of. I managed to swim in underneath the jetty. When they arrived at that spot, they tried to fish me out by hooking the gaff at my clothes. I slid further away under the jetty, keeping my mouth above water for air. They continuously jabbed in through the gaps with various tools. It was impossible for them to see me in the dark, but they had a feeling for where I might have moved to, because I was gasping and coughing.

For the first time, I was able to verify something that you could normally only take on trust, which is that drowning is the worst way to go. Swallowing oily sea-water in large gulps must be the most desperate feeling imaginable. Apparently there is a moment when the closing mechanism at the back of your throat opens up involuntarily. In the panic, you mistake water for air, inhaling the fluid right into your lungs. It was hard to understand why people chose drowning as a way of death. And I thought of how unlikely it would be for a woman to do this while she was pregnant, unless she was helped by others.

I made more and more noise. I was gulping in air, or what I thought was air, scraping underneath the dock above me as though it was a cage, keeping me down. Their tools struck me and sent me down further underwater. I knew there would be no ultimate proof of my injuries being sustained before or after drowning, above or below the surface.

The strange thing about drowning is that it's so close to surviving, only a few gulps away. There is even a diagnosis called phantom drowning or false drowning, which brought it home to me exactly how death by inundation of the lungs works. While fighting off the water you bring the worst on yourself. Instead of remaining calm, you voluntarily join the dead and drowned of all time. You already see them in the dark coming along the sea floor with their absent eyes open and their lipless mouths singing. They are no longer breathing and have become fully adapted to being underwater. You see their hair floating upwards and their starfish hands held out towards you in greeting. Their soggy clothes billowing and their heavy shoes keeping ballast. Sand and stones and bits of shells in their pockets. Their limbs half-eaten by the scavengers of the sea they keep for company. Hundreds of drowned people waiting at the mouth of the harbour like a large choir performing the great underwater lament.

The maggots have got your eyes. The crabs have got your lips.

There was not much more time left for me in my misery at that point. I managed to escape from the jetty, out to one of the yachts, but they followed me and I didn't have the energy any more to keep myself under the water.

And then it all came to an end. To me it seemed they just got tired of it or already thought I had joined the choir of the drowned.

What I didn't know was that Johnny had come out of the building to assist me. This was something I had been trying to avoid at all costs. But I realised it too late. After a period of silence, I took the courage to rejoin the living. I wanted so much to belong to this country and pulled myself out of the water, even though I expected them to finish it for good. I came out coughing up water so it took a while for me to take notice of anything.

Then I heard the gasping. The sound of sputtering coming from the jetty, close by. I turned to see that it was Johnny, lying on his back. The gaff was stuck into the side of his face. He was trying to dislodge it but there was no hope. Each movement caused him further agony and loss of blood.

I ran to him and held his head. He was covered in blood and could not speak. I tried to make him comfortable, taking off my wet jacket and placing it underneath his head for a pillow. Then I realised that it was not the gaff that was the problem, but one of my own chisels, stuck right into his chest. I could hear a siren in the distance, howling through the streets, and wished it would come faster. He was very quiet when the rescue services arrived and he didn't have long to wait before he was carried away. They brought him through the building and out the main door because the gates were all locked.

I was arrested and taken away, which is understandable because I had no business being in the boatyard and there was blood all over my hands and my clothes. Johnny was not able to speak up for me. No matter how much I explained the situation to them, I think my accent and my choice of expressions worked against me and made me look more like a culprit. In the absence of any other suspects, this seemed like a logical precaution on the part of the Garda to take me into custody. I insisted that I wanted my legal advisor and friend to be there with me before I would say anything.

They began to put words into my mouth, hoping that I would nod at least. But I shook my head like a real criminal and said I would give them nothing until my friend came to see me. They contacted him but he never came. He refused to stand by my side and I was left alone. They asked me if I wanted them to arrange legal aid, but I turned that down. Right into the early hours of the morning, they continued to try and get me to speak against my will, until my silent memory of events was finally corroborated by the video evidence.

31

It's impossible to forgive yourself for surviving. I heard it said once that the living sometimes envy the dead, and I only believed that after Johnny died.

He spent roughly three days in hospital fighting for his life. What troubled me most was the fact that it was my own chisel which had killed him. After my release from custody, I tried to go and see him in the hospital, but was not given permission to do so by the family. Nor was Helen. Strictly family only, according to the nurses.

He didn't regain consciousness, so maybe there was no purpose in speaking to him, only for my own sake and for my guilt. While he was still alive, I wandered around the streets in a terrible heap, worrying and blaming myself again for bringing such disaster with me to this country. When I heard the news that he was dead, it became even more difficult. It was not something you learned in school, was it? How to grieve. It was not like you took lessons in letting go of people you love who are taken from you by force.

The one good thing to come from all of this was that I had reunited the family. Though it was difficult to rejoice, it was great to know that the Concannon family were now grieving together for their father and you could allow yourself to be happy at least that this tragedy had brought them closer than ever before.

'Johnny, Michael, Máire Concannon. Furbo and Dublin. Beloved husband and father, dearly missed by his wife Rita and children, Kevin, Jane and Ellis, as well as brothers in Canada and the USA and friends at home and abroad.'

In death, he had come home at last. He had returned to the land that would always love him, as they say in the song. He never made it back into the house, but there was a nice bed made up for him and he was surrounded by his close family when he gave his last breath in the hospital.

The details of the funeral arrangements were published in the newspapers. The death notice was accompanied by the remark 'funeral private' as well as a further request that there should be no flowers sent to the church or their home, and that the money should be given to charity instead.

By 'private', I accepted that the general public was not encouraged to take part, but I would never have considered staying away from the funeral myself. I discussed it with Helen and she encouraged me to go because I was Johnny's friend. She had never met him and didn't want to compli-cate things for the family by appearing at this time. She sent her condolences by letter to Kevin instead.

The morning of the funeral was damp and still. The rain held off, only just, suspended like a tarpaulin above the mourners. There was quite a crowd in the church in spite of the request for privacy. The lifeboat men were there, as well as many of the people from the yacht clubs. The Garda on duty and some of the ambulancemen I had seen on the night came also, along with nurses at the hospital who had looked after him while he was dying. It was touching that they would all take time off work to go to the funeral.

From the back of the church I could see Rita Concannon in the second row, with Kevin on one side of her and the girls on the other. She had her arm around Ellis during the ceremony. As is customary, the son went to the pulpit to say a few words. The whole congregation of mourners was moved by the gentle tone of regret in his voice. He said his father was a great singer and a great hurling player and a great Irish speaker and that there was something about him that represented a time gone by which would never come again. His absence from the world would be a loss not only to his family but to many of his friends and to the country as a whole. He had entered into our memory now where he would live for ever.

It felt as though he was speaking directly to me, even looking right into my eyes. I found myself nodding back and believing that this tragedy had finally reconnected us and brought me back into the family as well. But I was only deluding myself.

There was a special song chosen for the occasion, sung by a young girl who was related to the Concannons, a cousin. Her voice was unique, a breathy echo in the back of the throat that I had never heard before and was not even discovered yet by any pop star I knew of. Because it was an old, familiar song, sung by such a young person with a strong, new voice, the frailty in the words broke everyone's heart.

'Bring flowers of the fairest, and roses the rarest.'

Afterwards, the mourners were gathered outside the church. There are no lessons you can get for how to behave and how to approach the bereaved, so I decided not to go straight to Rita but over to Rosie first, her next-door neighbour. The family were all mobbed by neighbours and friends, so the idea of this being a private ceremony had been ignored completely.

By 'private', they had possibly only meant to exclude the unwanted. People were heard saying what a lovely man Johnny was and what a crime it was for him to be taken away from us in such a brutal way. One of the brothers from Canada had come back and he looked very like Johnny but more well dressed and healthy. People talked about other things and told stories that had nothing to do with Johnny's death. In other words, life went on with great speed at the same time.

When I got to Rita finally, she stalled in front of me and I didn't know what to say.

'I'm very sorry,' I said, because I didn't have any better words and the rest of my thoughts stopped in my throat.

I could remember the funeral of my own parents and all the mourners around me, suffocating me and using up the air outside the church. I could remember wishing they would all go away and not impose their grief on me. I could not understand the process of bereavement, because you don't get lessons for losing your parents overnight and dealing with the guilt of their deeds left behind on your conscience.

I never really went along with the belief in the afterlife either. It was nothing more than a poetic explanation for the void created by the dead. We are the afterlife, I thought to myself. Us, the people left behind.

I could understand the difficulty that Rita had in speaking to me. It takes courage to accept warmth from people. I also think you have to have warmth inside you in order to receive it. Rita Concannon gave me her hand, finally, and then she wanted to say something that didn't fully come out in the right words because she was crying at the same time.

'I was so unfair to him,' she said, but then she seemed to change her mind again because Jane started pulling her by the arm.

'Come on, Mammy,' she said, her face as stern as ever.

It's terrible, the assumption you make that you can be of some assistance, expressing your condolences, trying to help the bereaved to be strong. It's the other way around, the mourners upsetting the grieving family and putting all kinds of rubbish in their heads. It's the bereaved carrying the rest of the world on their shoulders.

Kevin came cutting through the crowd directly towards me. He had been discreetly inviting certain guests back to the house for a reception after the burial. I didn't expect to be included and it would have been absurd to stand there eating sandwiches in the room that took me months to renovate, much and all as I would have liked to see it full of people. I wanted to reassure myself that the Concannon floor was solid. I wanted to be sure I had left enough bounce in the boards, but not too much. Awful that, when you walk across the room and the glasses on the sideboard jump. I had been in houses where the floor was more like a trampoline.

It must have been clear to everyone that Kevin had something quite personal to say to me. They knew that I was his friend. They also knew the circumstances of Johnny's return home and how he was barred from the house. But everything always turns out fine if the story ends well, isn't that so?

Kevin put his arm around me. It was like old times and he led me quickly towards the side of the church. I felt the great weight of his friendship resting across my shoulders.

'I'm sorry,' I said, but it was a mistake even to attempt anything in language.

We stood at the side of the church, with the granite wall so beautifully constructed beside us. There was a copper lightning conductor coming all the way down from the spire, passing us by and going into the earth. The metal was grey and green from verdigris.

He looked into my eyes. He rested his hand on my shoulder so that I was at arm's length. He paused and chose the words he wanted to deliver with all the care of his professional training, making sure they were clear and would not have to be repeated.

'How dare you turn up here,' he said. The bitterness sprang from his eyes. 'You have the nerve to go up to my mother after all this. You have brought nothing but disaster to this family since you arrived.'

I could not think of anything that might disagree with that. He was absolutely right, I had brought this whole disaster with me.

'You stay away from us, do you hear me?'

Placing emphasis on those words, he took hold of my shirt around the neck and pushed me right back against the granite. His grip was so tight that I remembered nothing but drowning.

'Don't let me see you ever again. If you come to the cemetery, I will call the guards, do you understand me?'

With that he swiftly brought his knee up into my groin. All I could do was to utter an involuntary vowel sound. The slow pain brought tears to my eyes. And maybe this was the real farewell to our friendship, a more solemn departure. His words could no longer be misunderstood.

He let me go and I protested, but not in a very effective way, bowing forward towards him with my hand on my stomach. I told him not to deny me the right to pay my respects like everyone else.

'Go and plant a tree somewhere,' he said.

He wore his lovely suit with a light grey tie. He stared at me as though I was a defendant in court. He was ready to walk away, but then he remembered one more thing. As if there was a handwritten word or two at the bottom of a notepad reminding him not to leave without making this final important point.

'If you go near Helen, I will fucking kill you.'

'What are you saying?'

'You were always a sponger, Vid. One eye on the money and the other eye on the woman.'

'That's not fair enough,' I said.

'If you even as much as lay a finger on Helen, I will personally come and kill you, that's for sure.'

It struck me to tell him that he was too late. But he would find out sooner or later and I didn't want to speed on that revelation.

It was clear that he regretted ever meeting me in the first place. He despised himself for all the information he had given me and for taking me so intimately into his confidence. He was withdrawing all of that now in one go. All the stories he told me, all the fun we had, all the jokes. Every one of the pubs we were in. All the pints we consumed together. The fishing, the travelling, the landmarks he pointed out. The entire map was being taken away from me. The story of my brief time here deleted. It was the saddest place to be, not knowing where I stood any more. When he disappeared back into the crowd and finally drove away in the black limousine, with one arm around his mother and the other around Ellis, I felt nothing but emptiness, as though he had even taken away the right for me to be lonely.

The pain began to spread at the base of my stomach, as though I had not eaten in a month. But it had nothing to do with food. It had nothing to do with being kicked either and everything to do with having the ground taken from underneath me with such force. I stayed out of sight and waited for a while. Then I straightened myself up and put my finger on the lightning conductor, just out of curiosity and having nothing better to do.

Helen was the only person I wanted to speak to. I may have been a guest here in this country, but I had no intention of staying away from her, even at the risk of his rage coming down on me. I phoned her and she said it was a disgrace to ban me from paying my last respects to a man who died saving my life. She insisted on driving to the cemetery and walking with me on her arm right up to the small gathering of mourners. The coffin was resting on its trellis with carrier bands ready to lower it down. The priest going over the last-minute prayers and everyone saying goodbye for good.

I was glad to be there, because otherwise I would not have heard the priest say a few words in Johnny's own language, in Irish. We stood far enough away not to attract attention, but close enough to hear the words in Irish coming across the cool autumn air towards us. Helen translated them for me before they evaporated.

As the coffin was being lowered, she whispered and asked me to look at Ellis.

'There's something wrong,' she said.

'Why?' I asked, because I thought they were the perfect family now, all holding on to each other, supporting their mother and letting her know that she was not alone.

'It's not like her,' Helen said. 'Something about her standing there with her family like that.'

'Do you think she's had the termination?'

'Unlikely. Not with all this happening.'

'So maybe she's going to keep the baby?'

'Look at her,' Helen said. 'Not like her to be so obedient.'

It was true. Ellis had become docile and distracted. Looking away at a crow landing on a headstone, at the windows of the houses outside the perimeter wall of the graveyard, at the grey fire blanket that sat on the funeral. She was in her own world, as far away from this consecrated place as it was possible to be.

They were throwing bits of gravel on to the coffin. It sounded like beads falling. Ellis playing like a child, wanting to throw more gravel into the grave until Kevin took her away quite forcefully, I thought, making sure that she didn't slip from the grasp of the family again.

There was nothing stopping me now from saying farewell to Johnny. When the mourners were all gone, I stepped up to the grave and looked down at the coffin. I took out the paper with which he had wrapped the gift with the hurling medal inside. I promised to keep the medal, but I had the wrapping paper with me, neatly folded in my pocket. I opened it out and let it go. The Galway colours floating down without a sound after him.

32

This was where I entered into the story of the country at last. I became a participant, a player, an insider taking action. Not letting things happen around me as if I was still only an immigrant and it was none of my business. I was not trying to make a name for myself or anything like that, but I was entitled to play my role as an ordinary inhabitant who belonged here.

Helen described it as a distress call. On the night of the funeral, we agreed that we had to do something to rescue Ellis. There would be plenty of time to waste on talking for the rest of our lives, but now was the time for intervention.

'We have to help her,' Helen said. 'She's not answering her phone.'

I knew exactly what to do. We arrived late at night, when the funeral guests were gone. Helen drove past the Concannon house and there was a light left on downstairs, probably in the kitchen at the back, a glimmer of sleeplessness coming through the fanlight and the frosted-glass panels. She parked the car down at the end of the street, close to the seafront, pointing away from the house to enable us to get away quickly.

As we passed by the house once more on foot, I noticed the

security camera installed over the front door. A movement detector switched on automatic security lights, illuminating the entire front garden like a football stadium. We walked into the laneway at the side of the house and around to the back. I got a foothold in the granite wall and managed to look across. Rita was still up, reading something on her laptop in the kitchen or maybe just staring at it and not reading at all. Her face looked blue. There was also a light on in the room where Ellis slept. We agreed that I would gain entry to the house first and then I would let Helen in by the front door so she could go up and get Ellis.

Strictly speaking, this was breaking and entering. I was fully aware of the penalties for trespassing. I was not so worried about fingerprint evidence, because my prints were already everywhere in the house. Cameras had also been fitted at the back and I didn't like the idea of ending up in court again, this time with the Concannon family testifying against me.

I put on a baseball cap and a scarf over my mouth, then climbed up on to the granite wall. From there I made my way on to the kitchen extension, taking care to shield my face from the camera and also to make no more noise than necessary, like a cat crossing the roof. I had very good information about the house, such as the window to the mid-level bathroom not having a lock. It was easily opened and I even remembered the point at which it jammed. I would have fixed this, along with a lot of other things around the house that were crying out to be done, if I had been allowed to continue working there. The lead pulleys needed to be replaced inside the frame and I had all kinds of plans for routing out the wood and putting in double-glazed panels.

It was nothing to climb through the window. I had to be

cautious not to step on to the toilet bowl or lean on the sink for support, because these were old fittings that would not take much weight. Also, the floor. You tend to have an instinctive memory of house sounds, so I had to rely on that intuitive recall of creaks and expansion sounds as I walked out from the bathroom on to the landing.

Remembering the floorboards was probably not unlike the way music operates and how singers remember the words of songs without any effort once they are in motion. I read somewhere about a test carried out on concert pianists which proves that they know some micro-seconds in advance when they're going to make a mistake. But it's already too late by then and they cannot correct it. Something like this happens when you step on a creaking board. The important thing is to carry on with confidence and not let on that you've made a mistake.

The house remained silent. Which is not really an accurate way of speaking about a house at night. It was full of shouts on the stairs, full of absence, full of words and memories and laughter and crying noises left in the rooms. All that was ever said and unsaid in the family. Even the sound of my own voice included, as well as all the hammering and squeaking of wood and de-nailing yelps that came with my work.

What we had not noticed initially while we were passing by was that Kevin's car was parked on the street. I could see it now, through the fanlight as I made my way down the stairs. Was he in the house asleep, or was he out somewhere, on the night of his father's funeral? I gave him the benefit of doubt and assumed that he was present, upstairs in bed.

There were other unknown factors, such as the alarm system. I expected the front door to be triggered for part-guard. When I opened it to let Helen in, I was very surprised that the alarm failed to go off.

Helen wore her leather jacket over her head like a head-scarf so as not to be recognised on camera. I closed the front door with a click that was so minuscule, it could have been the sound of a snail falling out from a cavity in the granite wall outside. I guided her up the stairs, pointing to all the places where she was permitted to place her feet. She was much lighter than I am, so that helped.

We stood on the landing, outside Ellis's door. Helen quietly opened the door and disappeared inside. Rita was downstairs in the kitchen and I had the urge to go into her bedroom and switch on the light, just to see if the black ash wardrobes were really as bad as I thought they were. And since I was a genuine intruder now, I thought I might as well steal the letters from Johnny Concannon that were sent with the ice-cream money. But I did nothing of the sort, only waited until Helen came out with Ellis, all dressed and ready to go.

Ellis smiled at me and was about to talk, but Helen placed her index finger on her lips.

We made our way down the stairs, but then something happened that every musician must fear most. Laughter. Something in the tension of the performance that triggers off a temporary inability to take what you are doing seriously any more. It's the weight of concentration pressing down and the trapdoor of comedy letting go underneath. A moment of sheer relief in which you see only the funny side of things. You laugh precisely when you tell yourself not to. It always happens in solemn places, at interviews, in church, in police stations. Even during sex. Like sheer blasphemy. Situations where you are least expected to laugh but where you are confronted with something that is not unlike vertigo, when you give in to the urge to throw yourself over the ledge into the disaster of bottomless laughter.

Ellis could not help herself. It was the idea of being freed from her family that must have gone to her head. The dizziness of liberation, just before the escape was complete and she was not yet out of danger. Nerves, that's all, letting go of the restraint. She had to hold on to the banisters with one hand and Helen's shoulder with the other, trying to contain herself as well as she could, but unable to get her own legs to carry her any further. Helen frowned to remind us not to blow it, but that only made things worse. We were on the last set of stairs, prevented from making that final stretch to the front door.

Ellis laughed so much that she sank down on to one of the steps with her right knee. The worst thing you could do in a situation like that was to look at each other. But it was already too late by then, because Ellis saw into my eyes and the highly infectious quality of laughter spread to me instantly. I began going down like a collapsing housing block, detonated for urban renewal. Helen gave me a clout on the back of the head and I looked at her with such an expression of surprise and offence that she could not stop herself laughing as well.

So that was it. The three of us stalled on the stairs, laughing as silently as possible until Ellis could not hold it any longer and moaned as though a loose nail had gone up through her foot.

Light burst into the hallway and the laughter stopped as abruptly as it started. We looked down and saw Rita Concannon standing in the doorway to the kitchen.

'What's going on?' she said.

She was wearing her dressing gown and I could see the unevenness in her chest, with one side flat from her operation. I felt really sorry for her. She had lost everything and now we were taking Ellis away. Her eyes were narrowed and her lips tight. The pattern of her life-story accumulated into one stare.

'Kevin,' she shouted. 'We've got trouble here.'

Nobody knew what to say, on the day of a funeral, so I took it on myself to speak up for everyone, just to calm things down.

'She'll be back,' I said. 'You'll see, Mrs Concannon, she won't be away for long.'

'Intruders,' she shouted.

'We're not abducting her,' I said. 'She wants to go with us, to visit Furbo.'

It was not about freedom of movement so much. We just wanted Ellis to come with us on a journey to see where her father grew up and where the drowned woman was found on the island. It was hard to explain all that to Mrs Concannon in one go.

'Ellis,' she said, speaking past me. 'You need help through this.'

Ellis told us later that she was already booked into a clinic in London which specialised in family planning and terminations. Flights and all taken care of. Kevin had promised to accompany her. She had agreed with these plans but then changed her mind on the stairs.

'I'm going to have the baby,' she said, which was as much of a surprise to herself as anyone else.

'You haven't thought this through, Ellis,' her mother said.

'You'll be glad,' I said to Rita, like an expert in family counselling.

'Don't listen to them, Ellis.'

'I've made up my mind,' Ellis said. 'I've never been more sure of anything in my life.'

They stared at each other and I was afraid that Ellis would start laughing again.

'A baby makes everything right,' I said. 'Wait till you see.'

I could have pushed the point and said that babies correct all our mistakes. They are the great correctors of the world. They repair everything going back in families for hundreds of years, all the way back in history, everything that's ever been broken. This was her chance to look forward into the future instead of looking back all the time.

But there was no need to say any of that because Rita Concannon had already made the conversion. All we were waiting for was her to come and embrace her daughter.

There was movement in one of the rooms upstairs. The sound of bare feet across the floor above us. It was Jane. Then it was Kevin, too, woken by our voices on the stairs. It's hard sometimes to say what happened first. Did we bolt or did we wait until Kevin was on the landing? My guess is that it all happened at once, the way you would strike a match or begin a song.

'It's all right, Kevin. Let them go,' said Rita.

By that time, we were already out the front door and down the terracotta path, through the gate. Outside on the street, as we were running away, I looked back and saw the casement window. I even stalled for a moment to reassure myself what a beautiful job myself and Darius had made of it, knowing that we had left nothing unfinished. I saw Kevin running out the front door, putting his coat on and stepping with his bare feet into his shoes. Rita was at the casement window, looking down the street after us.

I thought of what he was going through. All that guilt going around inside his head about not accepting the medal from his dad and walking away from Helen and turning his back on me when I was the only friend he could trust. On top of all that, he must have known that I was the cause of his violence. He must have seen something happening between Helen and myself on that first night we met. And now we were taking Ellis with us.

Helen pulled me by the arm and we continued running.

His car was pointed in the wrong direction, so he came straight down the street after us on foot. Even then, I wanted to stop and explain to him that we were not stealing his sister, only taking her on a trip to the islands. But there was no time for words and he would not have understood my point of view without using his fists.

We got into the car and Helen did all the right things, fumbling with the keys in the ignition and starting the engine at the last minute and driving away just before he reached us. There may have been the bang of a fist on the glass. Ellis looked back with great concern through the rear window and Helen asked her if she wanted to stop.

'Go,' Ellis said, so we carried on and I didn't have the heart to look at him, standing in the street with his coat open and his bare legs and his bare feet inside his shoes.

We drove only for a very short time before stopping again because Ellis had to be sick. She stepped out on to the pavement and Helen supported her under the arms while I kept looking back into the street with my usual premonition of things to come. By the time they got back in and Helen drove on again, Kevin had caught up with us in his car. We raced away. Ellis screamed. I knew there was no point in trying to escape. He had a faster car and he was more dangerous, more immortal, more willing to give up everybody's life and drive us all into the sea to make his point.

Within seconds he had overtaken us. He swerved right in

front and forced Helen to pull in so hard, the car bounced on to the pavement and came to a stop. The engine cut out. It was a quiet street, with trees and houses set back from the road so far that nobody would hear a thing.

We sat still, waiting. We watched his car door opening and saw him stepping out, chest bare under his coat. His sandy hair came up gold under the yellow lights. He started walking towards us, taking the time to stand right in front of Helen's car in order to recognise each one of us individually, staring us right in the eyes. There was time enough for us to go back over all the good things we remembered about him as well as all the bad things. Time enough to wish that he would accept things the way they were now and not feel diminished by giving in and being generous.

He pinned us back with the force of his intellect, each one of us facing the full charge of his accusation in open court. He was so good with words that he had no need to say anything. He had the lawyer's confidence to wait and allow guilt to come running towards him with both hands up. He stared at Helen in the driving seat, then at me in the passenger seat, drawing out our silent confessions while he made up his mind how to bring the full impact of his justice to bear on us with the best of his violent abilities. He took in a deep breath and ran his hand through his hair. The tension in his eyes was spring loaded. So much potential rage waiting to break free. He was searching for the most imaginative way of exacting punishment.

He came towards us and walked around on my side of the car. Then he opened the back door. Ellis looked up without moving. She let out a tiny, scared sound from the back of her throat, maybe a weird kind of giggle.

It was clear that none of us would put up any resistance

and Helen put her hand on mine to make sure I understood that.

Kevin placed his elbow on the roof of the car and leaned inside, pointing at Ellis.

'If you're going to have this baby,' he said. Then he seemed to lose his vocabulary. It took him a while to search for the correct words that would pin down exactly what he wanted to say.

'That's what I came to tell you,' he said. 'Everything is going to be OK, Ellis. Whatever you decide is right.'

He stood back and paused for a moment. Then he closed the door and walked away. He didn't wait for any reaction. He was so confident that he didn't need to look back. A concert pianist who required no applause. He didn't want our admiration. He had made the big leap across his own doubts and pulled off the most brilliant performance I had ever seen. He got back into his car and drove away, leaving us behind, unable to move.

33

We drove with the light coming after us. Helen and Ellis were talking in the front seats while I stayed quiet in the back, trying to gather up what I had learned about this country and wondering if my first impressions were still valid.

The motorway seemed to take all the glory for itself, distracting from the landscape. The sun was paused behind the clouds, spreading like a cobweb across the wet fields. The light came seeping through the hedges, distributed at such a low intensity that you might have thought there were pieces of silver foil behind the trees. It felt as though we were driving through an interior space. Everything seemed so close. Smaller. Cattle and horses within reach. Hardly any shadows. Even the houses in the distance had an energy-saving sheen coming across the roofs.

There was something sad about the landscape, I thought. But it was not a question you could ask: Why is your country looking so sad right now? I assumed it had to do with the light, or the absence of light, or the absence of people, and I wondered if that was how they compensated for it, through talking and joking, through friendship.

By the time we got to Furbo in the afternoon, the sky had

lifted and there were blue patches breaking through the clouds. We walked up from the main road and came to the house where Johnny Concannon grew up. It was a two-storey cottage, now derelict. Some of the furniture was still left in the kitchen, some chairs and a rusted toaster. A sofa in the main room with an old TV lying upside down. The house had lichen growing on the front and the pink of the plaster showing through the gable walls. There was a mound of turf at the back which had become overgrown with grass. And scraggy fuchsia hedges, rigid from flinching against the constant wind off the sea. We walked around the house and Ellis said that she would love to restore it and come to live here when the baby was born. It was a good thing to say, the day after the funeral. Promising to teach her child the language left behind by her father.

We made our way down to the shore and saw the usual bits of debris lying around that were given back by the sea. I found a faded blue hemp rope wedged into a crevice between two rocks. I was like a shore-ranger, trying to lift it out. But the rope was jammed in so tightly by the force of the waves that it seemed to have taken root almost. I could not dislodge it, otherwise I would have it with me now.

We came to the beach and stood looking out for a while. There were long, parallel lines of foam drifting on top of the water. We saw the islands lit up in the distance and the ferry coming towards us, cutting through the waves. None of us spoke. We were in no hurry, watching the tide coming in around us. There were no sand-hoppers out. Only the waves spilling across the sand, carrying strips of loose seaweed, and Helen pulling Ellis by the arm to make sure her shoes didn't get wet.

We drove to Ros a' Mhíl to get the ferry out to Inishmore.

We parked the car and walked down to the quay, the three of us, Helen and Ellis linking arms while I got the tickets. There were lots of boats docked, but only one of them sailing because it was low season and there were very few visitors left. A couple from Berlin drinking cans of beer to control the effect of the boat lurching from side to side. Some younger French people with dreadlocks and haversacks, reading a map. People from the island as well, returning from a day shopping in Galway, speaking Irish to each other and talking about some TV personalities. Helen told me that one of the men was making fun of the women. He kept saying 'Do you know something I've noticed about you?' but never actually saying what it was until the women turned their backs on him and said they didn't care what he thought.

The sea was rougher than we expected. The boat was rocking so much that whenever you looked through the window the land could be seen dropping out of the sky and going down into the sea and rising up again past the window. It was an illusion that was not worth trying to work out because it would make you seasick. Which is what happened to Ellis, even though she had eaten nothing. There were paper bags provided at the back of all the seats, but Helen decided to bring her upstairs on deck where her thin vomit was carried away by the wind. The sea calmed a little as we arrived into the shadow of the islands and came near to landing.

Helen had arranged to meet a friend she knew on Inishmore. He stood on the pier waiting for us. Michael was his name and he was the principal at the school in Kilronan. He spoke to her in Irish at first and he knew exactly where to take us. He drove out along the road to where none of the tourists ever went and where nobody had much reason to go. He stopped at a place where the narrow road ran out, where there was nothing more than a stone wall and the wide shore of jagged grey rocks on the far side.

He spoke to us about the drowning of Máire Concannon. He told us that he had heard about the event from his own father. There was nobody alive now who could remember it first hand, but he went through all the versions that were told and all the rumours that were washed in by the waves down the years. There were sharp limestone rocks all around and you could see how they were ideal for making the tall stone walls for which the island was famous and so often photographed. You could never lose your mistrust of the weather, so they said. The walls could stand up to any storm the Atlantic threw in at them.

Michael pointed across the bay to Furbo, where we had been earlier. We wondered how long it would take for a drowned body to make its way over on the tide. He said it would be hard to estimate such a thing, but it was better that she had arrived here, because he had experience of bodies being washed up on the other side of the island and they were in very bad shape, often totally dismembered. There were times when they could find nothing more than a hand or a limb at the most. A foot inside a trainer, left unidentified, God knows where from.

I could hear Michael talking behind me and the distant sound of waves crashing in front, like being in between two conversations. The shoreline was too far away and rocks were too jagged for us to walk across. There was no way of telling where exactly her body was found. But then Michael led us towards a wall separating the shore from the first field. There was a flat rock set in like a step jutting out on each side. We crossed over and followed him along the inside of the wall until he stopped.

'Here,' he said. 'This is where she is buried.'

He pointed out two rounded, granite stones set deep into the earth, parallel to the wall, just a metre inside. The stones were white and smooth, emerging about two feet over the ground and surrounded by grass. The distance between them was approximately the length of a human body, six feet, maybe a little more.

'This is the first place where there was earth deep enough to hold her remains,' Michael said.

Ellis had one hand on her belly and she rested her head on Helen's shoulder. We were standing only a few feet away from the hastily dug grave into which Máire Concannon had been put to rest. It seemed like only yesterday that she was found on the rocks and brought here on a board, all bashed by the sea. And maybe you could say this was her real funeral, only in delayed time. Two plain rocks in the ground to mark the place where she lay. It was impossible to tell which one of them was the headstone or which way the body was turned. But you had to assume that the men who buried her under cover of night so many years ago would have done their best to place her head pointing back in the direction of Furbo, where she belonged.

Afterword

The story of the drowned woman found on the Aran Islands was first given to me by the Irish artist, Páraic Reaney from Carraroe at the opening of an exhibition of his work in Galway in the summer of 2008. He, in turn, heard the story from Michael Gill who is the principal at Kilronan Secondary School on Inishmore in the Aran Islands. In the autumn of the same year, I revisited Inishmore, where Michael and Olwyn Gill gave me the full story of this event, separating the facts and the rumours. Michael brought me to the place at *Pointe* (Point) on the headland of *Carraig Fhada* (The Long Reef) which is marked with two rocks, gone slightly white. He had heard the story from his own father and confirmed that the place is known on the island as *Bean Bháite* (Drowned Woman). Michael and Olwyn were also in a position to tell me that the drowned woman's name was *Máire Conceannain* (Mary Concannon) and that she was from *Na Forbacha* (Furbo) in Connemara. Olwyn spoke to me about meeting a relative of Máire Concannon who had come back some years ago from the US to visit Inishmore in order to investigate the circumstances around her death and also to visit an ageing aunt in a Galway hospital who could still recall the events.

It is possible that further evidence may emerge at some point in the future, but apart from the oral record, there seems to be no factual account in writing anywhere, apart from a brief mention of the place called *Bean Bháite* by Tim Robinson in his great work on the Aran Islands.

In a poem entitled *Athrú Trá* (Tide Change), Michael Gill draws a link between the drowned woman and the rocks that mark her grave. Her body was brought in on the north wind and her gravestones were brought in on the melting glaciers. Granite boulders are a geological anomaly on the islands, known locally as 'Aran visitors'.

The only definitive proof of her name and the circumstances around her death exist in folklore, passed on by word of mouth. It is difficult to put an accurate date on the events now, only to point out that they occurred recently enough to have been remembered first hand by an old woman in a Galway hospital around 2000.

There is nothing to be found in newspapers about Máire Concannon, no inquest or police reports and crucially, no death certificate. The Irish language writer and social activist Pádraic Ó Conaire, for whom there is a statue erected in Eyre Square in Galway, spent time living in London in the early 1900s. He cast some light in his writing on conditions in the west of Ireland and reported that there were no less than eight hundred prostitutes from Connemara working in London around that time. The drowning of Máire Concannon does not appear in his writing. There is also a more famous book about the Aran Islands written by the Irish writer John Millington Synge which begins with the words 'I am in Aranmore, sitting over a turf fire, listening to a murmur of Gaelic that is rising from a little public-house under my room.' There is nothing in his book either about the drowned woman or the place where she was found. It seems unlikely that Synge would have missed a story like that. If he had known about it, he might have written a play on the subject or mentioned it in his travel writings at least. So her death must have occurred sometime later, after he stopped visiting the islands, possibly even after his writing life ended abruptly in 1909.

Many thanks to Michael and Olwyn Gill, to Páraic Reaney, to the Serbian writer Dragan Velikić, to Sister Máire at the Presentation Convent, Rahoon, Galway, to Baibre Ní Fhloinn at the Folklore Department, University College Dublin, to Peter Browne at RTE, to Siobhán Ní Laoire at DIT, to Professor Tom Inglis at UCD, to Frank Hamilton, Brian J. Cregan, Pat Johnston, Alice Friend, Timothy O'Neill, Thomond Coogan, Jerry Parr and especially to Nicholas Pearson, Georg Reuchlein, Peter Straus and Petra Eggers.

The line of Samuel Beckett is taken from *Krapp's Last Tape*. The songs quoted in the book are the traditional hymn 'The Queen of the May' and also the traditional Irish drowning lament entitled *Caoineadh Liam Ui Raghallaigh* (The Lament for Liam Ó Raghallagh, or Willie O'Reilly). It is sung in Irish by Darach Ó Catháin on an album called *Reacaireacht an Riadaigh*, which is published by Gael Linn, an Irish language organisation where I worked promoting Irish music in the 1980s. The rest is fiction, as they say.

Mo mhíle buíochas arís, go tháirithe le Michael agus Olwyn Gill, Cillrónáin, Inis Mór, Oileann Árainn.